Red Shoes for Rachel

Judaic Traditions in Literature, Music, and Art
Harold Bloom *and* Ken Frieden, *Series Editors*

Red Shoes
— for —
Rachel

THREE NOVELLAS

Boris Sandler

Translated from the Yiddish by
Barnett Zumoff
With a Foreword by Mikhail Krutikov

Syracuse University Press

Syracuse University Press
Syracuse, New York 13244-5290

First Edition 2017
17 18 19 20 21 22   6 5 4 3 2 1

∞ The paper used in this publication meets the minimum requirements of
the American National Standard for Information Sciences—Permanence of
Paper for Printed Library Materials, ANSI Z39.48-1992.

For a listing of books published and distributed by Syracuse University Press,
visit www.SyracuseUniversityPress.syr.edu.

ISBN: 978-0-8156-3507-9 (hardcover)   978-0-8156-1087-8 (paperback)
978-0-8156-5406-3 (e-book)

Library of Congress Cataloging-in-Publication Data
Names: Sandler, Boris, author. | Zumoff, Barnett, translator. | Krutikov, Mikhail,
    1957– contributor.
Title: Red shoes for Rachel : three novellas / Boris Sandler ; translated from the
    Yiddish by Barnett Zumoff, with a foreword by Mikhail Krutikov.
Description: First edition. | Syracuse, New York : Syracuse University Press, [2017]
    | Series: Judaic traditions in literature, music, and art | Halfway Down the Road
    Back to You and Red Shoes for Rachel are English translations of their respective
    Yiddish works, which appeared in Royṭe shikhelekh far Reyṭshel, while Karolino-
    Bugaz is an original work, not previously published in English or Yiddish.
Identifiers: LCCN 2017004004 (print) | LCCN 2017005100 (ebook) |
    ISBN 9780815635079 (hardcover : alk. paper) | ISBN 9780815610878
    (pbk. : alk. paper) | ISBN 9780815654063 (e-book)
Subjects: LCSH: Sandler, Boris—Translation into English.
Classification: LCC PJ5129.S246 A2 2017 (print) | LCC PJ5129.S246 (ebook) |
    DDC 839/.134—dc23
LC record available at https://lccn.loc.gov/2017004004

Contents

Foreword

A String of Beads

Boris Sandler's prose occupies an unusual place in today's Jewish literature because his impressively diverse oeuvre does not fit easily into its compartmentalized, genre-oriented structure. As a Yiddish writer with rich life experience in the Soviet Union, Israel, and the United States, Sandler remains faithful to the classical legacy of Sholem Aleichem, Y. L. Peretz, Sholem Asch, and David Bergelson. Sandler might perhaps too easily be marked as a traditional realist, but this does not do justice to his original style and fertile imagination. One obvious problem with finding a place for him in contemporary literature is the widely shared but mistaken belief that Yiddish is irrevocably dead. Therefore, a Yiddish writer could only appear as some kind of a ghost, a *dybbuk*, perhaps a figure from Isaac Bashevis Singer's fiction. And a Yiddish writer from the Soviet Union seems an even bigger oddity, because wasn't Yiddish culture in that part of the world eradicated by Hitler and then finished off by Stalin? So how can Yiddish still be alive as a literary language, and how is it possible for a contemporary Yiddish writer to emerge from that part of the world? Isn't his writing merely a curiosity that by default belongs to an exotic cultural niche? And what can this "ghost" from that obscure corner possibly tell us that can be relevant to our present?

To understand this apparent anomaly, we need to look closer into Sandler's background. He was born in 1950 in the town of Bălţi—Beltsy in Russian, Belts in Yiddish—not to be confused with Belz

in Galicia! At that time, it was part of the Moldavian Soviet Socialist Republic, which, after the collapse of the Soviet Union, became
the independent Republic of Moldova. Belts is a shtetl in the historic
region of Bessarabia, which was a province of the Russian Empire until
1917, belonged to Romania between 1918 and 1940 and, in 1940, was
occupied by the Soviet Union. Before World War II, Belts was not different from many other Jewish towns of Eastern Europe. What makes
it exceptional is its postwar history. Of all the former Soviet republics,
Moldavia had the highest proportion of Yiddish speakers, and Belts
was one of its major Yiddish centers. Yiddish was a language of daily
communication, used not only by Jews but also by some of their Christian neighbors. This unusual situation is a result of the particular historical circumstances of this region during World War II. When the
Romanian army, with the help of its Nazi German allies, recaptured
Bessarabia from the Soviet Union in 1941, it took brutal revenge on
Jews for their supposed Communist sympathies. Jews were deported
across the Dniester River to the ghettoes of so-called Transnistria,
a territory in southern Ukraine that had been ceded to Romania by
the Nazis. The subhuman living conditions, epidemic diseases, floods,
hunger, and cruelty of the Romanian occupiers killed more than half
of the ghetto population, but the Romanians did not exterminate Jews
in small towns as they did in Odessa.

After being liberated by the Red Army in the spring of 1944, Jewish survivors were able to return to their homes and rebuild their
lives, which is how Moldova became the stronghold of Yiddish in
the Soviet Union. Although Yiddish was officially recognized by the
Soviet state as *the* Jewish language (as opposed to Hebrew, which was
effectively outlawed), unlike other minority languages, it was not
taught at any educational institutions. To maintain the appearance of
acceptance, the Soviet authorities supported two Yiddish periodicals
and even permitted the publication of a few Yiddish books every year.
A significant part of their print run was also exported abroad to show
the world that Yiddish was thriving in the Soviet Union. In the Soviet
Union, this literature was read by the rapidly diminishing audience of
elderly people who received their Yiddish education before the war.

Moldova was also still a place where many Jews of the postwar generation could speak Yiddish, although most of them did not know how
to read and write.

Boris Sandler grew up speaking Yiddish, but the language of his
education was primarily Russian. It was in Russian that he first read
Sholem Aleichem as a child and immediately recognized literary characters among the family and neighbors. Since then, Sholem Aleichem's
writing has retained its spell over Sandler's artistic imagination. A
career in Yiddish was of course out of the question for a Soviet Jewish boy, and Sandler chose a popular Jewish profession: he became a
violinist with the Moldova State Symphony. But his love for Yiddish
and interest in literature remained strong, and he found a mentor in
Kishinev Yiddish writer Yekhiel Shraybman (1913–2005). Shraybman
began writing in the 1930s in Romania, and in his elegant prose style
seamlessly integrated the juicy Bessarabian dialect with high literary
Yiddish. He drew his inspiration from his childhood in the provincial
shtetl of Rashkov, on the banks of the Dniester. Shraybman tutored
Sandler and a few other aspiring young writers in Yiddish literary craft
and promoted their writing. With Shraybman's support, Sandler's
first Yiddish novellas appeared in the Moscow literary journal *Sovetish
heymland* (Soviet Homeland) in 1981.

At the turn of the 1990s, along with Shraybman and his circle,
Sandler became the pivot in the revival of Jewish life in Moldova. He
served as the head of the Society of Jewish Culture, edited a bilin-
gual Russian-Yiddish newspaper, ran a Yiddish television show, and
composed two documentary screenplays. His social engagements and
literary interests have always been twofold, directed toward preserv-
ing the past and building a future for Yiddish. He published valuable
documents on the Stalinist persecution of Yiddish culture in Soviet
Moldova after World War II, and in his fiction, he began to explore
history in search of a foundation for a new Yiddish revival.

When Sandler immigrated to Israel in 1992, he invested more
of his energy and talent into the revival of Yiddish culture, and the
Soviet experience of self-reliance proved to be no less useful there. He
taught Yiddish at the Hebrew University and initiated a new Yiddish

magazine for children, *Kind un keyt*. Using his very limited personal resources, he carried through an ambitious time-sensitive project—recording video interviews with Yiddish writers and scholars—which are now available on DVD. In Israel, too, the magic lenses of his fiction became sharper and more focused, enabling him to see the past through the present across the geographic divide.

Sandler moved to New York in 1998 and soon took over the editorship of the Yiddish *Forverts*. He came with a vision, energy, and determination—qualities he had developed in the Soviet Union and honed in Israel. He revitalized the Yiddish paper by bringing in new creative forces and expanding the readership beyond its traditional age brackets. He modernized both the form and the content, using new digital technology and formats.

Notwithstanding all the political upheavals and relocations that Sandler has experienced in his life, there is a remarkable continuity in his career. From his teacher Yekhiel Shraybman, he inherited an unwavering faith in the future of Yiddish and a strong dedication to making it happen. Sandler's diverse and powerful imagination grows from his close attachment to his Bessarabian Yiddishland, which is alive in his soul and memory. He has no peers in contemporary literature, and this unique position perhaps makes it difficult to appreciate the originality of his works for an outsider. But in the context of American Yiddish culture, Sandler's trajectory and career look natural, even though unusual for our time. His imagination is rooted in the landscape of his native Bessarabia, and he gives voice to the collective memory of his *landslayt*. His characters come from the *shtetlekh* and villages of Podolia and Bessarabia, the old Jewish regions on the two banks of the Dniester rich in nature and history. But they are also haunted by the horrors of the Transnistrian ghettoes and camps. Their stories are barely familiar to a Western audience, for whom the Holocaust means Auschwitz and Treblinka, or the ghettos of Warsaw and Vilna. The horrors of the Tulchyn ghetto and the Pechora labor camp remain part of the local memory, still preserved by the few survivors and their families around the world who remain afflicted by that trauma and pass it on to their children.

This transnational community of survivors of Transnistria and their descendants is the source of Sandler's creative imagination. He often captures his characters in critical moments in their lives, when the past suddenly catches up with the present. The older generation is personified by Sarah from "Halfway Down the Road Back to You," one of many simple Bessarabian Jewish women whom Sandler has known from childhood. Her life story is typical for that time and place. A happy middle-class childhood in a provincial corner of prewar Bessarabia abruptly ends in historical catastrophe. The yearlong Soviet occupation is followed by the Nazi invasion, Romanian occupation, the deportations and horrors of the Tulchyn ghetto and the Pechora camp. When survivors come back to their ruined homes, they must quickly readjust themselves to the Soviet regime, which leaves no room for mourning the Jewish losses. The collapse of the Soviet Union pushes them to immigrate to their "historic homeland" of Israel, and once they gain momentum, it is difficult to stop. Israel may be good for the old people, but their ambitious children are eager to explore new opportunities in Canada and Germany. For centuries, these Jews had been firmly rooted in their native landscape, but once their roots are cut off, they seem to be unable to settle permanently. The Jewish *goles* continues, and now the Jewish state is part of it: "They were all now on the road, refugees, without a place to call their own—walking homelessly throughout the world." Past experiences shape our attitudes and sensitivities, Sandler tells us through the life stories of his simple characters. Their past traumas stay with them for life and are transmitted from one generation to the next. Like Sarah, they have "something to tell," but cannot "find the words and the strength to tell it," leaving it to Sandler to perform the important work of storytelling for them.

Yashe, the hero of "Red Shoes for Rachel," personifies the postwar generation of Bessarabian Jews. His fate is also typical: unable to fit into the system as a child of a traumatized single mother, he found his safe niche in chess, the "Jewish" sport in the Soviet Union. Rather than use his skills for career building, he retires to the provincial town of Bender. His role model is his teacher, Isak Yefimovich: "the chess kingdom was the only place where his first chess teacher could hide from his past, in which his whole family had been killed, and from his lonely present; and perhaps he was trying to save Yashe and his other students from tomorrow?" But life in the Soviet Union is not chess where one plays by strict rules. To succeed there one has to be flexible and know how to cut corners.

We first encounter Yashe after his immigration to America. In Brighton Beach, the Russian-Jewish shtetl on the narrow strip between the land and the ocean, he meets Rachel. Although born and bred in America, Rachel is also entangled in the traumatic past of her parents: "Ever since she had begun to understand what her parents went through during the war, Rachel had felt punished." She is doomed to carry her father's guilt for the death of his first wife, whose name she bears, and their daughter. Rachel sacrifices her life to the service of her paralyzed mother, whose past, now condensed in the Podolian shtetl's name Mezritsh, "remained tucked away in her memory, like a dried flower that was pressed somewhere between the pages of a thick book she had once read." Rachel's romance with the hapless Russian immigrant Yashe is an attempt to break through the captivity of family memory, but instead, it brings her back into the past, which is now embodied in a real Jewish immigrant from Bessarabia.

Sandler's characters tend to gravitate toward small secluded spaces, alcoves. In a traditional shtetl Jewish house, the alcove—*alker*—was a small windowless space adjacent to the main living room, which usually served as a bedroom. In Sandler's stories, *alker* becomes a spatial metaphor for escape from the surrounding world. His characters have a strong instinct for survival by hiding, which they seem to carry in their genes. It saved them in the Holocaust, and they continue to seek *alkers* wherever they go. Rachel's father eventually withdraws into the small alcove in his store: "Whenever he had a moment free from work in the store, he would sit hunched over, not even turning on the light, like someone being punished." The alcove is the place of self-reflection and self-destruction, where the father is alone, face-to-face with his past: "At times one could hear a suppressed murmur from the alcove, and it wasn't clear whether her father was talking to himself or praying." Sandler artfully uses ordinary spaces and objects as imagery for the representation of the psychological and spiritual state of his characters, transforming mundane reality into sophisticated metaphors. His characters come from the world where material objects were more durable and valuable than human lives. People are disposable, but their property could be of use for new masters.

The last novella in this collection, "Karolino-Bugaz," can appear somewhat disconnected from the previous two. Unlike them, it starts in a major key. Bella and Mark, a successful Russian immigrant couple who have made Brooklyn their new home, are about to celebrate their thirtieth anniversary. Their memories are bright and happy, they did well in the Soviet Union, and they have realized their "greatest dream" of settling in New York. It seems that they have finally managed to break through the spell of the past and liberate themselves from its burden. Bella's alcove in the bedroom has a purely decorative function: "the broad niche deep within which there stood a small, inlaid table on thin, elegant legs; above it, attached to the wall, hung a large oval mirror." But in this novella as well as in the previous two, the alcove turns out to be the space where one faces one's fate. Looking into the mirror, Bella notices Mark's note, which changes her life. The past, like a "dark shadow," rises behind her back in the mirror. The material success turns out to be illusory and misleading, merely an obstruction of the view. In the chain of generations linking Mark's grandfather Mordecai, who was murdered in the ghetto and whose name he bears, to his son David, who becomes religious in New York and joins the Chabad community, their easy happiness is a mere episode, an illusion of freedom from the fate of their kin.

Sandler's prose offers rich material for diverse interpretations. One can look into the psychology of characters, analyze the use of literary devices and narrative techniques, or study the representation of Soviet Jews at historical crossroads. Sandler deliberately resists the temptation to play into popular stereotypes. His writing has no "smell of borscht," which excites some American critics in new Russian-Jewish immigrant writing, nor does he indulge in narcissistic celebration of personal success in America. His storytelling is tightly controlled, with its intertextual fabric carefully woven thread by thread. The novellas in this collection form a cyclical trilogy, whereby the ending of the last story unexpectedly but logically brings us back to the opening of the first one, as they trace generations of Bessarabian Jews on their way from one historical station to the next. As a former Soviet Jew, Sandler is skeptical of utopian projects that promise happiness by means of unburdening us from the past. A Jewish future will never be able to get loose of its past, and history inevitably conditions everyone's life. We have freedom of choice, but we should also remember that we always carry our *alker* with us. To quote the ancient Jewish sage Rabbi Tarfon, "you are not required to complete the task, yet you are not free to withdraw from it" (Pirkey avot, 2:16).

Mikhail Krutikov

Acknowledgments

The author would like to thank Jordan Kutzik for editing the English text.

———

Grateful acknowledgment is also due to the following publications:

"Red Shoes for Rachel" originally appeared in Yiddish in *Forward* as a serial in January–March 2008. "Halfway Down the Road Back to You" appeared in Yiddish as a serial in *Forward* from February to April 2007. Both can be read online in Yiddish on *Forward*'s website, Yiddish.forward.com.

"Red Shoes for Rachel" and "Halfway Down the Road Back to You" also appeared in Yiddish in Boris Sandler, *Royṭe shikhelekh far Reyṭshel: tsvey noveles un a dertseylung* (New York: Forverts, 2008).

An excerpt from "Red Shoes for Rachel" was published in April 2015 on JewishFiction.net.

Part of Mikhail Krutikov's foreword is adapted from his essay, "The Spirit of Sholem Aleichem Thrives in the Work of Boris Sandler," which appeared on May 11, 2016, at Forward.com, http://forward.com/articles/340424/the-spirit-of-sholem-aleichem-thrives-in-the-work-of-boris-sandler/.

Halfway Down the Road Back to You

– 1 –

Precisely cut slices of white bread were lying lined up on sheets of newspaper spread out everywhere; there was an empty space on the little cabinets around the sink and on almost the entire kitchen table; even the only chair was covered with a page on which six or seven crusts of bread were huddled together. The kitchen was open; it was not separated from the front room by a fourth wall but looked like an alcove for preparing food. Eating, however, took place in the "salon," as they called the living room. It sounded high class, one could even say aristocratic—"salon," but even in the living room, the white slices, like mushrooms after a rain, had captured every surface on the sparse furniture, including the narrow little sofa and the few empty bookshelves attached to the wall; not even the top of the television set had been spared, and the slices had spread out freely on the windowsill.

It was a pleasure to look at such a salon and kitchen, flooded with such fresh-smelling mushrooms, and old Sarah, more happy than tired, leaning her elbows on the table and still holding the knife in her hand, looked slowly around at the lines of bread, not omitting a single slice, as if each of them bore a distinctive mark so that only she could arrange them in a certain order and uncover the secret of a hidden inscription.

Sarah had firmly decided: she was going to go visit them, and how can one set out on a visit without well-dried slices of bread. No sweet crackers whatsoever can compare to them; they break up into crumbs and creep into everything, and afterward they stick in your throat. A well-dried slice of bread is something quite different, especially white bread! It's always ready to be eaten, with a little boiled water or thin potato soup, or even simple ice-cold water right from the well, to say nothing of a glass of milk. It doesn't scrape your throat, it doesn't stick to your gums, and as you're eating it your tongue doesn't get tired so fast from mixing around the chewed-up bread in your mouth. A delicacy! As she remembered that word, Sarah smiled and she again swelled with pride at the work that her hands had so skillfully accomplished.

They would surely be satisfied by her gift, Sarah figured, but a thought kept nagging at her: would they recognize her? So many years had passed—a whole lifetime, one could say. On the other hand, all those years hadn't gone anywhere—they had melted into her blood, poured over her body. Her memory had absorbed everything, down to the last detail. True, she felt that it was getting weaker with each passing day; she was starting to forget things—faces, even words. Recently she had forgotten her daughter's last name—her landlord had telephoned her two days ago and had asked her for the name, because the telephone was listed under that name. For a moment she had forgotten it—the first name of her son-in-law, Misha, was right at the tip of her tongue, but his last name, which was, of course, also the last name of his wife, her daughter, seemed to have fallen into a black hole, no matter what she did. She did remember it later—Weissman— a simple last name, but the incident left her with a feeling of helplessness, as if she had suddenly lost her way on a strange street, or in a foreign city, or country.

It wouldn't take long, a few hours, till the slices of white bread got to the texture they should have. Everything dries quickly here. When the word "here" crossed her mind, a barrier immediately appeared by itself, and it responded with an echo: "there." The "here" referred to almost seven years, but, as Sarah now thought about it, that was almost completely eclipsed by the "there," a full seventy-three years. "Here" meant Israel, the city of Nazareth Illit, the apartment her children had rented for her. The lostness was something she had felt earlier, even "there" in her hometown, Beltsy, when they were just beginning to talk about going to Israel.

In the beginning she took the talk about Israel to be vague rumors that had been circulating in the air for quite a long time, like a sort of infectious childhood disease such as measles: you get sick once in a lifetime and then you forget about it. She thought that in this case, too, people would get over the measles and forget about the plague, the talk of going.

But that's not the way it turned out—it became something more: the words started to become reality. They sold a lot of things from the house, and if the things they were selling were being torn out by the roots, as it were, together with a piece of history of the house and the family, the brand new things they were buying, often still packed in hard boxes stamped on all sides with warnings: "Do not throw!", "Do not strike!", "Glass!", "Open here!", "Caution!", "Handle with care!", frightened her. She was afraid to touch them and just wanted to get out as quickly as possible from her bedroom, which was filled from floor to ceiling with packages and cartons of various widths and lengths. It was Fira, her daughter, who took care of all that. The mother just sighed and felt that each new day left her less of the mission that she had so faithfully and devotedly carried out during her family life: to be a housewife, to run her own home. At night, she used to practically sigh to David: "But they're turning our whole life into dust!" Her husband didn't answer, though Sarah knew that he wasn't asleep; she could tell that from the way he was breathing, the way a good doctor could tell everything that was going on inside a patient simply by putting his ear to the patient's heart or chest. She knew that David felt the same way she did, but for now he couldn't find any words to explain it all and justify it. One time he did indeed answer her, but that didn't lift the stone from her heart. "They're right, Sarah," David said quietly. She held her breath and waited for her husband to continue, which God knows was appropriate from his word "right." But he just repeated it and added: "because they have a choice."

Sarah was now sitting on the edge of the little sofa reading a newspaper. A few minutes earlier she had carefully squeezed herself into the last bit of free space amid the spread-out newspapers with the slices of bread on them. It was like the way she used to go over to her child who had fallen asleep on her bed and take a nap next to him. At first it was her son, Ilik, and afterwards, six years later, it was little Fira. A thick packet of newspapers lay right next to the sofa. She had collected them after reading them; every Friday morning she bought the newspaper at the kiosk across the street, from the Moroccan Jew Yossi, and she read it unhurriedly during the course of the week, a page at a time. Yossi knew Sarah very well, and as soon as he saw her, he would yell in Russian: "*Babushka, gazyeta!*" ("Grandma, newspaper!")

She was dressed warmly: over her long flannel robe she wore a sleeveless fur coat; on her feet she wore heavy socks and winter boots; on her head, a green kerchief tied with a loose knot under her chin, which, as if deliberately, kept moving up to her lower lip, trying to hide the old lady's mouth. When they were packing their things, David had once reproached her: "Why are you dragging along those old rags of yours?! You would do better to take the opportunity to buy a new wardrobe." Perhaps he was actually right; there always comes a time when everything you've saved turns to ashes and dust, as had happened to their home. However, the "old rags" had definitely been of use to her. The new country was indeed a hot one, and in the summertime, it was impossible to sit inside without a *masgan*, as they call an air conditioner here, but in the winter it got very cold in the apartment, and there was no heating here as there was there. It was possible that winter was warm somewhere in the country, but in their house in Nazareth Illit the cold was piercing. It crept into your bones, especially from the stone floor. She had begun to hate those stone floors immediately, from the very first day. No matter what she wore on her feet, she felt the poisonous cold pour over her body.

So now she was sitting, swathed in heavy clothing, with a thin blanket on her lap and her feet on a small pillow, also brought from "there." When Fira was still a child she had loved to play with her little pillow, which was embroidered with colorful flowers and decorated with a green silk ribbon around it. She used to fall asleep more quickly if she laid it on her head and hugged it with her pudgy hands. Even later, when she was already old enough to be a bride, Sarah occasionally found her sitting on the sofa, deep in thought, pressing the embroidered pillow to her belly. Her mother knew that it was a sign that something had happened to her. Later, of course, she forgot about the pillow; got married, had a son, moved into her own house, and became a skilled housewife herself. The green silk ribbon had long since been torn off and the colorful cotton thread had faded and gotten rubbed off, but the pillow still protected her old, careworn feet from the cold that constantly rose from the floor.

No, she had no interest in reading today. Of the few Russian newspapers that could be purchased at Yossi's kiosk, she bought *Novosti Nedeli* (News of the Week). She got onto that one while living together with her children. Actually the news is the same in all newspapers. Here they don't make it easier to stomach or censor it. On the contrary: they keep repeating the truth till one's heart grows heavy. They have no pity whatsoever on themselves. But the main thing in it was the supplement: *Yevreyski Kamerton* (Jewish Sounding Fork). That section put one's heart at rest. She loved to read the beautiful, moving stories of Jews of her generation. On the pages of *Sounding Fork*, one could find a piece of what every one of them had survived "there," but of which they had only been able to talk here.

She took off her glasses and put them in a pocket of her robe, and folded the newspaper precisely. Her gaze once again rested upon the white slices. She touched a piece of bread lightly, with her fingertip, then moved the knot of her shawl down. With her mouth free, she softly said out loud: "Another hour or hour-and-a-half and I can hit the road."

–2–

Two weeks earlier, right after Sukkot, a woman had called her on the telephone and asked whether she, Sarah, had heard about the video interviews with Holocaust survivors that were being conducted by the Spielberg Foundation. "You were in the ghetto, weren't you?" the woman asked, as if she were unsure of it.

That had annoyed Sarah. The whole business of receiving compensation from the Germans was still fresh in her memory. She herself had no use for their money—it was covered in Jewish blood. Her daughter Fira, however, had insisted; a half-year after they came here, she, through an acquaintance of hers, had sought out the address of some sort of women's organization that helped new immigrants from the Soviet Union prepare the paperwork to get the "German pension." They could, of course, have hired a lawyer, but Fira declared that lawyers tear your guts out, and anyway she could do what they do herself. She had had plenty of experience with Soviet bureaucrats, so she would be able to cope with the Israeli and German ones too. "They're all cut from the same cloth!"

She went to Jerusalem with her mother and took her to the office of that women's organization, where she had to sign a stack of papers, and only then did her troubles begin. Letters would arrive, asking Sarah to indicate exactly where she had been and who could confirm in writing that she had indeed been there. And there were other such questions that caused her pain and made her feel that they didn't trust her, as if she were "slyly" fooling them or trying to get money that was not due her. That didn't bother Fira; she was a practical woman and "didn't let her emotions lead her astray." She wrote to various authorities, sent an inquiry to an archive in Vinnytsia, and got what she needed. Sarah saw the document herself and a cold shiver of horror ran through her body: her only witness, who was crying out to her from that murdered world, was also a bureaucrat, as Fira would call him, who once wrote her name in the camp commandant's office ledger, saying that she, Sarah (here he entered her maiden name), together with her sister Chaya Hershko-vitsh, had received a bundle of wood on November 15, 1941.

It didn't make sense to her that after so many years the document that confirmed the bitter truth of her fate was lying around somewhere amid the thousands of files arranged on shelves, squeezed between other faded, yellowed papers and notes.

And here she calls, the woman, and asks whether she can come to see Sarah so she can tell about those years. Sarah certainly had something to tell, but where could she find the words and the strength to tell it? Her hair stands on end whenever she reads what people survived during the war in the *Sounding Board*. The woman from the Spielberg Foundation should talk to them! But the woman on the telephone was insistent—each person had to tell his or her own story so that the coming generations would remember it. The stranger spoke inspiring words—Sarah had thought very little about it previously. There had never been an occasion to tell her story, and there had been no one to tell it to. Should she have gone and told her own children about the hell she had survived? It was bad enough that she had experienced it herself and had carried around the pain, locked inside her, all her life.

Nevertheless they came at the agreed-upon time—the woman who had talked to Sarah previously on the telephone—Edith was her name—and two young Israeli men from the local area. When their equipment was set up, the men immediately began giving orders, acting as if they were in their own homes; they spoke loudly, in Hebrew, and when they needed something from Sarah, Edith translated it for her. The first thing they did was move the sofa and place it facing the window, and then they unpacked their equipment and plugged it in.

While the film crew was preparing, Sarah sat on the sofa where they had placed her, and looked at everything that was happening around her with mixed feelings: she felt both curious and lost. She couldn't believe that the entire hustle and bustle was really for her, the old, unknown woman who had come here from the distant provincial town of Beltsy, where she had lived for some seventy years. She had prepared for this visit: she had put on the cream-colored rayon gown with three golden buttons in front—David had bought it for her half a year before they emigrated; on her feet were her dark brown shoes, which were still quite new—she had worn them perhaps three or four times. She had left her green kerchief in the bedroom; she had tied her hair back on her neck and had inserted her gold-ornamented semicircular bone comb, which had been a gift from her son for her seventieth birthday.

Edith, a dark, charming woman with plump lips, about forty like her Fira, sat down next to Sarah, stroked her hand, and said:

"You don't have to relive it," she said softly. "I'll ask you questions and you answer me. You don't even have to look at the camera—look at me and tell me the story."

"Will they show it on television later on?" Sarah asked.

Edith smiled. This apparently wasn't the first time she had heard those words.

"For now, we just have to complete the work, but in time somebody will certainly be interested in the material. In any case you'll get a copy of what we do today."

They turned on the lights on both sides and aimed them at Sarah, as if the bright lights could peel away the distant corners of her memory, all the hidden days and nights that she herself had tucked away there and locked up with seven locks. Then she heard the first questions:

"What is your full name and when were you born?"

Edith was sitting on a chair, facing her. On her knees lay a notebook open to a fresh blank page; she had apparently chosen to write down Sarah's answers herself. Sarah answered in Russian, as she had for the dozens of surveys that she had filled out for various authorities that she had had occasion to deal with there, and now here too.

"Wechsler, Sarah. Born in 1924, in the city of Beltsy, Bessarabia."

"Who were your parents?"

"My father was a worker," Sarah continued in the same formal tone, but suddenly she stopped, and after a moment she started over: "My father, Zelig Nusnboim, was a merchant, a well-known and distinguished person in the city. I remember my mother telling us proudly that when our father went into the municipal bank, the bank manager would meet him at the door. My mother, Dobe Nusnboim, didn't work; she ran the house and brought up the children, me and my elder sister Chaya. We spoke Yiddish and Romanian at home. In addition to those, my mother knew Russian pretty well because she had lived in Bessarabia when it belonged to Czarist Russia—only after the civil war did the territory become part of Greater Romania. We lived very well, quietly. A maid helped my mother with the housework, but my mother always did the cooking herself."

"And did you observe the Jewish traditions?" Edith asked.

"Yes, we kept kosher. For Passover, we had separate dishes, which we kept in the attic in a wicker basket covered with a thick piece of cloth. I don't remember my father going to the synagogue; on Rosh Hashanah and Yom Kippur, yes—arm in arm with my mother, both of them beautifully dressed—but in general, no. Jabotinsky's portrait hung in the front room of our house; for a time, my older sister hung around with Zionist youths, and when they used to get together at their meetings, she would take the portrait with her. My mother, as I recall, was active in community affairs; she was a member of a committee to help poor children who were attending the ORT schools. Do you know what kind of schools those were? The children in the upper grades both had conventional studies and were taught a trade. The girls were taught to be seamstresses; the boys could become carpenters, for example. Once a week my mother had a "tour of duty": she checked on how the children were dressed and whether it was clean in the classrooms; she tasted the food, because the children used to eat lunch there. We kept chickens in our yard, and one day my mother ordered that ten hens be butchered and taken to the ORT school."

Sarah sighed.

"I'm remembering trifles," she said. "You probably want to hear other things from me?"

"Did you experience any anti-Semitism at that time?"

Sarah thought about that for a while. She understood the question, of course, but her memories relating to the years of her quiet childhood under the warm wings of her parents and the short time of her blossoming womanhood just didn't contain a trace of human hatred and wildness.

"Anti-Semitism? Certainly there was anti-Semitism then too. It's simply that in those years I still understood very little about such things. We lived on Church Street in Beltsy. Wealthy people, mostly Jews, lived there. We had a big house with four rooms. Across the street lived a certain Russian immigrant and his wife. He had fled from Russia after the revolution, and he had a soap factory. People said that he was an anti-Semite. They had no children, and since they were childless the wife used to ask my mother at times to let me go for a walk with them. Apparently she liked me. She treated me very well, bought me candy . . . Of course, later, in the thirties, when the Romanian fascists came to power, there were bitter rumors that the anti-Semites were girding themselves to attack the Jews. At that time I was already a student at the Romanian Gymnasium, and the Jewish students at my school knew that the Romanian literature teacher, Mr. Constantine, was a member of a right-wing extremist group. Then the Soviets came. There was great jubilation; many of the Jewish youths who had been studying or working in the larger Romanian cities came back home. By the second or third day—I don't remember exactly—they changed the currency, and everything, down to the last pin, was seized from the stores. My father, who was a smart man, quickly understood who our "liberators" were. Late one summer evening—my bedroom door was open because it was very hot—I heard my father telling my mother: "Mrs. Nusnboim, we are not destined to have a peaceful old age." He always used to address her that way: Mrs. Nusnboim. Soon thereafter, Chaya brought home her fiancé, a Jewish boy by the name of Semyon Hershkovitsh, who had come with the Red Army. He worked for the City Council as a bookkeeper, and immediately declared that he would not accept a wedding canopy or any other religious trappings. They would register in the Citizens'

Registry, as was appropriate for proper Soviet citizens. We were all sitting at our big table, on which the white Sabbath tablecloth was spread, and were drinking tea with jam. I watched my father listening to what the prospective bridegroom was saying, and with each word the blood drained from his face, drop by drop. Of course my mother had noticed that even before I did. She slowly slipped her hand into my father's and squeezed his fingers. She began speaking as soon as Semyon finished. Her first words seemed to adjoin his last words, with not even a narrow gap between. She didn't speak loudly, but it was the only time in my life when I heard her speak that way. Her words still ring in my ears to this day: "Of course my husband and I understand little about today's life, but without a wedding canopy there will be no marriage!"

Sarah drank a little water from the cup that Edith had prepared for her. She wiped droplets of sweat from her upper lip with her finger and then continued with her recollections:

"And that indeed is how it went: after they registered in the Citizens' Registry, we set up a wedding canopy in our house late in the evening and the dyed-in-the-wool Komsomol member Hershkovitsh said the *harei at*, as is appropriate for a Jewish bridegroom. Only later did we learn that his father had been a ritual slaughterer in a town in Ukraine, and that the anti-Soviet Whites had killed him when Semyon was only a child. In general, he was a good person. He was very helpful, especially when they started purging people and exiling them to Siberia. I believe that it was only thanks to him that they didn't bother my father."

About four hours passed. During that time, one of Edith's two young assistants asked Sarah several times to interrupt her narration while he quickly changed the tapes in his machine. Between the brief interruptions, they both sat on their chairs while Sarah was talking; the one who was operating the video camera read a book, and the other one, who had previously been puttering around with the lights, also started to leaf through some book but then dozed off. Later, when she was once again alone and only the heat from the mighty lamps remained in the air, she recalled the two Israelis; it was a shame—she had just baked delicious crumb cookies (her grandchildren loved them) and she had completely forgotten about giving them to the visitors. Deeply immersed in her own recollections, she had sort of separated herself from all her surroundings, allowing herself to be pulled away by the power of her memory.

She remembered that for a long time after the horrors of the war itself had ended she would get a sudden blast of heat in her face in the midst of the daily hustle and bustle, exactly as if space had split open before her eyes and was showing her fragments of pictures from that dark time. But immediately after the glowing heat, a cold shiver would pass through her body and her breathing would seem to stop, her heart pounding so hard against her ribs that she felt like tearing the clothes off her body. She had learned to hide the fragments of her past from strangers, and even from David after they got married. Time heals, she had heard more than once, but she kept asking herself: why don't my wounds heal? She had found her own remedy for that horror: her children, her home, her work; Sarah's life rested on that fundamental tripod of a woman's fate. She stopped working prematurely; Fira was writing a dissertation and Naum, her little son, would go to kindergarten one day and then stay at home for a week, having caught some kind of illness. So his grandmother had to take care of the child. Sarah's house stopped being her home as soon as she locked the door for the last time and turned the key over to the new mistress. Her children? Where were they now? Ilik and his family had gone to Germany, and Fira, with her Misha and Naum, had left for Toronto nearly three years before.

"Let them all be well where they are," sighed Sarah, and she hoped that they and their children and children's children would never have to live through what she had survived.

-3-

Now she was puttering around in the drawers of the kitchen table. She was looking for the key to the other room, which she didn't use. In her children's apartment, which they had all rented when they came to Israel, there was also a certain windowless room, or more correctly, a windowless alcove. The children called it the "security room," but she had a different name for it: the "you-shouldn't-need-it" room. Back in her parents' house, that's what they used to call things that they always kept tucked away from daily view—in some pigeonhole or in the shed—and remembered only when something bad happened. She remembered from those years a sort of strange piece of machinery that they called a "pump," and as her father explained it, they couldn't do without that pump should there be a fire, God forbid—"you shouldn't need it!" There were other things there too: rat poison in a dark-green bottle; the cardboard alms box; the medicine chest, as her mother had called it, which had been stuffed with various packets of cloth and gauze and several small bottles of iodine—"you shouldn't need it!"

But there had been other things in the house that they had kept hidden from her and her sister, and little Sarah couldn't begin to understand why they belonged in the category of "you shouldn't need them." After all, they were so delicious! Little glass jars with preserves—thick stewed raspberries, either mixed with sugar-powdered currants or cooked syrup and sour cherries—all of the jars were covered with hard white paper and wrapped at the edge with heavy silk thread, and her mother kept them in a compartment on the top shelf so even their maid, Manya, had to stand on a stool to take down a jar of "you shouldn't need it." They used them when someone in the house wasn't feeling well: a slight cold or loose bowels and so forth. Sarah continued the custom of keeping such sorts of "you shouldn't need them" in her own home after she got married. In her daughter's house, however, she didn't see them. Fira was more wrapped up in her studies and her work, and thoughts of such "little jars" were the last things on her mind. Furthermore, her mother could bring them whenever she needed them, God forbid!

Here in Israel, they didn't know about such things; they simply weren't here—no sour cherries, no thick syrup, no currants, and not even raspberries. In the beginning, she wondered about that. How could it be that in Israel, where oranges and lemons grow everywhere, you couldn't get "a handful of syrup to ensure a full recovery?" But there was no lack of other things that "you shouldn't need." They actually kept them in dark alcoves, amid the baggage brought from the old country, which was still wrapped till "later," when they would have their own apartment. There were four gas masks, one for each person, a white box with a red Star of David on the top, and a dozen or so bottles of mineral water . . . Sarah also arranged for several packages of salt and ten pieces of soap to be stored there. Her son-in-law, Misha, couldn't let the occasion go without needling her: "What's up, mama— are you planning to set up a laundry in the security room, too?"

She had emptied out all the trifles from the table drawers but hadn't found the key. She clearly remembered having put a silver-colored key there. Perhaps Valya, her aide, had taken it? Her daughter had gone to the Social Security office before she left to arrange for an aide to come to her; Sarah herself hadn't wanted that—she was still strong enough to take care of herself. Nevertheless, they had sent the woman Valya, for four hours a week. She came once on Monday and again on Thursday. She had been there the day before, Sarah recalled. Valya called her no less than Sarah, using both full names the way Russians do. Valya had come to Israel from some small town in the Ural Mountains, together with her Jewish husband and two sons. No, she had no complaints whatsoever about Valya—she was definitely a very fine woman—but she didn't want anyone to bathe her or clean up her house. So they worked out between them that Valya would walk with her a bit in the morning, and if Sarah needed her, she would help with the shopping.

Why would Valya suddenly find the key to that door useful? Sarah moved things about in the table drawers again, and suddenly recalled that she had put the key in a different place yesterday. Now certain in her movements, she opened the small cupboard above her head, and immediately felt the lost object. Her face glowed: there—the key is lying there and saying nothing! She wasn't completely senile! She squeezed the key into her hand and felt its substantive iron coldness. Without thinking, as if her feet had decided by themselves, she went over to the door of the alcove and stood in front of it. Again she had forgotten something; a thought rolled around in her head that interfered with the other one: actually the slices of bread should be dry enough already. Apparently the door to the "you shouldn't need it" and the slices laid out in lines had some connection. She was preparing to go into the bedroom to get a pillowcase in which to place the fine white mushrooms, but just at that moment the telephone rang. With all the preparations, Sarah had forgotten that her daughter Fira called her at this time on Tuesdays. Ilik called too, but not every week; it was usually on Saturday or Sunday afternoon.

Misha had started the whole business about moving to Toronto. His cousin lived there, so Misha and Fira had gone to visit for a week. When they came back, they were reinfected with the travel virus. But why? They had hardly gotten settled here—he works, she works, Naum had finished school already. No, people live more peacefully there, and Naum will have "better prospects." Sarah just shrugged her shoulders. What could she say now, and who needed her comments anyway? It would have been different with her David—he certainly wouldn't have kept quiet. But it was understandable that whenever another choice became available they would leave here. For Naum, there would certainly not have been any prospects at all here, despite all the "pull." But there? It's not easy, of course. They work hard, but after all, they're the ones who wanted capitalism! To be sure, Fira and Misha have survived—one day Naum finishes school and the next he has to leave for his military service. Naturally their hearts ache, but they knew where they were going and that it was far from a quiet little corner of the world! What's the use of talking—Sarah knew very well, from her own life, that refugees are like shadows in daylight: you don't stay overnight where you sleep and you don't sleep where you stay overnight.

As a rule, Sarah didn't speak for long on the telephone with her daughter. After all, it costs a fortune to talk, and one doesn't pay with shekels but with dollars. How is she feeling? How can a woman her age feel? As long as she can stand on her own two feet! What does she do? She doesn't conduct any important business; she cooks, cleans, and reads the newspaper. She understands, of course, that it is by no means easy to move to Toronto; status-shmatus—Fira will find a way, with her own status. As long as the children put roots down there and Naum has better prospects. He's already a student in a college . . .

Today's telephone conversation revolved around the same things as usual: the daughter asked her questions and the mother gave her answers. When they were already near the end, Sarah asked:

"Is Naum at home?"

"It's two o'clock in the afternoon here now, Mama, and Naum comes home when it's already late at night where you are. Why do you ask?"

Sarah was silent for a moment, and her daughter was silent too. Apparently both women needed a short period of silence to separate the chatting about everyday matters from the few unsaid words, the way it used to be between them long ago. Then everything was clear without words—a look, a gesture, a grimace explained a lot.

Fira broke the tense silence. Her voice changed immediately, departed from the forced "everything's all right."

"Mama, your voice doesn't sound like usual today. What happened?"

"Calm down, Fira, I just wanted to hear Naum's voice."

"He'll call you, mama."

"You shouldn't spend money unnecessarily. Just tell him that he should remember his old grandmother. After all, I raised him . . ."

They said goodbye to one another. Sarah sat by the telephone for another few minutes, with her hands on her knees as if she had just lost something on the floor because she didn't have the strength to hold it in her hands any longer. A certain weariness came upon her and descended to her legs. She decided she wouldn't go anywhere today. Who sets out in such a mood? She would just put the bread in the pillowcase—she couldn't leave it lying there all night . . . Yes, she shouldn't forget to take her pills. Her head felt very weak.

$-4-$

They say you should unburden your heart. The charming woman Edith had told her that they travel around Israel this way almost every day, and people like Sarah who had survived the horrors tell their uncut stories. And the same thing takes place with all the survivors who speak other languages—both here in this country and throughout the world. "This is that kind of project," Edith told her with a certain dignity, as if this project could squeeze into itself all the thousands and thousands of hearts waiting for someone to pour out their pain to, at least at the end of their lives.

"And so?" thought Sarah. "Will they collect all the films in one place and show them on television so everyone can see the Jewish pain, hear it, sniff it like a certain jar of 'you shouldn't know from it,' and then throw it out?"

Yes, the world gives good advice: Unburden your heart. Time heals. Troubles make you stronger. So why is it that when Sarah sees a bloody shoe lying in the gutter not far from a bus that has just exploded, a charred shoe with smoke still coming from it whirls before her eyes—a reminder of what was left of her father?

———

By the day after the war began, Sarah's father had rolled up the three big woolen rugs, packed up the silver utensils and the winter tools, and arranged with a coachman to have them taken to a former employee of his who lived near the Kishinev Bridge. His reasoning made sense: At one end of Church Street, where Sarah grew up, was the military hospital; as recently as a year ago, it had still been Romanian, but when the Red Army had marched into the city, a Russian sanitation brigade had moved in with them. Sarah's father had remarked even then that government buildings don't remain empty. He was certain that the first thing the Germans would do would be to bomb the hospital and the houses where the Russian soldiers were staying with their families. Several such families lived on Church Street, in houses whose true owners had been removed and exiled by the military.

The Kishinev Bridge district in Beltsy was at the end of the city, and the poor Jews of Beltsy lived there. "It's a sin to waste a bomb on those 'toy houses'?!" was the bitter evaluation of the former wheat merchant Zelig Nusnboim. He was also certain that the war would end even before the winter mud appeared. He was indeed a smart man, but Hitler and Antonescu—those two dogs—had their own plans. They sent their airplanes to blow up precisely those streets and alleys in Beltsy where the Jewish poor had lived out their poverty, generation after generation.

Sarah's father and his wagon got to the place first, and Sarah, her mother, her sister with her baby in her arms, and Manya lagged quite a bit behind. Chaya's husband, Semyon, had been mobilized on virtually the first day. After the wedding, the young couple had continued to live with their parents, who gave them two rooms with a separate entrance.

The year under the Soviets was a good one for Sarah. She finished her first year at the Pedagogical Institute with high marks. True, learning Russian was very hard for her, but the fresh winds of a new life seized her and her comrades and whirled them in its enthusiastic dance. Semyon quickly became an intimate in the house; he helped his father-in-law get settled at work. In that way, the former "bourgeois element" Nusnboim began to carry the honorable title of "Soviet worker"; he went to work every morning wearing black calico satin sleeve protectors that his wife had sewn for him. Manya, the maid, remained with them. She herself wanted to stay because she had no one in Beltsy. Semyon had already figured everything out: how to justify her social situation so she could live with them.

It seemed that their lifestyle was almost unchanged, except that my father developed a strange habit: before he said anything, he first looked around and his voice became hoarser and softer, as if someone constantly had him by the throat.

It was very early when they left their house. Her father told her mother, in his very polite way—Madam Nusnboim—take only the things you need with you. Her mother got completely confused; poor thing, she didn't understand what that meant—for a good housewife, everything in the house is necessary. The art of evaluating things came later, on the roads, in the ghetto, in the camps. Her father wanted to take Manya, who limped on one leg, on the wagon with him, but she refused: "I'm not some aristocratic lady!" Chaya, with her child, immediately announced that she too would go on foot, and added, with a certain decisiveness that didn't fit her at all: "We have to stick together!" From the time she was small, they had considered her the quiet one; their mother was not happy about that, and once, in a moment of anger, she had even said: "You could wipe the floor with her." Now she was insisting on staying together.

The sun had already poured out its heat across the whole sky; you couldn't raise your head because the light stung your eyes. They were all only drops in the river of humanity that ran through the streets, without a clear knowledge of where the stream was carrying them and where it would end up. The further they descended from the highest part of the city, the lower and more closely packed the houses became, with low clay porches in front. The windowed doors almost reached the road, and astonished women and children looked out from them, as if they were not alive but were cut from colored paper and placed in those "toy houses." It looked as if they weren't even thinking of abandoning their four walls, covered with reeds or straw. Sarah, who had been born in this city and had lived here for almost seventeen years, suddenly realized that in all those years she had never gone so far from her Church Street; she had hardly imagined that in her city there could be such little streets and houses. In a few minutes, she was also able to see, with her own eyes, how quickly and thoroughly all of it had been burned up. It seemed to her then that she was standing all alone in the middle of the fire and smoke; she didn't hear anything, but she smelled the nauseating odor of burning feathers and skin, as if Manya were standing in the middle of the Kishinev Bridge and constantly singeing chickens that had been slaughtered and plucked for the holidays. In her head a single word kept rattling around: "Pump, pump!"

———

That evening, after the Spielberg folks had left, Sarah had the feeling that she was again standing somewhere in the middle of a road, all by herself, and just couldn't decide whether she should walk straight ahead or turn back. She tried to understand what walking straight ahead meant under her current circumstances, for previously, at the beginning of their hellish wandering, they, the exhausted souls dragging themselves along the road, had known that to stop walking and tarry on the side of the road meant to remain lying there forever, as had happened to Manya.

Here in Israel, in the city of Nazareth Illit, where she didn't go out of the house without her aide Valya—where everything was strange and distant to her, all her roads crossed on the piece of rented territory of her current loneliness. From there, from her parents' home, she had carried away the frightening word "homeless." "God forbid that you should be homeless," her father used to say, like a curse. At that time she more imagined than understood what the word meant: not to have a place of your own, a roof over your head—to have to turn to strangers. She understood the full meaning of the word right after that first bombardment of the little Jewish streets near the Kishinev Bridge. And now, after so many years, the forgotten word, "homeless," and everything that goes with it had unexpectedly again emerged from her mouth and fallen to her feet, as if someone were saying: "Come, now I'll be your guide."

That same night, Sarah dreamed about her mother. She was dressed in her festive dark-blue silk dress, with its soft, white collar; between the two points of the collar, there was an oval silver brooch with a piece of amber in the middle; on her head she had thrown a thin, loosely knit kerchief. That's what her mother looked like on Yom Kippur, and her father, in whose eyes her mother's figure and his love for her were reflected, used to remark, half-jokingly: "Madam Nusnboim, in such a garment, the Almighty will surely inscribe you in the book of life." Sarah saw her mother's face as close as in that dream perhaps only when she, as a tiny infant, was suckling at her mother's breast, with her little nose pressed up against it. Could such a thing engrave itself in one's memory? In her sleep, the old lady swallowed her saliva as if she were refreshing herself with her mother's milk. The deep bitterness of the day slowly left her. "I know," her mother's soft, calming voice appeared. Her lips were closed, but her words reached her daughter soundlessly. "I know everything about you, even what you wouldn't want me to know. I'm your mother, after all, and you know yourself that it's hard to hide anything from a mother. You long for your yesterday. We long here too, but for the tomorrow that they took from us. We will soon meet somewhere halfway between our two longings . . ."

Something rustled in the darkness, and Sarah woke up. She rubbed the tip of her nose as if she wanted to convince herself that she was still here, and that the weak sunshine that fell onto her bed from the window was of this world. But perhaps the opposite: perhaps the traces of cold on the tip of her nose were the remnants of her mother's touch. She again heard a soft rustling noise coming in through the open door of her bedroom. Because of her age, her eyes didn't work right, but her ears were always on guard, like those of an old cat. No, so far as she had heard there were no mice here in these houses. Maybe it was some sort of bug?

———

Almost all her life, except for the three and a half years of her war-induced homelessness, and later during David's work in the village, she had lived in her parents' house. Her father had been mistaken: ironically, danger lurked over him not on wealthy Church Street but on a faraway little street that Sarah wasn't even sure had a name. After returning to Beltsy in May 1944, they found that their street had suffered very little damage. Here and there a door, a window, or a shutter was missing—wooden items. So she moved back into her ancestral home, and later also brought her husband, David, there. Every now and then she would wake up in the middle of the night because of a rap on the windowpane, and she would lie there on her back with her eyes closed, listening to the sounds of the house. After what she had experienced, after the homelessness, she understood that one's own walls are not just bricks and mortar; they absorb the living breath of the people in the house. The walls themselves breathe, or else they fall ill, become covered with mold, crumble, and finally collapse. Her first act after crossing the threshold of the abandoned house was to spread mortar and lime on the walls. She had never before had occasion to do that, but after her first clumsy movements the work went smoothly for her, with a sort of special zeal, as if she had grown up not in the house of a wheat merchant but in a peasant's cottage. They told her that several Romanian officers had lived in her father's house during the period of her wandering and imprisonment. The mortar, mixed with stinking horse manure, and the harsh, thickly cooked lime, were supposed to eat away and carve away from every little crack and nick in the walls and ceiling every memory of those temporary owners. She cleaned the plank floors with boiling water mixed with red pepper, and only then scraped them with a kitchen knife, as if she could thereby peel away the traces of their boots.

Sarah remembered that after everything was done she had sunk down in the middle of the freshened, empty living room, precisely on the spot where the whole family used to sit down at the table every Sabbath and holiday, and burst into tears. She had realized that she would never be able to carve and peel away the traces and marks, the nicks and scars on her heart and memory. Where could she get a tool that would be capable of sealing away her pain, so the world shouldn't ever need it again!?

–5–

Right after Fira's telephone call, Ilik called from Germany. His sister had told him that she didn't like the way their mother sounded. Sarah listened to her son's voice and tried to picture his face. She hadn't seen him for more than six years. His father-in-law and the whole household hadn't wanted to hear about emigrating to Israel; it was either America or Germany. There wasn't anyone to sponsor them in America, so the Germans took pity on them. Ilik had proposed that his parents and sister should go with them too, so as not to break up the family, but David had answered him: "I was there once already, and one doesn't jump into the same river twice." Did the son understand that his father meant the river of blood that the Germans had shed, Sarah wondered? Whether he understood or not, he went. Sarah herself would have died of horror looking out the window every day and seeing German faces.

And yet Ilik remained the apple of her eye. With his birth she had taken revenge on the desolate, dark forces that wanted to eradicate the Jewish people from the world. It's possible that at that time she herself didn't mean to go that far, but in her heart, that's how she felt. Ilik didn't constitute just one life; above all Sarah saw in him a continuation of her nephew, Chaya's little son.

"I'm very glad you called, Ilik—your voice has filled me with joy." She pushed aside her kerchief with the telephone receiver and pressed it even more strongly to her ear, so her cheeks felt the pressure. "You don't have to be upset. Of course I miss you all, but tell me, rather—what did the doctor tell you? Well thank God! Here they write that eating fried green nuts is good for cholesterol. Do you have green nuts where you are? And how does Rima feel? When is she due? Any day now? Let's hope that everything goes well with her."

The loose knot on the green kerchief got even looser and came away from the two corners. The cloth slowly slipped down and remained hanging on a shoulder. Her precisely cut hair became rumpled.

Her mother's heart swelled with pride: with God's will, her Ilik would soon become a grandfather. He himself had been just a little rascal not so long ago. She used to see him running around the courtyard in his red pantaloons, all excited, riding on a stick. At that time they lived in the town of Sîngera, not far from Beltsy; David had been sent there to set up an elementary school. Ilik's pantaloons apparently got the turkey excited; it ran around the courtyard all puffed up as if it owned the place. They were almost the same size, Ilik and the turkey. By the time his mother came running out of the house, the turkey was sitting on her son, but the little fellow wouldn't surrender—he called out for help and waved his stick around trying to hit the turkey on the head.

"Do you remember your red pantaloons and the turkey, Ilik?" his mother asked, a question unexpected by her and even more so by her son. But she quickly recouped—that was not what she had intended to say. "I wanted to ask you to remember that your father did a lot for you, and if, God willing, Rima has a boy—hear me out, Ilik—David is a very beautiful name, even in Germany. As you know yourself, Ilik."

It had already been a few seconds since they had said goodbye, but Sarah was still pressing the telephone receiver to her ear. The brief monotone sounds removed her farther and farther from the somewhat nervous voice of her son. He had always been hot-headed, easily excited—not an easy child even when he was very little. Of course David would have found some remedy for that.

She continued the conversation, but now with herself. Ilik had had a good head for studying, and though Sarah had never known when he was doing his homework, the teachers praised him at all their meetings. His behavior in school was another matter. She used to get frequent notes from the teachers saying that Ilik had interrupted the geography lesson or had had a fight during intermission, that they had caught him and two other boys smoking in the bathroom, and that he had run away from classes several times. Sarah used to hide the "good tidings" from David, both because she wanted to spare her husband—busy and exhausted at work, day and night—and out of fear that her husband's punishment would be too harsh. Given Ilik's character, that could lead to even more harm. But suddenly Ilik seemed to change—in eighth grade he fell in love. The girl, Bella, was a year older than he, but she was a student at the same school. Sarah knew her parents well, as often happens in small towns. Her father worked at the market, in a buffet restaurant, and his wife helped him there—not a very distinguished pedigree. On the other hand, who was thinking about things getting very serious at that point? Young children—today they fall in love, tomorrow they get disappointed! Youth is like a fresh breeze: it touches you, then runs away. Sarah herself had once felt the touch, but it was a fiery wind, not a breeze, and it turned her whole generation into ash and dust.

After finishing school, Bella went to Siberia to study medicine—her two older brothers had already studied there. About a year later, Ilik went there too, essentially chasing after her. Even David couldn't talk him into studying somewhere closer to them where they wouldn't be separated, especially since he had received a gold medal upon graduating from school. And now, with God's help, their little daughter, Rima, would soon become a mother.

Sarah put the dried slices of bread into a clean pillowcase. She did it slowly, looking at both sides of each slice as if some sort of blemish could make her work unkosher, God forbid. Shaking her head in satisfaction, she moved with short little steps down the line of bread slices—from the kitchen to the salon—and again thought to herself: she had good children: Ilik, Fira. Both had received a good education, had become skilled specialists in their professions, had married successfully, and had stood up on their own two feet . . . For a moment she stopped, as if the lines of dry bread had suddenly scattered and crumbled and thereby interrupted the cheerful course of her thoughts. Where was she now? Oh, yes—homelessness; the word had swum up again, like a blob of oil on the water, and had hidden their dear names and faces. They were all now on the road, refugees, without a place to call their own—walking homelessly throughout the world. Was this the option that her David (may he rest in peace) had claimed was the only one they had?

-6-

She had known David since their childhood; they were even sort of relatives. He lived with his parents in Ungen, a hop, skip, and a jump from Iași. Actually she had seen David just once, and she remembered him as a skinny, bashful young man with big, round glasses and a high forehead, upon which an oily forelock fell. He was older than she was, and even before she saw him she had heard two things about him: "he's a genius" and "the whole family is reflected in that young man." What those two expert opinions meant, Sarah sensed rather than understood; her father had sort of squeezed the words out, with heartfelt emotion—they had virtually welled up out of him, something that happened very seldom. That sentiment had actually aroused her curiosity.

The guests from Ungen didn't stay very long; they hurried to the railroad station, which was three blocks away from their house. Such "passengers" used to look in on them frequently. They would say hello and sometimes have a glass of tea with jam. Why her father was so taken with that young man, Sarah didn't understand; he sat there the whole time the older folks were discussing things and picked at crumbs of cake from the slice that was lying on his plate. Except that her father had once said: "A boy is someone who can say Kaddish for you, and two girls won't even be able to say a single Kaddish!"

The bashful boy went away and Sarah quickly forgot him, as one forgets the whistle of a departing train. Later she heard a few more times about David—also with special pride in her father's voice— that the young man was now studying in the best gymnasium in

Iaşi, among the 2 percent of Jewish children that were permitted to be accepted there. "You remember him, of course, Sarah?" her father asked, and the girl, making believe she was trying hard to remember, shook her head no, and added: "I don't remember." Just before the Russians came, her mother told her that she had received some not-so-good news from Ungen. "Little David (you know whom I mean) has been arrested by the Romanian secret police," and added in a whisper "He was hanging around with leftists." The Soviets saved David from being sentenced. Sarah found out about that years later, after the war. David was demobilized from the army and came to Beltsy to look for work. At that time, Sarah was working as a cashier at the city mill. He too barely remembered the single meeting with Sarah's parents in their house, but his father, who had remained in Ungen, had given him the address of their relatives in Beltsy, just in case. He really didn't know whether any of the Nusnboims were still alive.

They met in her house. Dressed in his army khakis and boots polished to a purple shine, and a dark, narrow-shouldered civilian jacket, David looked like many other demobilized Jewish fellows that one could encounter on the streets of Beltsy. Returning to the surrounding villages where they had grown up, they found empty, burned-down remnants of their parents' ravaged homes, and they also heard from their Gentile neighbors half-true stories about the murder of their families. With permanently entrenched pain and choked curses for their surroundings, they abandoned the places where they had suddenly become distanced strangers and set out on a path where only memory could embrace them, there to hide on their thousands of twisting paths. There, in their memories, they erected the strongest of headstones for their parents, little sisters and brothers, aunts and uncles, and numerous cousins—headstones that were absent from the mass graves overgrown with tall, succulent grass. In mourning, they came to the larger cities to look for a new beginning.

Sarah and David had tea, with cookies that she had recently gotten at work as a gift in honor of the thirtieth anniversary of the October Revolution. David took off his glasses and set them down next to him on the table. That was what the head bookkeeper, Abraham Katz, did at work too before he looked into the thick ledgers, because with his bird-like nose, his glasses almost slid right off when he looked down. Sarah barely restrained herself from asking why he wore glasses since he could read without them, but she was afraid of him because he was very strict and didn't have any sense of humor.

David didn't look strict, but sitting there late at night with a strange young man, just the two of them, even if he was a distant relative, created a certain tension between them. She suddenly recalled how years ago they had been sitting at the same table this way and drinking tea: her parents, Chaya, and Chaya's fiancé, Semyon. Her mother had later called that tea-drinking episode a "Soviet-style engagement contract." The memory that had come up made her head whirl, as if she were looking at a splinter from a broken mirror. Sarah started trembling and burned her mouth on the boiling water. Tears welled up in her eyes. She pressed her palm against her mouth, not knowing, poor thing, what to do next, so foolish did the whole thing seem.

David raised his head to her. He put on his glasses and exclaimed: "Rub your left earlobe a couple of times with your right hand." Sarah, like a good pupil, carried out her assigned task precisely. She rubbed her ear that way for a while, and suddenly they both broke out laughing.

That joke remained in their family permanently, and when one of the children, Ilik or Fira, would burn his or her tongue, you could hear right away: "Rub your left ear with your right hand!" But that late autumn evening was the beginning of their further path, which at that time looked like a very smooth one. About a week later, David found work in the sugar factory, and a week after that they registered as husband and wife. They brought David's father to them from Ungen, and life went on. But, as Sarah's mother, may she rest in peace, used to say, even the smoothest road is full of stones at the beginning.

Soon they sent David to a village not far from Sîngera to agitate the peasants to sign up for the collective farm. Rejecting such an important mission didn't even occur to him—he was, after all, a Communist, and he had received his party card during the thick of things, at the front in 1943. Though the village was not far from Beltsy, they had to part. Probably she didn't understand, with her woman's brain, some of the things that her David surely did understand, but Sarah had heard in the mill office where she worked that the peasants were putting up resistance. Pending the final establishment of the collective farm, the authorities picked up whole families in the villages and took them by night, on little wagons, to the railroad station, where freight cars guarded by soldiers were already waiting for them . . .

Sometimes, on Sundays, David came home. Blackened and exhausted, he would take a bath in the big, wide zinc tub. Sarah never knew for sure whether he would come on a particular Sunday or not, but she always had a store of hot water standing ready on the stove. Sidling up behind him, she would pour warm water over his bony, slightly stooped shoulders, and then would scrub them with a hard, heavily soaped sponge brush. David would groan, clamp his lips shut, and gradually come to himself. Then, when he had recovered somewhat, he would fall onto the bed like he was dead. In the middle of the night he would wake up. Sarah would be lying there with her eyes shut, half-dozing, trembling, and longing for him to touch her. A single touch was enough for her body to respond immediately and embrace him lustily.

The pale dawn, like a feeble bandit, would break in through the window of their bedroom and slowly move from the floor to the wall next to their bed. She knew that only a few minutes remained for her and her husband to share their closeness. Time would run out and he would get up and say again, as he did every time: "There's no other choice." And that's the way it went for months.

Meanwhile, Sarah was pregnant, and her father-in-law, Nakhum, with whom she still used the formal form of you but called Dad, helped her a lot with the housework. Those times were difficult. In the summer, it was dangerously hot, the fields became parched, and even the bit of reserve supplies that the peasants had stored and hidden were confiscated, down to the last corn stalk, on account of the plan that the newly created collective farm had to present to the government. A terrible famine took hold in the villages. In the city, on the streets near the railroad station, there appeared crowds of Moldavians with thin, home-knit feedbags over their shoulders. Their woolen caps barely stayed on their heads, which were more like dried-out skulls with a mop of hair. They ran their hands through fences, which excited the dogs, who apparently had a special taste for beggars who were looking forward to something more to chew on than a coin.

One time when they were returning home from work, Sarah encountered a person who was sitting on the ground and leaning back against a tree. Her first thought was that he was a drunk, but when he raised his head toward her with great effort, she immediately understood everything. When she got home, she looked for the big, cast-iron five-liter pot and started cooking a *mamelige*. Her father-in-law was astonished: "What happened? Are you expecting a lot of guests?" Sarah mixed the *mamelige* with a rolling pin, and she felt anger rising within her, like the *mamelige* in the pot. She herself couldn't understand why such anger was bubbling up, and didn't know whom she should let it out on, so her father-in-law became an innocent victim. She screamed her heart out, not looking at him: "People in the streets are dying like flies, and nobody cares!" David's father certainly understood what Sarah meant. He could probably have remained silent, or agreed with his pregnant daughter-in-law, but when she turned her head toward him, he, looking her in the eyes, quietly but firmly said: "And when many of their people were butchering our women and children, did anybody care?"

Her father-in-law carried the pot with the cooked *mamelige* outside. Sarah had already prepared a stool covered with a white handkerchief, onto which Nakhum poured out the *mamelige*. He then bent over the golden loaf, which was still steaming, and cut it into pieces with a thick white thread, as any Bessarabian would have done. Straightening his hat on his head, he went over to the door, which had just closed behind his daughter-in-law. *Mamelige* now appeared at the courtyard door two, or sometimes three, times a week, as long as the half-sack of cornmeal that Sarah had received as a supplement to her pay lasted.

$-7-$

Sarah was now lying in bed, covered by a quilt that she had brought from "there." She had to listen to her family's biting comments about that too: "Who needs such a warm thing in Israel?" And even if I don't need it, the housewife had thought to herself, can you waste such a quilt? After all, the quilt had preserved the closeness of the two of them, Sarah and David; how many secrets had it kept? How many terrors had it hidden? And now she was sharing her loneliness and her memories with the quilt . . .

They lived in Sîngera for five years. Sarah went to live with her husband after Ilik was born. By then they had transferred David to a new job: to set up the local village school. And he, as was his custom, got fervently involved in the new mission. Within a year, the school was the best in the district. They started sending David to various teachers' conferences and seminars; delegations kept constantly coming to the village "to learn from their experience" and the school's principal, a Moldavian woman, would boast about the achievements that were supposedly hers. Of course that annoyed David, but he never showed it; only at night did he "bring it under the quilt."

After a governmental teachers' seminar in Kishinev, he received an unofficial recommendation to study at the Beltsy Pedagogical Institute. He received it with joy, because studying was his greatest dream. Sarah also didn't sit still; she finished accelerated courses for teaching elementary school and became a teacher at the kindergarten that David had established at the school. And Ilik was also always under her supervision. They were happy and satisfied in those days. It appeared that it was precisely in a village that Jews had avoided going to after the war that the Wechsler family could find a home. They lived in an annex to the school—actually it was a rather large classroom separated from the main corridor. Later the city council gave them their own little house, with a courtyard and a little stable where Sarah kept several chickens, two ducks, and a turkey. Who knows—perhaps they would have settled in Sîngera permanently. David was particularly pleased to be part of the "village intelligentsia," as he called it. The parents of the schoolchildren frequently came to him for advice, and David, with his total seriousness, would receive them and listen to them, though their questions had more to do with what was going on in the vicinity than with the children's studies. But at night, under the quilt, seeing David turn from side to side, unable to fall asleep, his wife would quietly whisper to his back: "I beg you—be careful with your words. They'll soon see that you . . ." David would remain silent, and his silence frightened her even more.

And that, indeed, was what happened. They say that a man thinks with his head and a woman—with her heart. Did Sarah not feel that David's openness and belief in what he was doing would end up working against him? It seems that only he, David, didn't see that the principal was already green with envy because the school was actually being run by her surrogate, the Jew Mr. Wechsler—the students loved him and the teachers came to him for help. Well—they didn't have long to wait for the denunciation. One day they called David into the district center; they sent a car for him and immediately removed him from the school . . .

Old Sarah curled up under the quilt and held her breath, as if she could hide from the dark days that had flown in like birds when she herself had stirred them up and let them out of the cage of time. Now they had burst in on her current loneliness from those distant sleepless nights when she, having laid her son, who had fallen asleep, down in their bed, would lie down next to him, still in her dress, just taking off her shoes.

———

She needed to feel Ilik's breath on her face; she was like a watchdog ready to throw itself upon and tear apart anyone who presents a danger.

When she found out that they had taken David away, the accursed heat immediately gave her a headache. Was that bestial fear for one's life now going to return? She looked at Ilik, who was playing on the floor with a toy car, and her first thought was: I won't give the child up!

A few days later, they let David come home. That miracle occurred because the denunciation fell into the hands of a person who had known David during his prewar underground days when they were cellmates in prison. Now that person occupied a high position in Kishinev. He told David that he had been accused in the "alarm" letter of "Romanian nationalism." It was written in black and white that he had supposedly made fun of the Moldavian language, saying that it was, after all, only the same old Romanian language but littered with Russian words, and that substituting the Cyrillic alphabet for the Roman one was nonsensical.

In those days, such a denunciation was enough to cause the accused to be sent to the distant North for many, many years. David's highly placed friend told him to leave the village and go back to Beltsy; there he would help him find work, but he should forget about doing any further teaching.

They went back home to Beltsy. During all those years, David's father had ruled the roost there alone; only occasionally would he pop into the village to spend a little time with his grandchild. Sarah decided to rent out the two rooms in which Chaya and Semyon had lived after the wedding and in which their son had been born. Why let them stand empty when many people needed a roof over their head, to say nothing of the fact that the bit of rent would come in handy? And it did come especially in handy during the first days after they returned to Beltsy, when they had to begin a new period of their life.

David's friend kept his word; he helped David get a job in a construction firm, as a warehouse manager. That was just the first step on his new road, which also had plenty of stones. About a year later, Fira was born. Even during the pregnancy, Sarah's father-in-law pleaded with them to name the girl—and he was certain it would be a girl—after his prematurely deceased wife, Fira. "After all, David became an orphan at the age of ten," he told his daughter-in-law. "His mother has been lying in her grave for so many years without having anyone to carry on her name." Sarah was moved, though her own mother didn't have anyone named after her either. She had known that David had lost his mother very early, but the way her father-in-law spoke about his wife elicited memories of her own father. Sarah had never heard her father raise his voice when he was speaking to her mother— Madame Nusnboim—though her mother had been capable of exploding suddenly, getting red in the face, to the point that it took a while for her to calm down. Sometimes when Sarah happened to be present at such a scene, she would tremble as she looked at her father: would he yell at her mother too? But her mother's voice would echo for a few moments and slowly fade away as she remained silent after her sudden outburst. Only then would she hear her father's soft voice: "Madam Nusnboim—don't yell so! You'll awaken God, heaven forbid!" and her mother, with a wave of her hand, would say, now in a completely different tone of voice: "Go already, go!"

Nakhum died two weeks after Fira was born. Suddenly. One afternoon he was seized by a sudden pain in his chest; he took a heart pill, lay down on the couch, and never got up again. Sarah, having now lived a lifetime herself, thought: "Even in dying you have to be lucky." Her father-in-law had had an easy death—he had hardly felt anything. Her father had been lucky too, he had felt nothing at all. But his special good fortune was that he hadn't lived to see his Madam Nusnboim die in great pain and suffering; it was a great privilege not to live to see a loved one breathing her last. Sarah didn't have such luck; she was fated to see the death of many of her loved ones. Was that punishment, revenge, or perhaps payback for the fact that she was the only one in her family to remain alive?!

———

Sarah had a sudden slash of pain from her neck up to her right eye. She had indeed taken her pills, but on the other hand, pills that could help people forget their troubles had not yet been invented. Her doctor in Beltsy had told her that many years ago. She had been lying in the hospital for a whole month, paralyzed by a stroke. Too many things had come together in her life at that time for her to find her way out alone and remain whole. Fira had a difficult pregnancy; no matter what she ate, it immediately came back up and she vomited bile. She and Misha were then living in Kishinev, and Sarah had had to ask each time for leave from her work in the kindergarten and run to help out. It couldn't go on that way for very long—how long could they go on using substitutes for her, despite her good relationships with the other teachers and the kindergarten's administration? But it was not only that . . .

It had been quite a while now that she had been walking around with heartache. No stone on her road had been as heavy as the one she had been carrying in recent days and nights. And if the burden got lost amid other worries during the day, it rose up again at night. The bitter coldness between her and her husband was still lying frozen on their bed. Sarah knew the woman who was apparently the culprit; she worked in the municipal library and had a husband and a grown daughter. Sarah was probably guilty herself for David's having a whirl with the librarian. True, she had no time to read books and magazines, except children's books that she got at work and read to her children. She also never put on pretty clothes, to say nothing of expensive creams. Her little bit of lip pomade lasted her a whole year. Her dresses and underwear? She wasn't going naked, God forbid, and she wouldn't allow herself to waste money on rags. First Ilik was going to university, and then Fira. To provide enough for children to be far from home was not easy. Then to marry them off . . . True, her David had gotten far, had been appointed to manage the whole construction company, but hadn't she played a role in that?

Nevertheless, she didn't dare speak to him about the librarian. Something held her back, but exactly what she could never explain, and truth be told, she didn't want to. She just swallowed it—God forbid if the children find out—so she waited and waited . . . That's how things were going for her in life, one stone brought out another one. She collapsed at work and when she awoke she was already in the hospital. Her right side was paralyzed and her face twisted. David was the first one she recognized. He stroked her hand, but she could neither feel it nor his stroking. His face and the white hospital gown he had thrown over his shoulders were the same color. He smiled to her, with a sort of teary smile, and she didn't understand right away what he was saying to her: "Little Fira has given birth to a boy. They're calling him Naum, Naum, after my father Nokhum . . ."

– 8 –

Her neck was aching. She drew her head down into her shoulders, the way one corks up the narrow neck of a bottle; perhaps that would help quiet the pain and not let it spread throughout her body. Holding her breath and half closing her eyes, she squeezed into bed and waited for the spasm to pass. It was apparently a little clot—the old lady tried to picture what was happening in her brain—that it had gotten stuck in a little artery and didn't let the blood pulse through her brain. After her stroke, she had been haunted for quite a while by the fear that at any minute an arm or a leg would be taken from her. She would immediately start to rub her fingers and pinch her body till it hurt, but ironically, feeling pain would calm her. With time, she forgot her fear. In addition, she learned to accommodate to her pain and the illness she was avoiding. Sarah was always sickly but in the end it was David who died first.

David had started feeling sick several weeks before they were supposed to emigrate. At that point they had already sold the house in Beltsy and had moved to Fira's place in Kishinev. She immediately took him to the best doctors and put him in the best hospital; one test, another test—the doctors were still not sure, but they suspected he had liver cancer. Then came the day to fly to Israel, and Israel suddenly began to look like a remedy. Sarah remembered that once, when she was a child, a poor man had come to their house. He was an old man with a long, gray beard, like something from a story. It turned out that the man was a distant relative of her mother's, a Hasid of the Sadigura Rebbe. Her mother immediately sat him down at the table, gave him something to eat, asked questions, listened. When he was about to leave, the old man pulled two slender, red strings out of his breast pocket and gave them to Sarah's mother. Those strings, he explained, had been given to him by another Hasid, who had brought them from Israel, from the holy city of Jerusalem. For quite a long time, Sarah and Chaya carried the little red strings close to them, as a "means of assuring a favorable eye," as their mother put it.

After learning that David was dangerously ill, their emigration to Israel, which till then had made Sarah tremble, acquired a completely different aspect—a hope that they could save David there. There they should have the best Jewish brains and the best medicines. She clung to Israel like a little red string that helps with all problems.

From the airport, they took David immediately to a hospital not far from Tel Aviv, and they took the family to Nazareth Illit. Fira and Misha visited him in the hospital a few times, but Sarah never saw him alive again.

Sarah's thoughts started getting confused. Perhaps she would actually fall asleep. She had been unable to fall asleep at night ever since the beautiful Edith and the two young Sabras had visited her. During the day, she could still doze off while reading a newspaper, but the nights were tearing her to pieces, sucking the life out of her. Sleeping pills didn't help, and they made her confused. After the night when she saw her mother in her dreams, strange things had actually started happening to her. First of all she had realized that she didn't know where Fira had hidden the key to the "you-shouldn't-need-it" room. Why she needed that key, Sarah didn't yet understand. She just thought it would be nice to know where the key to that door had gotten to. After that, she remembered that she had awakened one night because she heard a rustling noise. She had begun looking all over the almost empty apartment, searching in corners, moving the couch, and looking in the kitchen cabinets. She hadn't found anything, but nevertheless Sarah had thought, and even said out loud, that she should have Valya buy insect repellent. While wandering around that way with her broom in her hand, Sarah stopped in front of the locked door, and again something struck her: where in the world could she have hidden it, that darn key? She felt that the door was starting to attract her, like her mother's jars in the old days, with their sweet snacks "you shouldn't need them." Only that night did the old lady first remember where the key might be. She immediately went over to the closet in her bedroom, took a dark brown, lacquered basket down from the shelf, and with a trembling heart opened it. In the inner, sewed-in pocket, she touched the key with two fingers. She glowed like a child who had found a lost toy while playing find the treasure. She used to divide the children in her class into two groups: one group hid the treasure and the other one had to find it. Sarah herself used to get caught up in the game, and like the children, she would go searching for the treasure. Her many years teaching kindergarten became part of her daily routine; it became part of her character and behavior; it could be seen in her relationships with people and things, and was part of her habits, thoughts, and speech. Her own children had long been out of diapers and had themselves become parents, but Sarah still reminded them to wash their hands before they sat down to eat, or to go to the bathroom before leaving the house.

She would press the treasure she found to her heart and praise herself the same way she praised the children: "Good girl, Sarah—she who looks, finds!" She went to bed satisfied and fell asleep immediately.

She snapped out of her noisy puttering around—after all, she had searched and swept out every corner of her apartment. Except the "you-shouldn't-need-it" room. She pricked up her ears and turned them in the direction from which she had heard the rustling. For a moment there in the dark she thought there was a thin wire that ran from her ear to the door through which the sounds on its other side vibrated. The wire made them louder, doubled them, and by the time the rustling reached Sarah's ear they had grown into a terrible screeching. She cried out briefly and covered her ears with her palms . . .

The old lady sat down on her bed, with her feet hanging down, and silently swung them back and forth, like a mourner who had already wept all her tears. "Just look," she complained, "on one pan of the scales is a bunch of years, and on the other one is just one moment—and the moment has outweighed the years." For how many years had the dull sounds of screeching and scraping on walls followed her before she could drive them from her memory? And there you are: after so much time, they're here again. In a single moment, the frightful sounds had escaped from their imprisonment and started pursuing her.

———

Everything stood there before her eyes—as clearly as only a dream can be: her sister Chaya and her little child, Ilik. He wasn't able to walk yet, but he had learned to move: tucking one foot under him, he leaned on his little hands and got up on his free foot. He moved quickly, like a little animal with a broken paw, and when the two sisters weren't looking, he scampered up to the wall in the blink of an eye and made scratches on it with his nails. He scraped off the plaster and stuffed the crumbled pieces greedily into his mouth, so no one could take away his "food." His teeth had barely emerged, but he sucked the pieces of wet plaster and smacked his lips over them as if they were sweet candy, something which he had never in his short life tasted. His little fingers were bloodied, and his nails were torn off and broken. Chaya never scolded him; she would wrap up his injured fingers with little rags and repeat the same words every time: "The child wants to live!"

Ilik was born prematurely, about four months before the war began. It was a miracle that Chaya had enough milk; actually she had more than enough—like a milk cow after grazing. Her few blouses were always soaked with the sticky, turbid fluid that Ilik never stopped sucking. Chaya herself looked like a shadow with two bloated breasts— manna in the desert of hunger and sickness. During that first wartime winter, they all fell ill with typhus—first their mother, then Sarah, and then Chaya and Ilik. They had already taken her mother's body away by the time Sarah recovered. Barely able to lift herself, she saw next to her a little heap of rags with something stirring beneath them. Probably a rat, was her first clear thought after being out of it. But from amid the rags, the skinny white leg of a little child emerged; after that, a wrinkled little face was unveiled, with his blue lips clinging to Chaya's swollen nipple. From the corner of his mouth, lice were crawling over his neck like a black thread . . .

Sarah was still swaying on her bed, as if with that movement she could quiet down the suffocating wave of memories and rock herself to sleep.

"The child wants to live . . ." Those few words nourished and encouraged both sisters, didn't let them fall while they were being driven along the soaking wet, bloody autumn road that was slippery under their half-bare, injured feet like a giant, fat earthworm, that tried to throw them off and leave them lying in the narrow ditch at its edge. The bullets of a Romanian gendarme would soon console them and forgive everything. Their maid, Manya, was left lying in just such a ditch after two days on the road from Tulchyn to the Pechora death camp.

They stayed in the Tulchyn ghetto till the end of November. The rumors that they would drive the Bessarabian Jews farther, to some sort of camp near the Bug River, had been going around for a week already. After that, however, they heard that the members of the community council had given the commander a nice bribe and he had promised not to bother anybody. It didn't take long till they heard a knock on the window and someone was crying out, weeping: "Oh people—they took our gold and silver, made promises, and played us for fools!" Sarah tried to picture it: What does a camp mean? A piece of empty ground surrounded by a barbed-wire fence? Perhaps earthen huts or stalls? She knew the answer, though she stubbornly rejected it: "They're driving us all to our deaths!"

Dragging themselves along, they reached the village of Pechora on the third day. It had already begun to get dark. A white, three-story building that could be seen from all directions stood on a hill. It had once been Count Potocki's palace. After the revolution, Red Army officers had rested and recuperated there. The building was enclosed by a high, brick wall, and the newly arrived residents of the "sanatorium" were driven through an iron gate into its large courtyard. As they passed the portal, the Jews who were already there started to run toward them, looking for relatives, neighbors, and acquaintances. One shouted over the other. Hot tears and a bit of joy at seeing one another alive again warmed the cold evening. Jewish names, accompanied by sobbing and weeping, echoed in the air, but they were interrupted by angry, curt cries and commands by the camp police, who enforced their words with sticks and whips.

The mother, both sisters, and the child were driven into a narrow corner room on the second floor; there was probably room there to set up six beds, not more, but they stuffed about forty people into the former courtroom. They sat and slept on the floor with their legs stretched out; lying on their sides or bending their knees was impossible.

The next day a quarantine was declared. The peasants from the village were not allowed to approach the gate. The Jews couldn't trade for anything, not even a few potatoes, a handful of beans, or a bit of seed pressings. They weren't given any food, or anything to drink either. They could get water only from the river or from melting snow. There was no place to bathe or wash their meager clothing, to say nothing of getting a piece of soap. The lice ate people alive. Typhus and dysentery felled young and old. Often they couldn't open a door because a dead body was lying on the other side of it. Dead or dying people were lying around in the hallway and on the stairs. They had to run into the courtyard to move their bowels; they dug a broad ditch there for that purpose, but it was seldom that anyone got to use it—they would relieve themselves wherever they happened to be. There wasn't any air to breathe, for those who could still breathe; it seemed as if their noses, throats, and lungs were stuffed with excrement. The dead bodies were collected once a week; they were thrown onto little wagons and taken to a mass grave near the river. It got quieter and quieter every day. People stopped talking or arguing. They avoided talking about the homes they had left and family they had lost along the road. Seldom did any of the women mention what she used to cook. The word "food" itself sounded as if one were talking from fever. Ilik lost his strength completely; he even stopped crying. Their mother died during that first frosty winter. Neither Sarah nor Chaya could get up to accompany her to her burial, or even lift their eyes to see her being taken away.

– 9 –

The old lady walked around confused all morning. She was pursued by the sleepless night, and she kept throwing sharp glances at the "you-shouldn't-need-it" room. She even put her ear to it and held her breath. She stood that way for a while, then quietly, as if she were afraid to wake someone up or frighten him, tiptoed to the kitchen to prepare something to eat. Then the opposite: she began making noise with the pots—she pulled them out of the cupboard and set them in place; then she started washing the few dishes, though that made no sense whatsoever because they were already clean. When she finally turned on the faucet, the stream of water gave a powerful spurt into the sink. She hadn't done that since she came to Israel—water here was more expensive than milk. Here she had had to relearn how to wash dishes with as little water as possible. The knife slipped out of her hand and fell onto the stone floor. She had definitely not done that intentionally. "Is that for better or worse?" she thought. Sarah remembered that Manya, the maid, used to say that if you drop a knife onto the floor you should be careful of a sharp tongue.

She looked at the clock: a quarter to twelve already, and Valya had not yet come. It was Monday, wasn't it? She had begun to doubt whether it was really the day that Valya came to her. Where in the world was she? For a moment, the old lady felt lost. Maybe today was a different day? She looked around, searching for the calendar. She had always had a calendar in Belz hanging in the kitchen, next to the icebox. Every morning, right after she woke up and while she was still in her nightgown, she would go into the kitchen and tear off yesterday's sheet. Though she was not superstitious, she had a reason for tearing it off not in the evening before going to bed but at daybreak, when everyone else in the house, David and the children, was still dozing: at night, the terrors came—everything around her felt insecure; at night, the soul leaves the body, her mother used to say, and it comes back in the morning, or else it remains forever lost somewhere along the way (whether her mother meant that seriously or was being humorous remained hidden from her); but at the moment that Sarah tore off the sheet she felt that the night was over and a bright new day had begun.

Her gaze fell on the newspapers; there the date was indeed shown, but how would that help her? Having completely lost any hope of clarifying anything, she thought to herself: call Fira in Toronto or Ilik in Germany and ask them what day today is. They'll surely think that their mother has lost her mind. Suddenly she felt lost in her own thoughts and confusion, and she went over to the sofa to lie down . . .

———

Winter had passed, and after that spring had flown by, and now it was already summer outside. The sequence of time had not changed— everything remained the same as before the war: the trees in the garden had blossomed, the grass had grown, and the River Bug was still emptying its waters into the Black Sea, as it had for hundreds of years, even back in Count Potocki's time. The policeman Mishka the Cossack, always a jolly fellow, with a Cossack cap turned to one side so his mop of blond hair showed from under the cap's shiny brim, liked to say: "Why are you so sad, girls? Are things really that bad for you? There's more than enough grass—so you have something to eat! There are trees with which to hang yourselves—as many as you want! And the waters of the Bug are sufficient for you to have someplace to drown yourself! In a word—a spa!"

They were indeed allowed to go down to the Bug to bathe and wash their little bit of clothing. They would gather the branches and the fallen dry leaves in the garden and cook a watery soup on two hot bricks. The cooking was done in a rusty can that they had dug up on the river bank, a reminder of a past life. They usually cooked beans—a handful of beans was easier to smuggle in from the other side of the fence than a few potatoes. They cooked for almost a whole day. The leaves quickly burned up, but breaking off a branch, even a dry one, from a tree was not allowed—the guards would have mercilessly beaten their heads in with clubs for that. But the threat of blows didn't stop them because the power of hunger was even stronger. In the evening, the whole garden sparkled amid the trees with little fires glowing from another day of life.

At that point, Sarah and Chaya had already exchanged almost everything they had brought from Tulchyn for food. There remained only Sarah's coat and Chaya's watch, which her husband had bought her after their wedding. They had kept that for later, to exchange for a bit of food to have in their mouths during the winter. They decided to smuggle themselves out and sneak into the village. Chaya had already done that more than once while Sarah remained with Ilik. This time, all three of them went. Sarah couldn't imagine how she could stretch out her hand and beg, but the road didn't leave her much time to think about that; the danger of falling into the hands of a policeman or a gendarme, or just some peasant looking to score points with the authorities, was too great. This time they reached a point far away, perhaps twenty kilometers from Pechora, past the villages Tarasovka and Kobilyovka. They looked for paths in the woods covered by foliage and for roads that bypassed the larger villages, behind the peasants' huts and orchards, so no one would see or notice them, God forbid! By day, they sat quietly in the thick bushes, and only when evening came and the sun hid behind the mountains and the peasants returned from the fields did they go to the backyards and wait for someone to come out of the huts. Sarah never had the opportunity to stretch out her hand. When the little children saw them, they ran away, so frightening did they look. The older ones already knew who the tattered scarecrows were, and they immediately ran back into the huts. In a few minutes, a woman came out carrying a real treasure in her skirt: a piece of black bread, a few boiled potatoes, and tomatoes and cucumbers. They were even invited into the house. Watching the guests swallow everything they were given, the woman wiped away tears: "God, dear Father—when they finish with them they'll turn on us!" Ilik gorged himself like a grown-up—barely had he stuffed some jam into his mouth when he was pulling a plate of beans toward him. His little belly got bloated and hard like a drum. One could feel all the vessels in his yellowed skin, but he couldn't stop himself, poor thing— he grabbed and grabbed. At night, when they were lying somewhere in an orchard, they couldn't stop eating. They ate what had fallen from the trees: apples, pears, and plums. Their bowels got upset, but they found the strength to put up with the cramps and diarrhea.

They had their own method of smuggling themselves out of the camp. Ilik already knew that if his mother and aunt bound their white kerchiefs on their heads it was a good sign: "Giddyup, we're going to look for *mili*"—that's what he called milk. Usually they would go out after noon. Huddling in the grass near the path that led down to the river, they would wait till the policeman went into the building. When his back was to the trees, they would go onto the path and quickly go down to the Bug, managing to hide in the dense rushes till the police-man came back. When he returned to his post near the river, he would walk around for a while and then get busy with things "above him." That would be the right time: plunging their naked feet into the slimy muck of the river bottom, they would move along the bank, bent over and hidden from malevolent eyes by a wall of thick green rushes. In that way, they would get to the narrow path that led to the first huts in the village of Pechora. It was there that they were especially liable to be caught—the iron gate and the guardhouse next to it were right next to the road in to the village. Fortunately, the watchmen were almost always drunk; sleepy and dazed by the sun, they would fall over snoring.

Pechora, a large village, was always full of policemen and gen-darmes. The locals had already gotten used to the hungry residents of the "sanatorium," and they pretended not to see the sneaking shadows going back and forth. Only the dogs and the little boys would run after them, the former with angry barking and the latter throwing stones, as they had previously done with the Gypsies. What was important was to get out of the village as quickly as possible. More than once they had occasion to drop to the ground and wish it would swallow them up so they wouldn't fall into the hands of a local policeman or a

Romanian gendarme. Ilik knew that he mustn't cry—mustn't let out a peep. Only his little eyes, dark like his father's, shouted his fear.

Eight kilometers from the camp, after the village of Bortnik, they would come to the forest. There they could catch their breath. It was good to suddenly feel like a wild animal, completely free. Their feet, bruised from going barefoot, and their wounded bodies, bitten by lice and flies, were healed by the cool forest brooks. They would spread out their washed clothing to dry on the grass and stones, and they themselves, bathed and rinsed—clean as if they had just come from the Creator's hand—would loll in the sunny meadow that suddenly became transformed into a golden sailboat that had swum out of a dark dream. But any rustle they heard, like a wave of human hatred, would easily overturn and swallow up the sailboat.

After three or four days of wandering on the open roads and paths, they would go back to the camp. It only seemed that escaping to freedom made them free; actually the chain of their enslavement snaked through the dust after each of them. The high brick wall of the Pechora camp followed them step by step, and no matter how far away they got, they constantly felt its stony coldness on their foreheads, as if they were constantly leaning against it.

Sarah woke up. Someone was ringing the doorbell. She stood up with difficulty, went over to the door, and opened it. It was her aide, Valya.

"I figured that you had dozed off," were her first words.

Sarah looked both sleepy and astonished.

"Is today really Monday and not some other day?" she stammered.

"Definitely Monday. I did tell you last time that I would come this afternoon, because I had to go to the doctor with my Isaac."

Valya had now come into the room and unbuttoned her coat. But she didn't take it off—she kept talking:

"You know, my Isaac knows only three words in Hebrew: *toda* (thank you), *slikha* (excuse me), and *beseder* (OK), so I have to go to the doctor with him to explain what hurts him."

She herself burst out laughing, but quickly realized that she had nevertheless come to work.

"It's a beautiful day outside today, and here, with you, everything is closed up and stuffy. Come on, Sarah, get dressed, and meanwhile I'll open a window to air out the apartment."

The old lady didn't answer her. She remained standing facing the door and didn't move from the spot.

"Did something happen, Sarah?" asked Valya. "Do you not feel well?"

But Sarah acted as if she hadn't heard the question. Lost in her own thoughts, she exclaimed:

"I'm not going out today . . . and in general, I'd like to be alone today."

"Are you sure, Sarah?" Valya too felt tense. "Perhaps I could help you with something anyway, or if you need something . . ."

"Yes," Sarah remembered something, "Perhaps you could buy me five loaves of white bread."

"Five?" said Valya unbelievingly.

"Better six," Sarah confirmed, and pulled her purse out of the pocket of her robe.

The wonderment in Valya's eyes increased. Again she asked:

"Are you expecting visitors?"

For a moment, Sarah stopped rummaging in her purse, as if the question had returned her to her first abandoned thoughts. "I myself am going visiting," she said, so quietly that Valya, not hearing as she took the money from her, exclaimed, somewhat angrily:

"Good—if you don't want to answer, you don't have to!"

In about half an hour, she brought back the bread, and as she was leaving, she reminded Sarah:

"If you need anything, you have my telephone number. Call me and I'll come right away."

The next day, after washing up and having a glass of tea and a cookie, Sarah got to work with the knife, and soon the white slices lay precisely lined up on the breadboard.

– 10 –

The old lady had everything ready for setting out. The white pillowcase stuffed with slices of dry bread lay at her feet, and she
had the key squeezed in her hand. She wouldn't have to look for it any
more, as if she were playing "find the treasure" with herself.

The pain in her neck had quieted down; apparently the spasm
had passed. Sarah could now think clearly. Yes, of course the door to
the "you-shouldn't-need-it" room was the right address and precisely
tonight was the most suitable of all the sleepless nights till now to
open it. There she would definitely find what she needed. That's the
way it had always been, from childhood on: precisely the things they
hid in the "you-shouldn't-need-it" room came very much in handy
when you needed them. Sarah suddenly felt a surge of energy and
started to feel warm. The warmth rose slowly from the soles of her
feet to her knees and her hips, poured over her body, and filled her
empty chest with blood. She threw off her warm blanket, stood up
from the bed, and started to get dressed. She had prepared her cream-
colored dress in advance, and it lay precisely folded on the chair; also
there, under the chair, were her dark brown shoes. She didn't need
much time to get dressed, except to fiddle a bit with the buckles on
her shoes; it was hard to buckle them because her feet were swollen.
For a few moments she hesitated about whether to put on her green
kerchief or to stick the bone comb in her hair; in the end she put on
the kerchief and left the comb lying on the pillow. Pressing the white
pillowcase full of bread to her abdomen and encircling it with her two
arms, as she had done during the late months of her pregnancies, she

walked out of the bedroom, and with tiny steps approached the door of the "you-shouldn't-need-it" room.

———

This was their second winter in the Pechora camp. Sarah and Chaya had been lying huddled together on the floor for a week now, without food or drink or making any sounds. They had never lain so close together that the somewhat warmer breath of each one could graze the eyelashes of the other; Ilik had always lain between them, and they would give him their last bit of food and warmth, which both of them needed; their love had covered him on both sides like two wings, and they had guarded him tenderly. But a week ago, Ilik had died—he didn't cry, didn't beg for food. He became extinguished quietly, like a little star that had lit up out of its time and in a foreign sky.

The words "the child wants to live," which had, like an incantation or an oath, sustained the two sisters, crumbled into tiny letters that the millstones of their existence ground up and left as a pile of ash. They buried Ilik under a tree in the garden. At night, so no one would see, they dug a narrow but deep grave with a piece of tin and their own fingernails; they scraped away the half-frozen earth the way Ilik used to scrape plaster from the walls. When they returned to their sleeping place, they stretched out on the cold floor, hugged one another, and silently, each one for herself, concluded that they would never get up from that spot again. Enfeebled and forgetful, they lay for a week halfway between being and not-being.

"You must live," Chaya's voice was heard.

"What for?"

"To have a husband, children, a home."

"Do you believe that is still possible?"

"You must believe in that."

"What does believing mean? God?"

"Love—a lot of love . . ."

"The love of both of us couldn't save Ilik."

"We thought only about food."

"Hunger and cold are stronger."

"I thought so too."

"What has changed now?"

"Everything. I have outlived my son . . ."

The door to the "you-shouldn't-need-it" room opened easily—one turn of the key was sufficient. Leaving it in the lock, Sarah opened the door and crossed the threshold. She immediately saw the sunny meadow. She squinted, unused to such bright sunshine. Now she had to decide the direction in which to continue. She would surely not go back, so there remained only the way forward. Her mother's words from the dream showed her the way. She remembered: they would meet somewhere halfway down the road leading to each other.

"You must live, little sister." Chaya virtually breathed the words into Sarah's mouth and encircled them with a kiss. Sarah's dried, cracked lips surrendered—she absorbed the kiss. She felt that every blood vessel in her young body was thawing, returning to life. Her lungs drew in as much air as possible. "She needs fresh air," echoed in her ears like the distant echo of a past life. They were then on the way to the village of Kubolta for the whole summer—Sarah, her mother, and Chaya. There was a lot of fresh air and goat's milk, which a peasant woman would bring every evening in a green bottle plugged with a piece of corncob. Both sisters had to drink a glass of milk every evening at bedtime. During the morning they used to go down to the Raut River. Their mother would sit at the river bank and watch the children, and the girls used to play near the water with pebbles. Their mother strictly forbade them from going into the water alone. But one time Sarah saw a playful little fish turning and twisting in the transparent water just a yard from the shore. She was immediately enchanted by it—it turned and twisted faster and faster, as if it were in a whirlpool—now it was drawn down into the dark depths. Little Sarah stretched out her hand and was ready to catch the fish to save it, but she slipped on a round stone and fell into the whirlpool herself. She heard a whistling in her ears, her body began to expand, her blood vessels began to stretch out, and her throat went into a spasm. Sarah coughed and opened her eyes. She heard a choked cry in the distance: "Returned to life, dear God . . ."

Bending over her and smiling at her was an old woman with a green kerchief on her head. She reminded Sarah of someone, but for the moment she couldn't figure out exactly whom. Her mother? The moment that separated that recent dream from the present picture before her eyes was too long—it contained a whole lifetime.

"Who are you?" Sarah asked the old woman.

"I—am you. I've come from your future."

"Where is my sister?"

"She is no longer alive. The waters of the Bug swallowed her when you fell asleep after the kiss. It brought you back to life. It's now time to repay the debt. Come, they are waiting for us to come to them, the remnants of our yesterday."

————

It was already well into the day. The telephone had rung several times and then stopped ringing. Perhaps it had been Naum calling from Toronto, trying to reach her after coming back from a student party, or perhaps it had been Ilik calling from Hamburg, hurrying to give her the good news that he had become a grandfather, that his Rima had given birth to a girl.

Sarah is a very beautiful name, even in Germany.

September–November 2006
Brooklyn, New York

Red Shoes for Rachel

– They –

They were often seen together, the three of them: he, she, and the old lady, who was in a wheelchair. He and she were a medium-built couple, dressed modestly and in an old-fashioned way, at the age of people who had retired prematurely and were starting a new phase of their life. The old lady in the wheelchair looked like a dressed-up doll; the pink bonnet on her head, edged with a narrow red silk ribbon, suited her very well; her legs were covered by a dark-green, checkered blanket, on which rested her little fists, which were full of clumps of dark-blue veins. She would sit motionless, looking at her surroundings with two narrow, lifeless eyes, and only when the wheelchair swerved to one side of a nasty pit in the pavement or went over a pebble would her head shake slightly for a few moments, like that of a porcelain China doll, and then she would squint several times. One of the couple—he or she—would immediately bend down to the old lady, look to see whether anything had happened, God forbid, and would then smile at her, straighten out her blanket or her charming bonnet, and continue to push the wheelchair.

They liked to stroll on the long, broad boardwalk, which was made of narrow wooden planks and stretched alongside the very edge of the ocean. They particularly enjoyed the first warm spring days. Starting at eight o'clock in the morning, when the sun was already tempering its glowing rays in the cold water and the air was full of a salty freshness, their promenades would last about three hours, starting from the building on Brighton First Street where they lived and going nearly all the way to Coney Island, to the amusement park rides. Sometimes they would stop at a bench, put sunglasses on the old lady that hid half her face, and turn the wheelchair toward the sun. They themselves would sit down on the bench and cuddle, and with their eyes closed, they would push their faces into the breeze and enjoy the sunbathing.

The couple hardly spoke to one another; they understood each other with a single glance, a nod, a raised eyebrow, or a motion of a finger—the language of mute signs often took the place of the sound of words for them. Nevertheless, their ears were constantly on alert, pricked up in the old lady's direction. She had only to let out a little squeak or a groan, and one of her two companions would be next to her in a second, would look at her and touch her to see whether she was all right, whether something was hurting her, and they would take a small bottle of water with a nipple out of a small basket attached to the wheelchair and bring it to her little mouth.

They had been going out on such morning strolls for a long time now—he, she, and the old lady, and the passersby who saw them, especially the older folks, would look after them admiringly and sigh: "It should happen to us, to have such children . . ."

– She –

She, Rachel, was born in New York; if she had been born three months earlier, her birthplace would have been Eschwege, Germany, where her parents were in a displaced persons camp. Because she was still a child then, she could never say the name of the place correctly; even her parents seldom spoke that name—they preferred to make do with "there," and it was immediately clear which "there" they meant. What did engrave itself in Rachel's memory from among her mother's recollections was the name of the town where her mother was born and lived until the war. Mezritch—that's what her mother's town was called, and Rachel quickly memorized the name because it would often erupt from her mother's lips. The best and most beautiful things that had happened to her mother in her life had happened in Mezritch; in Mezritch the sun shone brighter and the air was cleaner; in Mezritch there were many goats and people lived happily . . . Rachel had swallowed her mother's stories together with her cookies that she steeped in milk, but the older she got, the more boring her mother's remembrances of the past seemed, and only the name of the town— Mezritch—remained tucked away in her memory, like a dried flower that was pressed somewhere between the pages of a thick book she had once read.

Rachel's father was the opposite of his wife. A morose and depressive person, he was nearly twenty years older than she. Her mother had once told her, as if to justify her husband's aloofness and closed nature, that before the war her father had had another wife and child, also a girl, and that they had both been killed.

In the grocery that her parents owned, her mother stood at the sales counter, spoke to and served the sparse customers, obtained their bit of merchandise, and kept the accounts, and her father worked as an assistant: bringing in and taking out merchandise, taking it down to the cellar, and packing cartons or boxes. He used to raise the heavy iron shutters outside the store every morning and lower them every evening and lock them with a big lock. He used to call the shutters, which emitted a rusty grating sound when they moved, the "accordion." What the word "accordion" meant, little Rachel didn't understand. In the evenings, when she would stand on the street and watch her father fiddling with the hook somewhere up above the store's wide window, and after his strong pull downward the iron "accordion" would unroll a bit, Rachel would be ready to dance with joy.

"Well—how do you like my playing?" her father would ask hoarsely every time, as he caught his breath, and his sunken cheeks squeezed out a pale smile.

Rachel would immediately run up to the heavy shutters that now covered the entire store and run her hands over the iron furrows; she could not imagine how the big, wide shutters could disappear into the narrow crevice up above, over the window and door.

She would rejoice after letting the shutters down; her parents would be free and would go for a little walk with her, holding her hands on both sides. Even if it was only for a few blocks, till they got home, it was still a walk together, and she, Rachel, was in the middle, like a ring that locks two other rings together. And yet the grocery never left them—it followed them step by step and reminded them of it by its smell, which penetrated her mother's hair, the thick skin of her father's palms, and their clothing. It was a mixed smell of laundry soap, herring, and mustiness. On the way home, her mother would always ask her father: "Did you check? Is everything locked up?" She asked, not because she couldn't rely on her husband, God forbid, but because more than anything she was afraid of thieves.

"For a thief, there are no locks!" her husband would answer—the same way every time.

Rachel's mother knew that very well herself, and indeed because she knew it, her fear was that much greater. She had taken upon herself the burden of running the business, and she clung to the bit of income with tooth and nail. Bearing a burden was nothing new to her. She had done that in the ghetto, at the age of barely thirteen or fourteen, after her mother died, leaving her with a younger sister on her hands . . . In her town of Mezritch, people used to say that you don't slaughter a cow so long as it still gives milk . . . Perhaps for that reason, when the murderers came, they were kinder to the cows than to the people. The grocery store was her Brooklyn "goat"—that's what her uncle Max had explained to her when he was helping her with the business. Uncle Max had gone to America long before the war, when Rachel's mother was a little child and he himself was still called Mordecai. He was actually the one who had tracked her down in the DP camp and brought her, by then pregnant with Rachel, and her husband to New York. The "goat" yielded only a very meager amount of milk, but the greenhorn grocery store manager wouldn't surrender. She taught herself how to be a merchant—she had no choice. There was also no place to look back to, so she occasionally stirred up sparks of hope and faith among the embers of the burned-up past, and warmed her present with them.

Little Rachel used to spend whole days with her parents in the store; she would find a spot amid the empty cardboard boxes and play "buyer-seller" with her doll, Sandra. She, Rachel, would be the seller, like her mother, and Sandra would be a customer. Her father also had his own little spot—the alcove, separated from a rear corner by two little walls. There they could wash their hands in the sink, which had a bronze faucet that was eaten away in spots by green rust; there was also a broom and a pail with a soggy rag for washing the floor. Little Rachel used to sneak into that place when she held it in so long while playing that she had to run there to relieve herself. The alcove was illuminated by a small bulb attached to the wall above the sink. When she was sitting on the potty, Rachel liked to look at the pictures plastered on the walls. Torn from cheap magazines—most of them had long ago yellowed—laughing faces of blonde women in splendid hairdos and clothing looked down at her. The girl of five or six had not yet heard of Hollywood or movie stars; at that time, she hadn't yet been in a movie theater at all, even once, but the radiance that emanated from the beautiful faces enchanted her and wrapped her in sleep-inducing warmth. Her mother's voice would pull her out of her sweet immobility: "Rachel, have you fallen asleep in there?"

One picture on the wall was that of a man. Wearing a bowler hat and with a narrow strip of mustache, he was leaning on a cane and smoking a cigar. Every time Rachel's gaze encountered the comical little man, she rejoiced anew: "He's here—he hasn't run away!" She never worried about the beautiful, dressed-up ladies—they always looked happy, or as Rachel's mother once said: "Their faces are full of life!" But by his comical appearance, the little man with the big, dark eyes introduced a strange uneasiness into the cramped, half-dark alcove. And suddenly she would feel that there were tears in her eyes. Why? What for? She herself couldn't understand whether it was because things were going well for her or because she had suddenly gotten sad . . .

And yet, no matter how long Rachel sat on the potty, the alcove was not hers but her father's little place. Whenever he had a moment free from work in the store, he would sit hunched over, not even turning on the light, like someone being punished. At times one could hear a suppressed murmur from the alcove, and it wasn't clear whether her father was talking to himself or praying. He wasn't religious, but Rachel had learned from her mother that as a young man he had spent some time studying in a yeshiva. "That man is eating his heart out," her mother would sigh. Rachel would shrug her bony shoulders, as if she wanted to ask her doll, Sandra: "How can someone eat his own heart out?"

Rachel liked to go to Brighton Beach with her father on Saturdays during the summer. Her mother would stay home—to clean up, wash up, and cook. "Go for a walk with your father—take him out into the sun. Maybe he'll come to himself." When they walked on the boardwalk, things were always lively—no matter when they got there, people were walking around. Rachel's father could have done without the noisy place—too many people together made him feel confused. He went there for the sake of his little daughter, and Rachel, all dressed up in her little blue dress with red and yellow flowers on it, her little red shoes, and a yellow beret on her head, glowed with happiness. She knew the way there very well, because the sweet-spicy smell of fresh, roasted nuts smothered in sugary syrup drew her to them the way a bee is drawn to nectar. They were sold from something that was both a little booth and a two-wheeled cart at the same time. The owner of that strange contraption, a skinny, sunburned man with a mop of dark brown hair and a narrow red sweatband on his sweaty forehead, would click his tongue loudly several times and suddenly emit two or three short words from his mouth that Rachel did not understand, but the rasping sound "r-r-r," like a thin little spear, would pierce the air and thread all those sounds together. The nut seller would quickly pass a narrow little paddle across the broad, glowing pan on which the nuts were being roasted, and, placing a small paper bag below it, he would push a portion of nuts into it. Rachel's father called him "Gypsy," and after giving him a few cents, he would take the little bag from him.

After they bought the little nuts, the Saturday stroll took on a special character. The nuts were round and they stuck to one another, but Rachel would separate them with two fingers and bring them to her mouth one by one. She was in no hurry to eat a nut. First she would touch its thin, white skin with her lips, then she would stuff its hard body into her mouth and play with it for a while—rolling it around on her gums with her tongue—and only after she had chewed it up and swallowed the delicious mush was it time for the next nut. "That's enough fooling around with it," her father would say, unable to stand it anymore. But that didn't bother Rachel, because she was sure that each little nut had its own flavor.

A few minutes earlier, when pressing the bag against herself, she had thought that there were a lot of nuts in it, and that she would lick her lips over them for a long time, all the way to Coney Island, but they ran out quickly and the bag got soft, like an ordinary piece of paper. When Rachel looked inside it, she saw only two little nuts, stuck to one another like two burrs for her mother at home. That was the end of the first part of their Saturday promenade. Their further path led toward the water. Throwing off her little red shoes and digging into the warm sand with her naked little feet, she started running toward the quietly playful waves. Her father could barely restrain her: "Don't get wild, don't run like that!" He clumsily placed one foot ahead of the other so as not to get sand in his shoes, but nevertheless by the time they got to the water's edge his shoes were already full. Rachel immediately dipped her sticky hands into the water and rinsed them for a while; after that she made a little boat out of her palms, and filling them with water she brought them toward her face. On the way, the water ran out, because the boat had a crack in it. Nevertheless, Rachel ran her wet hands over her syrup-smeared lips several times, and even stuck out her little tongue. After the spicy-sweet nuts, the seawater didn't seem so salty.

What Rachel liked best was to stand in the water up to her knees—her father wouldn't allow her to go in deeper—and look at the seagulls. The white birds with gray spots on their wingtips and strong beaks fascinated her, like those blonde, beautiful ladies in the faded pictures in the little alcove, but the living birds had a special power over her. Their short, throaty cries made her uneasy, made her feel as if her head were surrounded and constricted by a tight band, similar to the one the nut seller wore. But her band was hard and strong, like a narrow hoop that squeezed her head more and more tightly and painfully with each shriek of a bird. Her eyes closed and she saw before her a narrow, long tube that sucked her into it, into its black, deep emptiness, with weird speed and, in the blink of an eye, spit her out through its other end, far, far into the sky where the beautiful seagulls were already waiting for her . . .

As she trembled as if frightened, the momentary dark cloudiness melted into the clean, healthy ocean breeze like a black puff of smoke. The spots of sunshine flickered over the surface of the blue-green water, like myriad little crystal ships. Rachel couldn't tear her eyes away from the supple, peaky motions of the white birds. Her gaze fell on a certain gull and followed its soaring flight; suddenly the bird screeched and the marked flight path that only birds can see turned sharply downward. After a splash into the water, the gull immediately rose from the surface and continued to follow its invisible flight path, now with a little fish clamped in its beak. Rachel swelled with joy and pressed her damp palms to her cheeks, which had gotten red, both from the sun and from unrestrained joy. She returned to her father—had he too seen the gull's trick?—and ran to hug his dark, immobile figure. The fresh breeze ballooned out the broad trousers on his long, skinny legs and mussed the sparse hair on his head. He stood there as if grown into the sandy ground, but his eyes, deeply sunken in his prematurely aged face, were searching for a lost support somewhere far, far away, where the arc of the heavens comes together with the surface of the ocean. Rachel was already used to her father's not-here-ness, even though she could touch him with her hand. But why was his gaze always searching there in the distance when she, Rachel, was here next to him and loved him very much? Once when they were stand-ing that way near the water and Rachel was playing with the white birds, stretching her little hands out to them as if she could grasp the transparent thread of their flight and soar over the water like them, she heard her father call out: "Mirele." She turned her head toward him, with her hands still stretched upward. Her father again called out the same name, calling upon his lost far-off places, but he immedi-ately turned his gaze back to Rachel, and then, looking into her eyes, exclaimed: "Come, come to me, Mirele!" and stepped toward her . . .

Rachel knew—her mother had told her—that her father's first child, who was killed on the other side of the ocean, had been called Mirele. Lost, Rachel looked at her father. An audacious gull swooped quickly right next to her, almost touching the hair on her head, as if to show thereby that their game had not ended yet. Right next to her ear, the gull let out a cry in which Rachel heard the same name, but as a parody: "Mrrrl."

And again the avian screech cut through her brain; she grimaced, gnashing her teeth, and suddenly cried out angrily to her father and to the seagull: "I'm Rachel, Rachel!" Snatching her little red shoes from the sand, Rachel started running home, sinking her bare feet into the hot sand. From then on, the white seagull found a place in Rachel's existence. She would often come back to the edge of the sand and, walking into the water, stand there lost in thought. Perhaps she had invented the story about Mirele during one of these times. At such moments she would imagine that Mirele had been transformed after her death into a beautiful, white gull, and that she flew around here among the flocks on Brighton Beach.

–He–

He, Yasha, had been born in a very different part of the world, in a city called Bender, which is on the Dniester River. Surrounded since he was little by concern and love, which his mother shared with her two elder sisters, he saw his father only twice in his life: the first time was on that September 1 when he started school, and the second time was at his wedding, or, more accurately, at the Registration Hall, where he officially registered his marriage.

The three sisters lived in a little house, which they had inherited from their parents and which had miraculously remained intact after the war. There were two little rooms and a kitchen; the two sisters slept in one room and Yasha and his mother slept in the other one. When Yasha started fifth grade, the sisters agreed among themselves that the child was a big boy, *keyn eyn hora*, and had to have his own place, so they built an additional room onto the house. There Yasha was in charge.

In school, they teased him: "Yasha with his three mothers," because no one in his class could guess which of the three women was his real mother. One aunt used to take him to school, another one would take him home, and the third one came to the assemblies, or sometimes all three came to class together and squeezed onto a single school bench, on which Yasha and a classmate normally sat together. In addition, the sisters all looked alike—tall and skinny. All of them were slightly stooped and had identical short hair and pale faces. Even Yasha's teacher for the first four grades, Lyudmila Antonovna, was not always sure whether she was speaking to Yasha's mother or one of his aunts.

Yasha had never heard from his aunts that either of them had ever had children, so he couldn't imagine that they could have their own families and live apart. It was even hard for him to answer when someone asked him the hackneyed question: "Whom do you love more, your own mother or your two aunts?" It was just as if someone had asked another child whether he loved his mother or father more.

Nevertheless, Yasha once asked his mother why other children on their street had fathers and he didn't. Turning her head to one side, she answered quietly: "It was apparently destined to be that way." Yasha had occasion to hear the word "destined" quite often from his mother and his aunts; it was as if it were attached to their tongues. No matter what they were talking about among themselves, and no matter what happened, he always heard as a summary: "It was apparently destined to be that way." The word had a sort of a magical power—after saying it, sometimes with a heavy sigh, it was as if all the questions had immediately been answered. The expression became engraved in Yasha's memory, and not infrequently, after something went wrong, he used to console himself with a quiet: "It was destined to be that way," little understanding what that meant.

The day he crossed the threshold of elementary school for the first time, Yasha didn't recognize anyone. Everything around him looked too big and multicolored for him to be able to encompass it with his gaze or let his eyes rest on anything. He was dressed in a brand new school uniform—a gray wool shirt cinched by a broad belt that closed with a sparkling buckle; a hat that looked like a military cap with a device on it: an open book like a golden butterfly with spread wings; and a leather bag. The previous evening he had put everything he needed into the bag—he trusted neither his mother nor his two aunts to do it: the primer with the Russian ABCs; four notebooks, two with little boxes for arithmetic and two with straight lines for learning how to write letters and words; two well-sharpened pencils in a narrow pencil case; a yellow eraser; and a red wooden pen holder without a point, because first one had to learn to write with a pencil, and only then with pen and ink. True, he had also prepared an inkwell with a little glass full of violet ink, but he didn't take it to school.

That morning, Yasha woke up earlier than usual. His mother was puttering with his bag.

"I've put an apple in here," she said. "Eat it during recess."

Both aunts beamed with joy.

"You talk to him like he's a small child. Don't you think he knows himself that eating in class is forbidden?"

"A real student, *keyn eyn hora!*"

All three sisters accompanied him to school. Yasha walked ahead of them; he didn't walk—he flew. If not for his heavy bag and the flowers he was carrying outstretched in front of him, he would have walked even farther ahead of his companions. After all, he was already a grownup. A stranger stopped him for a moment not far from the school gate. He called Yasha by name, then went up to him and hurriedly, as if hiding it from strangers' eyes, stuffed something into the boy's shirt. Then he smiled to him good-naturedly, and lightly pushing him toward the school gate softly said: "Good luck!"

It happened so quickly and unexpectedly that Yasha didn't even remember the stranger's face. After taking a few steps, he turned back, but the man was already gone. In a moment everything was forgotten—carried away by the noise and hustle bustle of the festive day. Later, during the recess between first and second period, a friend of his, who was already in second grade, ran up to him, and, pointing to his shirt, asked: "What have you got in there?" Yasha was eating the apple his mother had given him to take along to school. Swallowing the piece he was chewing, he bent his head down, resting his chin on his hard, white collar. Only then did he see that between the top button and the second button there was something attached by a clip and hidden beneath the shirt. He grasped the narrow, silvery strip and pulled on it. He found himself holding a fountain pen in his hand, with some sort of inscription engraved with beautiful little golden letters on its dark-green, sparkling surface. In those days, one could only dream of having such a fountain pen. His little friend was ready to grab it from him but Yasha was on guard; he quickly pulled the hand holding the precious item behind him, and in order to get away as quickly as possible from the audacious boy, he gave him the uneaten part of the apple. The boy took the go-away bribe, but at the same time said in a needling way: "You won't be able to read what's written there anyway, shrimp!"

Yasha could hardly wait for the bell to ring during the final class of his first day of school. His teacher, Lyudmila Antonovna, noticed, of course, that her pupil's head was somewhere else. All of the children burst out laughing when she said that in front of the class. Yasha felt his ears start to burn. As a consolation, he again touched his pocket, where the beautiful green fountain pen, the gift from the stranger, was lying. It was he who had so quickly clipped the fountain pen to his shirt. Who was he to give Yasha such an expensive thing? Yasha again tried to remember his face, taking himself back in his thoughts to the moment when the unknown man had called out to him: "Yashanke!" indicating that he knew him well. But from where?

His mother picked him up from school. She glowed seeing her schoolboy. Taking his bag, she immediately started asking him how he liked school. Yasha made do with two or three words, then pulled the fountain pen out of his pocket. His mother's face changed—no trace of her previous joy remained. A coldness came over her expression and hid in the narrow corners of her lips.

"What's written there, mama?" her son asked, barely restraining his curiosity.

But instead of an answer, he heard her question:

"How did you get that thing?"

"Some man—this morning, near the school gate. He immediately disappeared somewhere."

His mother stopped, as if the earth would open up if she took another step. She dragged Yasha by the hand, bent down to him, and said to him severely:

"How many times have I told you not to take things from anyone!"

Yasha wasn't expecting anything like that. He pulled the visor of his cap down over his eyes so he couldn't see his mother's face, but her hot breath struck his cheeks and seemed to burn them.

"Did I tell you that or not?" his mother repeated.

Yasha tried to defend himself:

"But he pushed it on me himself—I didn't even notice."

His mother wasn't listening to him. She interrupted him, and like a command, angrily whispered into his ear:

"Never approach him again, and never take anything from him! Do you understand me or not?"

Yasha squeezed out a sort of "yes" and fell silent. He didn't know whether to cry out loud or silently, swallowing the tears together with the resentment that came surging up from within but remained stuck in his throat.

All the way home mother and son barely exchanged a word. Each of them, in his or her own way, was apparently trying to understand what had just taken place between them. At the very threshold of the house, Yasha's mother said calmly to her son:

"Please, Yasha—your aunts don't have to know anything about this."

Yasha was still silent. He remained resentful—only then when his mother had pulled him along by his hand did he realize the answer to his teacher's question for him: "that man was my father."

– He and She –

If they were trying to account for their meeting and acquaintance, they could probably have done it with a single statement that had ensconced itself in Yasha's childhood: "It was destined to be that way!" but it's hard to explain one's whole life with a single statement.

On that spring day, Rachel, as she did every morning, was strolling on the boardwalk with her mother. Suddenly a wheel from her mother's wheelchair got stuck in a crack between two boards. The wheelchair turned to one side and the old lady was at the point of falling out. Rachel lost herself for a moment; she grabbed her mother's coat with one hand and with the other hand she clung to the wheelchair so it wouldn't overturn completely. She felt that she wouldn't be able to hold out long that way, and wouldn't be able to free the wheel from the crack by herself. She was ready to cry out, to call for help, but an unknown man clumsily bumped into her with his shoulder, bent over to the wheel, and in an instant the wheelchair was again standing on the boardwalk on both wheels.

Rachel immediately ran to her mother, felt her all over, straightened out the bonnet on her head, and at the same time stroked her frightened face. A weak sound emerged from between the two thin strips of her compressed lips, which could have represented either a groan of pain or a capricious squeak from a spoiled child. Rachel smiled at her mother and excused herself for her clumsiness. She had to calm herself down, and after doing so, she straightened up and sighed, and only then did her gaze turn to Yasha.

He shrugged his shoulders and cast his eyes downward. It looked almost as if he were accepting guilt for the fact that a rotted plank in Brighton Beach's broad, long boardwalk had collapsed. She thanked him and excused herself for his having had to waste time here on her because she hadn't moved quickly enough when the mishap occurred.

"Without you, I really don't know what would have happened."

Yasha shrugged his shoulders quietly, rubbed his neck, and shook his head. Suddenly he pulled the knitted woolen sports cap off his head, and pressing it to his belly he began to knead it with his fingers. The morning breeze immediately took hold of his sparse yellowish hair and ruffled it on his pate.

Rachel interpreted his movements in her own way; she stuffed her hand in her pocket and reached for something there. For the first time, Yasha let his voice be heard:

"No, no," he confirmed his words by shaking his head "No."

They both stood there confused for a few moments. Then he raised his cap to Rachel and said goodbye to her. He also bent over to the old lady and gave her a wink.

Later on, sitting on the long bench against the red brick wall, he more than once replayed that morning's episode with Rachel and her mother, the way he always did after finishing a game of chess, especially when he had lost. And if when he analyzed his defeat he was quickly successful in finding his wrong move, Yasha was defeated in the game by both sides of the chessboard, because he saw himself playing against both the white and black pieces. He was suddenly seized by a feeling of shame and longing. Though longing was something he felt frequently, he had long since stopped thinking of such a thing as shame.

For Rachel too, after the momentary, accidental encounter with the "Russian," there remained a feeling of worry and distrust, just like the one her newly arrived Russian neighbors elicited in her. They now occupied almost all the apartments in the building where she lived with her mother. She knew the faces of many of them and greeted them; mostly they were older than she, and often they were very old people, like her mother. The young folks left early in the morning, to who knows where, "to look for something to put in their mouths," as

Rachel once heard one older woman explain to another. Rachel knew no Russian, but those words she understood because they were said in Yiddish. Her Russian neighbors also recognized and always greeted her. They behaved very politely, but only spoke to Rachel in Russian. When Rachel showed them that she didn't understand their language, the women would start to speak to her more loudly and more screechingly, adding hand motions, as if she, Rachel were hard of hearing. Often she grasped a few familiar words from their speech, similar to those she used to hear from her mother many years ago. She had almost forgotten Yiddish, the language of her childhood, and, together with the language, she had pushed bits of recollections, experiences, and feelings to the back of her memory. But now the few Yiddish words flew out, like bright butterflies of light from out of the darkness. On occasion, she received warm, empathetic looks when she appeared in the courtyard, pushing her mother's wheelchair ahead of her. But she didn't get too excited about that, and she didn't do it only because she was a faithful daughter. Her mother, who had lived and worked hard in America for some forty years, couldn't expect the same social privileges from the American government that the elderly Russians received from the day they arrived in the Golden Land—she had had to pay for her illness out of her own pocket.

Standing in front of the mirror, Rachel would say out loud, as if she were answering someone or making excuses to someone: "Go understand them!"

The next day, as she was passing the Moscow restaurant, she stopped and looked at the benches on which some three pairs of chess players were sitting, absorbed in the game. Several elderly men were walking around next to them, speaking Russian. On the previous day, before Rachel left the boardwalk after the accident, she noticed that the Russian man had left her to go to the bench. Perhaps he was here today too, among the chess players? Yesterday Rachel hadn't needed much to immediately evaluate the stranger's situation. He didn't look like a man who slept on soft pillows and put on a fresh shirt every morning. The collar on his dark-blue, checkered, long-sleeved flannel shirt did not look fresh, to say nothing of the jeans held up on his belly by a worn-out belt without a buckle. His pitiful appearance was actually the only reason her hand had crept into her pocket; she had done it automatically, especially when he had pulled the sports cap (which looked more like a dishrag) off his head. The beggars that she encountered in Brighton Beach often did that too. But her womanly instincts told her that yesterday's Russian was no beggar—rather, he was just an unfortunate person, a luckless fellow.

She didn't see him among the morning chess players and she continued on her way, which she used to do almost daily, as a need that was inseparable from her existence, from the fixed responsibility that she had borne since her mother had become ill. Since her mother had become paralyzed and Rachel had decided to remain close to her, she had become a slave to worry. Her hands, as if chained to the wheelchair, had become like two mechanical pieces without which the entire machinery could not function. She could have freed her hands and left her mother in an old-age home, where they would have looked after her, perhaps no worse than she herself did. But Rachel had immediately driven such thoughts from her mind, not surrendering to a seductive weakness, and it was hard to determine which was a more important component of her decision—her moral obligation and concern as a daughter, or a hidden desire to demonstrate, to herself first of all, that there could be no other path for her.

Yasha had sidled up to the two women so quietly that Rachel, not expecting it, began trembling slightly and stopped for a moment.

"Excuse me—I seem to have frightened you."

Rachel turned her head toward him. Something in him had changed, she thought; the previous day's beard seemed to have been shaven off, revealing a genteel, round face with naïve blue eyes. For a moment her gaze rested on his shirt; it was a different one, a clean one this time, though the collar looked wrinkled. Out loud, Rachel said:

"Just a bit, and do you know why?"

Yasha shrugged his shoulders and just listened.

"Because I was looking for you before myself."

She gave the wheelchair a push and continued slowly on her way. She didn't look toward him, but she sensed that he was walking alongside her, like a companion, or perhaps an admirer. Rachel started laughing. The word "admirer," like those little moths of Yiddish, had flown up from some hidden chamber of her memory. Yasha interpreted Rachel's unexpected chuckle in his own way:

"I understand—I look funny."

"No, no," Rachel caught herself. "Excuse me. I was just thinking of something silly. Have you been here long?"

"You mean in Brighton Beach?"

"In America."

"Three and a half years."

"So you're still a 'greenhorn,' though your English . . . Did you learn the language here?"

"Here, by practice—though I took English as a subject in school and later in the university."

"You studied in a university?" the question burst out of her with an astonishment that could also have meant: "How were you able to do that?"

She herself felt it immediately, and tried to gloss over her tactlessness:

"I meant to say that it was certainly not easy for a Jew to get to study in a university in the Soviet Union."

Yasha gave her no answer. He retreated into his isolation, but only for a moment. Again returning to the conversation, he said with deliberate playfulness:

"It's been almost a whole day since we met, but we haven't yet introduced ourselves. Doesn't that seem strange to you?"

"A little, yes." Rachel immediately responded to the playful tone, pleased that the brief tension that she had introduced had been resolved in such a way.

They didn't shake hands, they just looked at each other and each one said his or her name, adding, as is usually done: "Very nice to meet you." "Me too."

The spring day was pleasant. Cool streams of air, full of morning freshness from the ocean, blew over the beach, which was occupied by seagulls that didn't rest for a second—they quivered on the damp sand;

audaciously shoved one another; screeched; and widely opened their broad, pointy-twisty beaks, splitting them into two halves so their narrow tongues vibrated between them and gave their throaty calls an especially penetrating quality. They flew away into the heights, separating themselves from earthbound creatures—flew way into the sky, and there, with their narrow, sickle-shaped wings, tore the oncoming streams of air into shreds. At this time of year, the strip of sandy ground between the water and the boardwalk belonged to the coddled birds, whose chaotic hustle bustle spread throughout the neighborhood.

The official introduction gave Yasha courage, and he asked:

"I see you here almost every day. You're very faithful to your work." He added more firmly: "You do a good job."

That drawn-out compliment about her "job" irritated her, though she understood that her new Russian acquaintance meant it sincerely. Looking straight ahead, she said:

"This is my mother, but I do indeed do the job not badly."

Rachel suddenly realized that it had been quite some time since she had had such a free and open conversation, especially since she never moved even a step away from her mother; the words and concepts she had used during these last years at home related only to the constricted framework of actions connected with serving her mother. She had actually become unused to carrying on a conversation with anyone, because she usually only had occasion to speak to herself. She had gotten unused to posing questions, because she didn't expect an answer. The only words or brief speech that she uttered to her mother fell onto a mute emptiness, like pebbles thrown into a deep well from which the living water had run out.

Rachel was also listening to the voice of her new acquaintance, and though he soon fitted her name to his Slavic accent, that didn't bother her; furthermore, in his pronouncing her name in his own way—Retshil—she heard a distant echo of her childhood: her father had also been unable to pronounce his daughter's American name correctly.

They continued to stand facing the building where Rachel and her mother lived.

"It's already twelve o'clock," Rachel announced, as if she wanted to excuse herself. "We have to go home."

"How quickly the time has passed! I've almost stopped noticing it lately."

"You don't live far from here I understand?" Rachel asked.

Yasha broke out into a smile and answered as if the question had been quite different: "It won't be difficult for you to come here tomorrow?"

"No . . . if you wish, we can meet, like today, across from the Moscow restaurant."

"By all means—it sounds very romantic," Rachel agreed, and added: "Will around nine o'clock be good?"

Once she was in the house changing her mother's clothes, she recalled how she had picked the time and was now astonished at herself: Why in the world "around nine o'clock"? Why not simply nine o'clock? And she burst out laughing. She embraced her mother and gave her a kiss on the forehead.

The rain began during the night and continued throughout the morning. Two of the apartment's windows on the ninth floor where mother and daughter lived looked out onto the boardwalk, and farther, to where the horizon met the ocean. Rachel's mother had moved into the apartment about ten years before. There was a well-illuminated bedroom with a spacious living room and all the conveniences. For her mother by herself, it had been a successful purchase. Through decades of hard work and paying rent, she had saved up for a place of her own in her old age. Rachel wasn't living in New York at that time, but after she came back there to her paralyzed mother, the apartment became her home too. Though she felt pent up there, especially during the first half-year, the two windows that looked out on the always lively boardwalk and the spacious ocean sometimes brought hope into her enforced loneliness and occasional bitter depression. Standing thusly at the window, especially in bad weather, she used to suddenly have the thought that her gaze was searching for something far, far away, where there is no beginning and no end; there, where her father once used to search for his lost source of support: his destroyed home and his murdered little daughter, Mirele. Did she, Rachel, born in another world and time, have to share his fate? Be plagued by her parents' yesterday? She drove away those thoughts and stubbornly searched the cloudy sky for something that she could hang her hat on—something through which she could air out her own exhausted worries.

Going for a stroll today was out of the question. Rachel looked at the clock—a quarter to nine—and went over to the window through which she could better see the section of the boardwalk that led to the Moscow restaurant, as Yasha had called it. Did she expect to see Yasha there? But her heart was pounding nevertheless, and her gaze, which till now used to get immersed in the gray, cloudy distance, now knew what to search for. Rachel had felt that even during the night, perhaps with the first raindrops that rapped on the windows and woke her up. She slept in the same room as her mother, and with time had learned to listen for her mother's breathing while she was asleep. Raising her head from the pillow, Rachel pricked up her ears. The rain had gained strength, and had been transformed from a buckshot-like rapping into a steady hum, mixing with the high waves of the ocean. Her mother was quietly panting and smacking her lips in her bed. Rachel lay down on her back and closed her eyes again. She immediately started to sink into a soft, warm mass similar to the sand on the beach on a hot, damp night. Hanging over her forehead she saw a damp image of a masculine face, which was swaying slightly, as if on the surface of the water. Tender caresses wandered over her body, which was still wrapped in her nightgown, and they awakened forgotten womanly desires. She moved her lips toward the face, but it immediately moved away, as if excited by her. From her temples to the tips of her toes, a shudder of lust passed through her that captured every one of her limbs in its net. The masculine face was again hanging in front of her eyes, but it was now a clear one with features that she recognized immediately: "Nati, Nati," she heard her own quiet whispering, and like an echo, her mangled name—"Retshil"—tore through the noisy weather into her dreamy state.

Rachel awoke. As was her custom, she immediately listened to her mother's breathing. Weak and sweaty, she sat for a while on the bed, hung her bare feet down, and leaned over the edge of the bed. Day was beginning to break. She thought: "Today I won't see him," and stuffed her feet into her soft bedroom slippers. The awakened new day met her with the same worry wagon to which she had permitted herself to be harnessed and was pulling submissively. On days like this, when the weather was bad, she couldn't go outside, so she particularly sharply felt the loneliness and isolation from another life that might have been hers. On such days, instead of a stroll she would move her mother's wheelchair to the window, sit down in an armchair facing her, and read a book out loud. Reading aloud to her mother had remained a habit from her school years. Catching on quickly to the spoken language, Rachel's mother had had no time or opportunity to learn to read English fluently. But her curiosity about life in general and about the reality of her new home in particular sought an outlet. Buying a television set was, for the time being, a luxury, so one evening when Rachel was reading a book, she had asked her to read aloud. Rachel was astonished: "Why, mama? After all, this is just a textbook." "So I'll learn something too," her mother answered seriously. "I lost my chance to study in the ghetto." Her daughter liked the idea, so they used to spend their time reading almost every evening. Rachel would read and her mother would listen while embroidering a picture with colored cotton thread, silently so as not to interfere, God forbid, with the special closeness that had been created between her and her daughter by the reading. Only once in a while would she interrupt Rachel's melodious little voice to ask her to explain this or that word.

Recently they had been reading a thick book with the beautiful name *Evergreen*—a biography of a girl from Eastern Europe. Since Rachel had begun reading the book, a certain thought wouldn't leave her alone: that all Jews from the other side of the ocean were at all times divided into two categories—those who always dreamed of moving to America and those who had already done so but never stopped yearning for the old country.

The stroke had taken her mother's legs, arms, and speech from her, but had left her hearing. The doctors believed that her ability to understand was also limited, but Rachel had already noticed several times that her mother was shedding a tear while she was reading her a book. That was not an accident—her mother had been weeping in the right places, with understanding. And the few tiny tears on her sunken cheeks definitely encouraged her daughter—a quiet hope beat in her heart.

Rachel read not loudly but clearly and distinctly. On the other side of the window they could hear the stiff waves throwing themselves angrily at the shore, and after every such attack, they would capture another piece of sandy territory for a few moments. Unwillingly, they would then pull back to their boundaries, in their hurry dragging back everything that allowed it, and leaving behind fat, squiggly strips of foam on the sand. Sometimes the grating cry of a seagull, apparently looking for its flock, would cut through the angry roaring.

The little doors of the elevator that stopped across from their apartment opened with a bang, then closed, and it again became quiet. Rachel stopped reading and dashed to the door like a shot, leaving the book on the armchair. Not saying a word, she turned the lock. Wet and frozen, Yasha was looking at her from the other side of the door.

"Did I forget my umbrella here by any chance?"

– Yasha –

From the time he was small, Yasha had been surrounded by the love and concern of three women, his mother and her two sisters, who didn't have very much happiness in life. Furthermore, the gift package that is supposed to come to everyone in life, the one that the Almighty distributes to all his children—as Grandfather Frost used to do at children's New Year's parties—never reached them either. But did anyone ever hear a complaint from them? Not at all! They got away with their lives after such fires of war—wasn't that something to be happy about?! They found their house almost undamaged and settled back into it—was that not a piece of luck?! They earned enough for a piece of bread and didn't go naked or barefoot—so they should say thank you! And if anything wasn't the way they might have wished, they had something with which to justify it: "That's the way it was destined to be."

Such a "happy" life used to shine from the eyes of millions and millions, especially during the festive demonstrations twice a year—on the 1st of May and on the 7th of November, the day when the great October Revolution, which made it possible to create such a "happy life" on one-sixth of the entire globe, had taken place. That's, at least, how it was taught in school, and so was it etched into Yasha's memory: the long columns of dressed-up people with multicolored balloons and little red flags in their hands; the men carrying large banners, preceded by strict-looking people with dark expressions and streamers in the middle of every column. On long, red pieces of canvas stretched out over the lines of heads, just a few words were written with big, white letters. From one demonstration to the next, little Yasha could read them more and more easily, but what those screaming white letters meant he didn't understand, even after many years, till he stopped thinking about them at all.

In those late 1940s and early 1950s, everyone lived with one worry: no matter how bad things get, just don't let there be a new war. The fear of a new war trembled in everyone, and not only because they could still see before their eyes frightful scenes from yesterday—the fear also emanated from the little radio speakers on the walls, which spoke all day with hoarse voices like someone with a cold; even the songs they broadcasted sounded as if they were being played on rusty instruments.

Later on, after Yasha had learned to read, he used to take a look at the local newspaper *Pobeda* (victory), which the mailman delivered every Friday morning. Yasha already knew that if the dogs started barking angrily, it was a sign that the chubby man who walked like a duck (the heavy bag that he carried on one side pulled him down to the ground) and wore a cap with a shiny visor had already appeared on the street. Running out of the house toward him, Yasha would grab the newspaper and first thing would start to look for photographs in its four columns; only after that would he try to read the headlines with the larger letters. The pictures were dark and not clear, and the screaming headlines, pieced together from unknown words like those on the banners in the parades, emitted an acrid odor of ink. He would immediately start to sneeze, and he wanted to take the newspaper home so that his mother and his aunts would find it waiting for them after work. One evening, Yasha heard his mother, after putting down the newspaper, exclaim unhappily: "A whole newspaper, and there's nothing to read in it!" Yasha immediately felt his aunts' eyes upon him. One of them quietly but reproachfully said to his mother: "Don't talk so much!"

But that's the way his life remained, and whenever he picked up a newspaper, he immediately felt the acrid-allergic odor creeping into his nose and throat.

And yet, in those turbulent years when he was far from ever satiated, Jewish mothers pounded into their children's heads that even if something was not destined for them, they should at least get a good upbringing and education. To that end, they started the trend of teaching their children to play a musical instrument. Jewish mothers dreamt that their little son would play the accordion and their daughter—the piano. Why the accordion and piano exactly? They explained it very succinctly: because they're beautiful. To Yasha's good fortune, and the misfortune of his mother and aunts, the music teacher they invited to determine Yasha's musical talent, a tall, stooped man with red, watery eyes, told them: "Your problem is solved—I could more easily teach a bear to dance." If not music, it had to be something else, so they racked their brains; it was impossible that their little Yasha didn't have any talent whatsoever. But Yasha himself would discover his own talent.

One day, while strolling in the city park, he saw two men playing chess. At that time he had barely heard of such a game, but the black and white squares of the chessboard, and especially the beautifully carved figurines, fascinated him so much that he left his companions, his two aunts, and seemed to grow into the bench. His gaze followed each figurine, he watched how they moved, how they fought to capture their opponents' squares, and how they got killed. And suddenly he thought: It's a real battle, a war, similar to the one that the boys carried on every day in the street. But here everything took place on a chessboard, and two armies—black and white—fought to the last soldier. Yasha didn't yet know at that time that a soldier was called a pawn in chess language and an officer was called a bishop, and that all the figurines moved according to strict rules. At that moment, fascinated by the unfamiliar game, he stretched his hand out to a white figurine that resembled a little horse and moved it across the chessboard.

"What are you doing, little boy?" he heard, and trembled.

The man who was playing with the white figurines looked angrily at him.

"Where is your mother?" he questioned him further.

At that point, Yasha started crying. His aunts, of course, immediately came running and attacked the chess player, poor fellow, because he had frightened their child! And the child was standing there crying and still couldn't take his eyes off the chessboard. Finally, when everyone around had calmed down and his aunts wanted to leave the park, because the mood had been ruined anyway, a second chess player approached them. He bent down to the little boy and handed him the small white horse.

"Take it," he said softly, "and let it be a memento of your first chess game." He ruffled Yasha's hair and explained to the aunts who he was. His name was Isaak Yefimovich Schwartz, and he was the director of a chess club at the Municipal Pioneer Palace, which was located in the very center of the city. It was in an old and beautiful house that had belonged to a rich merchant before the war, when Bender was still a Romanian city in the province of Bessarabia. The Soviets had confiscated the house and the merchant himself; if he hadn't managed to flee, he would have either been exiled to Siberia or shot. That didn't bother the young pioneers very much. They knew from books and movies that to be rich is not good; one has to be equal to everyone else.

The pioneer palace was full of children's happiness, and the happiness was absolutely sincere. Children from the whole city used to gather there and immerse themselves in joy. The palace became Yasha's second home, to which he would run after school. Isaak Yefimovich, as it turned out, was not only a good chess teacher but an unusual person—the ten or fifteen children in the chess club treated him like one of their own. Yasha, who had grown up without a father, felt a particularly strong attraction to him. Isaak Yefimovich apparently felt it too; he invited Yasha to his home more than once. He had no family and lived alone in a rented room, in which there was, besides the narrow couch with a small table and a stool, a small étagère with books—his only treasure—off in a corner. It held dozens, and perhaps hundreds, of books about the chess kingdom, as the teacher called it. Years later—Isaak Yefimovich was then no longer alive—Yasha came to understand that the chess kingdom was the only place where his first chess teacher could hide from his past, in which his whole family had been killed, and from his lonely present; and perhaps he was trying to save Yasha and his other students from tomorrow? Once Yasha heard Isaak Yefimovitsh say quietly, as if only to himself, that the rules of chess were the most humane rules that had ever been conceived.

The game of chess fascinated Yasha. He found his friends and enemies in the chess kingdom, and knew how to behave with them. He took successful steps forward: by the age of fifteen he was already playing for the city's men's team in the all-Republic chess competition and he won second place. About two years after that he was included in the all-Republic men's team to play in the all-Union championship in Moscow. His mother and aunts, of course, became fierce fans of chess. They knew the names of many famous grandmasters, but not infrequently got them so mixed up that Yasha didn't know whom they meant. Naturally, in their honest opinion, all world chess champions should be Jews, but when the Jewish Korchnoi lost the chess crown to the Russian Karpov, Yasha's mother was not too disappointed. She said at the time, quite seriously:

"I'm sure that his real name is probably Karpinovich. But it's not appropriate for Jews to always be first."

Yasha always strove to be first, and experienced each failure painfully. Isaak Yefimovich, who already knew him better than his mother and aunts did, said to him more than once:

"Yasha—losing one match should encourage you to win two others . . ."

Of course, the old teacher was not just referring to chess—but wisdom like that comes with age. After finishing school, many of Yasha's friends, the Jewish ones who wanted to continue their studies, went to take entrance exams in distant cities in Russia, even as far away as Siberia. There, their parents claimed, it was easier to get into a university; there, they said, there is less anti-Semitism. Yasha was fortunate not to have to travel to study in faraway places; he took the exams at Kishinev University and was accepted. His mother and aunts were in seventh heaven with happiness and pride!

"If you have a good head," they boasted to their neighbors, "all doors will open for you."

In a certain sense, they were right, but Kishinev University's doors didn't open for Yasha because he did well on his exams but because of his accomplishments in chess. The university badly needed a player like him, so they ignored his Jewish background. He studied in the department of physics and mathematics and was supposed to become a teacher in those two subjects, but most of his time was taken up by preparations for the matches and the matches themselves. After barely reaching his third semester, Yasha decided that after the world student championship in Budapest he would leave the team for a while and spend all his time studying.

He was among the first on the list for the all-Republic team. This was supposed to be his first trip abroad, and he forgot everything and everyone and devoted himself only to his training. He would never feel as good and inspired as he did at that time. For his trip abroad, his mother and aunts "obtained" an "imported" suit for him.

"A trifle," said his aunts tremulously. "After all, you will represent the entire country there!"

But his mother just said: "Wear it in good health!" Her eyes were dry and sunken. She looked very weak after her operation; they all believed that everything had been taken care of and that she would regain her strength, but the illness did not leave her—it tormented and tortured her for two years . . .

The day before Yasha was supposed to leave, the team's head coach came up to him. From his expression, Yasha instinctively felt that something had happened, and that this something had to do with him.

"You can't go to Budapest," Yasha heard, and right after that he felt the trainer's warm hand on his shoulder: "But don't ask why . . ."

Yasha needed a few moments to digest the unexpected news, and suddenly, as if someone had whispered in his ear, he silently whispered:

"My Jewish mother bothers you?!"

The coach, who had already started to leave, turned toward Yasha and calmly answered: "I, personally, am not bothered by her . . ."

Yasha decided to leave the university, but he knew how badly his family, especially his mother, would take his decision. He also couldn't avoid not saying anything to them, because he wanted to go back to Bender. His physics professor, a Jew and a well-known authority in that science, gave him a piece of advice: "Transfer to a correspondence course; it would be a shame to abandon your degree so foolishly." He knew the real reason for Yasha's unexpected decision, though Yasha himself had blamed it, in the dean's office, on his mother's illness; his professor felt that ambitions should be expressed where they could be useful. "There, my friend, is where you'll have the opportunity to lay your head . . ." the professor told him. Yasha swallowed it. Several years later, Yasha accompanied him upon his departure for Israel, for good. When they said goodbye, at the railroad car, the professor gave his former student a second piece of advice: "Don't waste your time, Yasha—there's nothing for you here!"

To study by correspondence, Yasha had to work somewhere, so he went to the pioneer palace—still a pedagogical type of work. Isaak Yefimovich had already died by that time and the chess club that he had founded was barely gasping, so they suggested that Yasha direct it. Working with children fascinated him; it was as if he were again returning to his own carefree childhood years. He continued to live on the same street and in the same house, together with his family. He began collecting books, which contributed to his long list of debts, and he spent a lot of time at the book lovers club. He understood that just like Isaak Yefimovich in his time, he was looking for a way out . . .

But reading didn't save him. Worse yet: the books that he used to get for a short time and read secretly at night, so a stranger's eye shouldn't oversee him, God forbid, made him even more confused and drove him to despair. No, Yasha never considered himself a hero, though he knew that there were those who did not remain silent—they fought, risking their lives . . . He certainly understood that his former professor had been right—that there was nothing for him here, but it was not only Yasha who had to decide whether to leave. His mother and his two aunts didn't even want to hear about leaving.

"What's so bad for us here?" they said, and again mentioned the great good fortune that they enjoyed in their life. "It's our destiny!" they sighed. Yasha didn't argue, not only because his words wouldn't have convinced them but because he himself wasn't yet mature enough to make such a decision. Furthermore, he met Clara at that time, and that encounter suddenly changed his whole approach to life . . .

———

Yasha remained standing facing the building where Rachel and her mother lived. Yesterday they had said goodbye and decided to meet today—about nine o'clock. She had said it so naturally, Yasha thought, as if such an arrangement had been in place between them for quite some time; all they needed was to add "as usual."

The previous night it had taken him a long time to fall asleep. Bits of conversation came to his mind, words from the discussion during his stroll with his new acquaintance. He listened to her voice in his mind as if through its soft, somewhat muffled tones he could feel her breath and perhaps even the touch of her lips to his ear. Unexpected desire seized his imagination. He repressed the feeling, but he couldn't stop thinking about her. He was supposed to tell her and explain a lot of things, because she was from an entirely different world, the opposite of the world where he was born and grew up. On the other hand, was it so important for a man and woman who were both looking for someone to lean on, for a bit of warmth and concern for each other, to rummage around in their yesterdays? Yasha found no answer to that question, but his memories pulled him back every time, perhaps because there he felt on firmer ground. The rain that had begun and had rapped on the window with its first heavy drops had confused his thoughts and introduced an uneasy feeling into his shaky hopes that something would change in his present life.

The wet wind that blew over the slippery planks of the boardwalk seemed to latch onto Yasha's loneliness and indecisiveness. It was already a quarter to twelve, and it was clear that Rachel wasn't coming out today—she wouldn't leave her mother alone. The slender thread of his nighttime hopes was about to burst at any moment. A man came up to him and asked in Russian:

"Do you have a cigar?"

Yasha shook his head "no." But the passerby wouldn't leave him alone—he asked further:

"Perhaps you know someone who is looking for a dog to mate with a bitch? I have a Pinscher with a good pedigree—you could make a few dollars from it."

Only then did Yasha notice a small dog with a long, pointy face and round, black, bulging eyes sitting at the stranger's feet. Its two pointy little ears were shivering from the cold. The owner was holding it by a narrow leash and kept pulling at it as if he wanted to convince himself that his dog, his source of income, hadn't run away from him.

"What's your dog's name?" asked Yasha seriously, not understanding himself why he had to know that.

"Bolivar!" said the person in a dignified manner.

Yasha burst out laughing. The name of the little dog reminded him of the story by O. Henry about the two gangster friends who were left with only one horse, whose name was Bolivar. And Yasha said, like one of the gangster friends:

"Bolivar won't support both of us!"

The passerby with the little dog had apparently not read O. Henry, so he interpreted the words in his own way:

"Are you drunk, or what?"

And suddenly Yasha understood what he had to do next. In a few minutes he was at the entrance to Rachel's building, letting his gaze wander across the little black buttons on which the apartment numbers were written. Hundreds of numbers, but he needed only a single one. And again luck was with him: an elderly woman came up the stairs breathing heavily, and stopped for a moment facing Yasha. In her eyes, apparently, Yasha was very attractive, so she looked him over from head to toe with tense attention.

But Yasha didn't wait for her hospitality, and asked her good-naturedly:

"Rachel and I arranged for me to come with my car to pick her up and take her mother to the doctor, but I've forgotten the apartment number. You know her, of course?"

"Who doesn't know Rachel—such a faithful daughter," remarked the woman, now in a much friendlier tone. She pointed it out exactly, opening the entrance door with her key. "They live on the ninth floor, directly opposite the elevator."

The woman got out on the eighth floor, so Yasha had occasion while riding with her to think up another story in order to answer the question of how he had come to know Rachel and her mother.

After the door of the elevator closed behind him, Yasha realized that all his improvisations till then had been just chatter, but what would he say to Rachel? What was he looking for here, at the threshold of the apartment of this woman he hardly knew?

He started to feel hot. He felt how heavy his clothes were. Soaked as they were from the rain, they were pulling him down. At that moment, the door opened in front of him. Rachel didn't ask anything; she covered her cheeks with her hands, as astonished children often do.

As was his habit, Yasha shrugged his shoulders and said the first words that came to his mind at that moment:

"Did I forget my umbrella here by any chance?"

– They –

Rachel invited the unexpected guest inside, pointed to a chair next to the door, and told him to take off his wet clothing and leave it there. She herself went into the next room, and by the time Yasha had taken off his short coat and his soaked sneakers, she was back, holding a towel in her hand.

"Here, Yasha—wipe your face meanwhile," she pointed to where he should go and added: "There's the bathroom—I've already prepared everything for you."

Yasha obeyed her every word, walking clumsily and carrying his jeans so they wouldn't drag on the floor and get it wet. It was only a few steps to the bathroom, but Yasha walked there as if on crutches. Closing the door after him, he wiped the sweat from his face. The hum of the water that was filling the bathtub returned him to reality, for the few moments since he had crossed the threshold of the apartment had fallen out of his consciousness. He suddenly began feeling around, searching, not understanding himself exactly what for. "Your wallet with your documents," came the belated answer. His hands didn't find anything and remained hanging helplessly. He turned his head to the right, looked in the mirror, and encountered a lost face. His sparse hair was stuck to his sweaty forehead, his cheeks were sunken, and there were two dark semicircles under his eyes.

"Ku-ku, Yasha, ku-ku," a distant, soft voice called out. That's the way his mother used to play with him, looking into the mirror with him, when he was still a very small child. Perhaps "ku-ku" was one of his earliest memories. The hum of the water hadn't stopped—the

94

bathtub was already sufficiently full, so he turned off the faucet. He tested the water temperature with his hand. A bit too hot, but Rachel had said beforehand that he needed a hot bath. Yasha got undressed quickly and crept into the tub. He lay with his head under the water, his eyes closed, holding his breath as if he could remove himself from life, not feeling anything and not thinking about anything—melting into the liquid and becoming a transparent drop. He had once read that every human being consists of almost 90 percent water, so he was missing only 10 percent to turn into a puddle. But it was precisely that 10 percent that made him a human being, a sentient creature . . . Is that a privilege or a punishment?!

In Bender, they hadn't had a separate bathroom, so they used to go to the public baths once a week. On the other days, especially in the summer, his mother would warm a pail of water in the evening, place Yasha in the broad and deep enameled bowl—green on the outside and white on the inside—and pour water on him from a pot. Small rivulets of mud would trickle down his bony little body, sunburnt and dirty from running around and rolling in the dust with the other boys. His mother and his aunts had strictly forbidden him to run down to the Dniester with them to bathe. Later, when he was already in the upper grades, their forbidding and their threats that he would be dragged down into a whirlpool, God forbid, had very little effect on him; he ran off there throughout his summer vacations. One day when he was at the public baths and his mother had shampooed his head, little Yasha heard an unhappy voice above him, speaking to his mother: "Shame on you! Why do you drag the young man to bathe with you?!" Yasha opened an eye carefully: two fat pink thighs were rubbing against each other, separated from a fat, wrinkled belly by a patch of black hair. His mother didn't answer the woman, but after her further words: "He could have gone to the baths with his father!" she got angry and answered: "We can do without your advice!" Nevertheless, a week later she asked a neighbor to take Yasha with him to the baths . . .

———

He came out of the bathroom refreshed, wearing dark-blue silk pajamas with a thin black belt. It was a bit narrow in the shoulders, so the trousers hung over the cloth toes of the bedroom slippers. Rachel had prepared the pajamas and slippers for him to put on during the few moments when he was trudging alone down the narrow corridor. Yasha just stood there, not sure of what to do next. He called Rachel softly, but she didn't answer, so he went into a large room with two big windows. A crude sofa, covered with mustard-colored plush, stood next to a wall. Farther down on the same side of the room, closer to one of the windows, there was a deep armchair, also covered with the same mustard-colored plush. Separating those two pieces was an old-fashioned floor lamp with a tall, green lampshade and a narrow, round marble table. Across from the sofa, against the opposite wall, was a small, glass cabinet with dishes on the shelves—Yasha's mother would probably have given it the fancy name "servant," which he had heard for the first time when he was about twelve. His mother had come in one day, happy, and the minute she crossed the threshold had said: "Sisters—I just got a quarterly bonus, and we're going to buy a 'servant'!" Off in a corner, on a wooden stand, was a television set with a small screen, far from the latest model. Yasha's gaze also didn't omit the two framed pictures on the walls, beautifully embroidered with colored cotton thread. They, in turn, evoked memories of his mother's and aunts' house in Bender, when during the long winter evenings all three sisters would sit on their sofa and little Yasha would squeeze himself in among them. Cuddling with one another as if all four of them could grow together into a single creature, they would hold hands and look at the few yellowed photographs that miraculously remained from their severed youth . . .

And another large image on the wall, hanging right over the sofa, painted with oils by a firm, artistic hand, drew Yasha's eyes to it. Two raging forces of nature—the sky and the water—had thrown themselves upon each other; the excited waves, with angry, white foam at their edges, had risen up to the thick, dark clouds that lurked above them, spreading their godly power throughout space. And between the two natural forces, hanging like a torn-off ray of light, was a seagull carrying a red child's shoe in his beak . . .

He heard someone opening the door to the corridor. For a moment, Yasha felt lost; he wasn't in a position to ask who was coming, as if he were the master of the house, especially when someone was opening the door with his own key. It never occurred to him that it could be Rachel, but then she appeared with several plastic bags in her hands, with her face wet but looking pleased.

"I see I've come back right on time."

"Does that mean that I was alone in the house?" It still didn't make sense to Yasha.

"No, my mother was in the house, after all."

Rachel went into the kitchen with the packages and asked from there:

"What's the problem—are you afraid to be in a house alone?"

Yasha smiled. The momentary inner tension disappeared. He went over to the open door and looked into the kitchen—a narrow room with a little window—designed, apparently, only for a housewife with an elegant figure. Rachel was puttering around at the narrow table with the packages she had brought in. She arranged little cans and packages and put something in the refrigerator.

"I just thought," Yasha said, "that you were in another room with your mother . . ."

Rachel's eyes rested on him.

"The pajamas suit you," she said quietly, quite differently than before. "My father rarely wore them. He felt that only aristocrats wore pajamas."

"To tell the truth, I never had any pajamas before either, except that when I was still a child of about five or six my aunts sewed me a pair of pajamas. But I didn't want to sleep in them, because, I told them, 'one doesn't sleep in a suit.'"

They both broke out laughing. Suddenly, Rachel caught herself as if she had remembered something, and apologized:

"I have to leave you alone for a few minutes to see how my mother is doing."

Yasha, who was still standing in the doorway leaning his shoulder against the doorpost, moved to one side to make room for Rachel to go through. For a moment he smelled the same apple-scent of the shampoo with which he had just washed his hair . . .

They ate lunch together, in the kitchen, at the narrow table. It didn't bother Yasha at all—on the contrary, he told her a well-known Russian proverb and translated it into English: "Crowded, but in peace."

"You know of course, that you can get all kinds of Russian foods at the international store. But I don't understand anything about them; furthermore, the names of the dozens of sausages and pastramis drive me crazy—I can't wrap my tongue around them. Fortunately, I met a Russian neighbor of ours there, also an immigrant, and she explained everything to me."

"I must tell you, Rachel, that your Russian neighbor didn't mislead you. Everything is very delicious, especially since you did it just for me . . ."

"Are you sure?" the mistress of the house remarked playfully. "I'm eating these delicacies of yours too, after all, and I hope I won't get poisoned."

"Americans adapt quickly to the cooking of various peoples, especially here in New York with its worldwide menu."

Yasha, whose "Russian lunch" at Rachel's was his breakfast as well, tried not to show how hungry he was. But he was apparently unsuccessful in pulling off that trick, because the hospitable lady of the house kept constantly pushing more food under his nose. He noticed that, and as if to justify himself, said:

"I had almost forgotten how delicious these snacks are."

"You know what?" Rachel proposed unexpectedly. The "what" remained hanging in the air for a moment, till she pushed herself away from the table and opened one of the three cupboards. "I have a bit of Scotch here, it's certainly not vodka but still; I'm sure that won't interfere with your appetite."

She put out two little glasses on the table, and Yasha poured the alcohol. He raised his glass, and looking at the golden brown bit of Scotch, said quietly:

"I propose a toast to two things: the rotted board on the boardwalk, which caused us to meet, and the rain, which arranged today's meeting . . ."

"Very original mediators," Rachel smiled, and suddenly added: "*Nazdorovye!*" (To your health!)

One's tongue usually gets looser after drinking. With Rachel and Yasha, however, it was just the opposite. They sat there quietly, as if as if they wanted to listen to the noise of the rain—a partner in the group—and perhaps because the no-longer-young people needed the silent pause in order to search their souls again before continuing farther along the road of being destined for each other.

"As I understand it . . ." Rachel said, drawing out the words softly, as if she hadn't entirely made up her mind whether to ask or not:

"Do you live by yourself?"

"Yes," Yasha answered, ripping himself out of his own reverie, "it's been half a year now since my ex-wife and our daughter moved to Boston."

He reached for the bottle and filled his glass. Rachel didn't ask any more questions. She felt that Yasha himself now had to decide whether he should continue telling things or perhaps make do with the few previous words.

"Clara, my ex-wife, is a dentist—a golden trade in America. But she had to pass exams, of course, to obtain permission to work here. Even before coming here, we had thought that before anything else I would try to find some kind of work wherever I could and she would study. My mother-in-law and father-in-law, who came with us, have many relatives here, and one of them helped me get a job as a taxi driver . . . It was not easy, but we knew what we had come here for, and that there was no road back. I must say that her parents helped us a great deal, especially by looking after our little girl, Marina. She was nine years old then. Clara studied, and I—I turned the wheel, sometimes for twelve or fourteen hours a day. In short, after a year and a half, Clara obtained permission to work and quickly found a job in a private clinic. We rented another apartment, not far from her parents, and gradually began to stand on our own feet. I was already sick and tired of being a taxi driver, but for the time being I was unable to quit. Of course it got easier after Clara started to work, but the better you live, the more you want. So I thought to myself: I'll hold out for half a year, until winter, and then I'll take a computer course. After all, I'm no dumber than anyone else, and it's a good business, well-paying. And that's what probably would have happened—I'm a determined fellow. But one day I came home late at night. Clara, as always, gave me my food, and then just like that, sitting across from me as you are sitting now, she said to me that somehow she had fallen in love with another man, a doctor who lived in Boston, and they had decided to get together."

Yasha had a choking lump in his throat. He was still holding the glass of Scotch.

"Strange," he continued. "This is the first time I've told the story out loud. It probably sounds very trivial, no?"

Rachel didn't answer. She had also avoided looking straight at his face while he was telling the story. She knew herself, from her own experience, that one can often be torn to pieces by such pain, but when you tell it to someone else it elicits no more than a sigh of sympathy.

"You know what, Yasha?" she suddenly proposed. "Let's drink coffee."

She didn't wait for his "yes" or "no"—getting up from the table, she started puttering around at the stove.

"Do you know, Yasha, what a *finjan* is? A *finjan* is a kind of brass utensil in which one brews real coffee. I'm not such a great cook, but I can make good coffee—they taught me that in Israel."

"In Israel?"

"Yes, Yasha. I lived there for quite a few years."

"You definitely have to tell me about that."

Rachel turned her head toward him, now looking him straight in the eyes, and said:

"I'm afraid my story will also sound trivial."

At that point, Rachel was not inclined to expand on that theme, and taking advantage of her rights as master of the house, she said:

"Enough sitting here crowded in, Yasha. Take your glass of Scotch and the bottle and go into the parlor. You'll be more comfortable on the sofa than here. In about ten minutes I'll bring you the coffee."

Yasha sat down on the sofa, leaning his neck against its soft edge. He left the empty glass and the bottle of Scotch on the marble table under the green lampshade. He again held his breath, as he had earlier in the bathroom when he had immersed himself in the bathtub full of water. A weary weakness spread over his body and poisoned every limb, every drop of blood; only his head, as if it were separated from his heavy, weakened body, swayed slightly—back and forth, back and forth. Each of the old-fashioned objects around him contained its own special secret and magic, which were capable of awakening things and events from long ago and binding them to today, drawing human beings into a deceptive game of time. In his today, he could see no way out, so he looked for support from his yesterday, and there he encountered the porcelain toy that used to stand on a glass shelf in the house of the three sisters. Among themselves, they called the coddled thing "the Chinese Emperor"; the Emperor sat on his throne, with his legs in loose trousers and shoes with pointed, turned-up toes tucked under him; his arms supported his great, round belly, with his belly button showing. He sat there proudly and sedately, and only his shaved head with its short, black, brush-like mustache swayed slightly back and forth, back and forth . . . To little Yasha, it always seemed that the Emperor's eyes were following him and knew about all his mischief; that indeed was why he always looked so displeased and was constantly shaking his head—"ay-ay-ay." Yasha's gaze continued to search in the corners of time till it came to rest on another head, a little head, also of a doll but a living one, with sparse, black hair and unfocused pale blue eyes; she was sticking out her little tongue, which was the size of a thumbnail, and licking the drops of water off her lips: his week-old little daughter, Marina. They had named the child after Yasha's mother, whose name was Manya. Understandably, Manya was too old-fashioned, so Clara agreed to Marina—it sounded pretty. Clara and her mother were afraid to bathe the baby, so Yasha carried out his first paternal mission. Where did he get the courage and knowledge to bathe a tiny creature who was only as long as an arm from palm to elbow?

Rachel appeared in the room with a narrow, square, silver platter in her hands, and on it there were two small china cups filled with coffee.

"Well—here's my patented Israeli coffee."

Not receiving an answer, she bent down toward her guest and encountered his sleeping smile. She felt embarrassed for a few moments and then took the platter back to the kitchen. Then she brought a pillow and a thin blanket from the cabinet in the corridor. Going over to Yasha, she touched his shoulder lightly. He barely opened his eyes, looked confused, and murmured something, probably in Russian because Rachel didn't understand it.

"Go to sleep, Yasha—don't be ashamed," she said, interpreting the murmur in her own way.

Rachel covered him and quietly went into the other room, where her mother was waiting for her.

– Rachel –

Ever since she had begun to understand what her parents went through during the war, Rachel had felt punished. In the little apartment that her parents rented three blocks from their store, there was always a lack of light and air, not so much because those two things physically avoided their residence but because sorrow had settled into every corner, looking out at them with cold, lifeless eyes. Rachel always went around feeling frozen. She used to dress warmly in her father's coarse, dark-brown pullover with the sleeves rolled up and burrow deeply into the wide old leather armchair, already worn out in spots, which was a gift from Uncle Max and stood right next to the window. There, curled up like a cat, Rachel felt cozy and comfortable, as if the warmth of other people's behinds and backs squeezed against the soft chair were being transferred to her. She got to love her perch, as her mother called it, and quite often, after school, if she didn't have to go to the store to help her parents, she would spend her time in the old armchair, either doing her homework or reading a book.

Rachel felt that her father was distancing himself from her more and more; the dark little alcove in the store became his permanent abode. He sat there for days at a time, and as a result her mother had needed to hire Bolek to help her with her work. Bolek was a Polish immigrant. A tall and skinny man, his straight blond hair was always tousled; in contrast, he greatly pampered his yellow mustache, which hung down from the corners of his mouth and almost reached the top of the little dimple on his pointy chin. "He does everything one, two, three!" said Rachel's mother, swelling with pride about him. She spoke with him in Polish, throwing in English words. The customers liked him too, because he joked with them in his mixed language—they laughed more at his speech than at his jokes. Rachel's mother was very satisfied with him, but her father hated him. He screamed that Poles were all criminals and Jew-murderers, and that Rachel's mother should fire him.

One afternoon—Rachel happened to be in the store just then—her father came out of his dark little place and attacked Bolek with screams and fists. Her mother immediately went to her father and tried to calm him. She told Rachel to bring ice in a little bag, and she laid it next to his heart and rubbed his temples with her fingers. Rachel had never before seen her father in such a state: he sat next to her mother on a wooden crate, every drop of blood drained from his face, his hands trembling, leaning his head on her mother's shoulder; he sobbed like a child, without tears in his lifeless eyes.

Rachel's mother took him to the doctor, who said that they should put him in a certain hospital in East Flatbush or else the illness "would progress rapidly." But her mother didn't do that; she had a different view of the matter: "A person who has lived through so much should now be locked up in a madhouse?!" Two weeks later, her father had another episode, this time at home. It happened at night: he broke a windowpane and tried to jump out. Rachel called the ambulance and they took her father to the hospital in East Flatbush. The next day Rachel's mother told her that during the war her father and his first wife and their seven-year-old girl, Mirele, had hidden in a bunker with twenty other Jews. A day had passed quietly—the Germans didn't find them. At night, however, the girl had started crying—her belly had begun to hurt a lot. The crying could certainly have been heard above, in which case everyone would have been killed. Her mother took her outside. Everyone had remained silent, her father too. He had seemed crippled, grown into the earth.

"That picture has remained before his eyes: his wife, with the child in her arms, creeping out of the bunker. The weeping and the last cries of his little daughter follow him . . ."

"What was her name, Mirele's mother?" Rachel asked, shocked by what she had just heard.

"Rachel, may you live for many years—perhaps I shouldn't have told you, but after all, you're already a big girl and will be able to understand." She sighed and added: "By the time I was fourteen years old, I too had already seen death before my eyes, you shouldn't know from such things!"

Two weeks after that night, Rachel's mother took her along to the hospital. Rachel sat in the courtyard, on a long bench under a tree with long hanging branches, and waited for her mother to come back with her father. The courtyard was reminiscent of the corner of a park, surrounded by a high, stone fence. Straight, rather wide paths paved with dark red bricks divided the flat ground into measured-out quadrants covered by manicured grass. In one corner of each such square, a narrow, square plaque was sticking out of the grass—there were as many squares as plaques. Rachel peered at the closest of them and read: Maury and Rosa Lerner. She tried to figure it out: What could the sign with the two names mean? The thought that came to her mind frightened her. "Are these the graves of the sick people who have died here?" She didn't know what to do; she didn't see a living soul on the paths except a squirrel that crept down from a tree and moved close to her. Standing up on its hind legs and folding its forelegs on its downy, white belly, it leaned its flexible back onto its pointy little tail. The little animal fixed its shiny, black eyes on Rachel; turned its gray, velvety ears outward so they could remain on guard; and stood frozen thusly with just its sharp-pointed little nose sticking up in the air, sniffing, ready at any moment either to grab any food it had successfully begged for or to scurry back up the tree.

Rachel's expression changed immediately. The small creature, which trembled at any rustling sound, drove away her dark fear and brought joy with it. Rachel felt around in the two little pockets on her beautiful pink caftan—it happened not infrequently that she would find some sort of snack in her pockets: a piece of candy, a cookie, or a nut that her mother had stuffed in there, but this caftan had been bought for her by her mother only a day earlier and Rachel had worn it today for the first time, especially for the meeting with her father. She shrugged her shoulders regretfully, as if excusing herself to the little animal, but as she continued searching in her pockets the squirrel suddenly shook itself, turned its head back and forth, once again put all four feet on the ground, and ran in short zigzags to a distant corner of the courtyard.

Rachel understood that something had frightened the squirrel, and she looked around. She saw her mother walking at the other end of the path, leading a man who looked like Rachel's father. She had to think about it, because even from a distance the man looked older and different than her father—he was hunched over with his head sticking out ahead of him as if he were racing forward dragging his weakened body behind him, with Rachel's mother barely holding him back and following him with small steps. Was he racing toward Rachel, seeing her sitting on the bench, and should Rachel run toward him as she always used to do years ago when she was still a little girl? Rachel didn't move. Everything got mixed up in her head—the little signs sticking out of the grass, the squirrel that had run away, her father's sickly movements, and her mother's forlorn smile when she encountered her daughter's gaze.

Her father sat between them. Her mother wouldn't stop talking, as if she were afraid of forgetting something if Rachel's father interrupted her, as he used to do frequently, squeezing his ears with his broad palms and screeching: "Enough—enough of pouring it on . . ." Or perhaps she was afraid to stop because her silent gaze would then encounter the lifeless eyes of her husband or his open mouth from which his lips seemed to have forgotten how to bring forth a human word. He looked downward somewhere with a blank expression; he kept constantly trying to bend over, as if the laces of his shoes were too tight and he wanted to loosen them. Rachel's mother, not stopping her "pouring it on," pulled him back forcibly. At one point, he uttered an unhappy, choked sound from his throat, and thick saliva dripped from his lower lip. Rachel's mother was holding a handkerchief wadded up in her hand, so she quickly wiped her husband's mouth.

"Why don't you say something, Rachel?" she exclaimed, as if she hadn't previously noticed that her daughter too was sitting there with them on the same bench. "Don't you have anything to say to your father?"

Rachel got confused. Perhaps she did have something to say—she simply hadn't thought about it. Her father seldom spoke to her about her personal affairs; she, her father, and her mother all stuck to one area of conversation—their family. Her mother was always busy—in the store, in the house—so she, the child, used to spend time mostly with her father. That didn't mean that her father paid her any special attention, played with her, or told her stories; he did his own thing and Rachel did hers, and it was precisely their quiet busyness that united them both. He used to emanate such an air of quiet concern, which densely filled the space around Rachel that she could stay there for hours feeling calm and protected from all danger. That was also true later, when her father used to accompany her to school in the morning and wait for her at the school gate in the afternoon. The silent presence of one next to the other created such a spiritual bond between them that a superfluous word might have disturbed it. The artfulness of their mute-language grew along with Rachel's growth, and accordingly her Yiddish got sparser and sparser and it got harder and harder for her to talk to her father in his language.

She recalled that her father hadn't left her bedside for a minute when she was in bed for a whole week with a severe cold. She had had a high fever at the time, and sometimes, coming out of a sweaty episode of feeling burned by tongues of flame, Rachel would grasp her father's sunken face. Each time, he would put his fingers to her cheeks and forehead and whisper something. Rachel would strain to understand what her father was saying, but she didn't understand it—the words were not in Yiddish, and certainly not in English, which her father barely spoke. Later she more than once wanted to ask him about that, but something held her back till it was entirely forgotten, or, more accurately, moved back into a distant corner of her memory like many other questions that remained lying there, silently dying away without an answer. (Years later, when Rachel was living in Israel, she heard a familiar whisper next to her ear, and an answer to the forgotten question appeared: her father had been saying a prayer beside her sickbed.) The years had even further filled the relationship between Rachel and her father with a certain heartfelt-satiated feeling of things unsaid. It might have looked like a game; they would make do with a few words torn out of their day-to-day hustle bustle—when they were eating supper, were making a request of her mother, less often when watching television, and even more rarely during a stroll. Their promenades near the ocean on Saturdays became a rarity as time passed, and Rachel used to run there alone or with a girlfriend. There, near the water, she felt like a free, white bird. But even the few words between Rachel and her father became quieter and quieter; her father suffocated them within himself like the last sparks that connected his self to the outside world. The darkness of yesterday swamped and poisoned the reality of today and left not a single bright spot for a tomorrow. Until the nocturnal episode occurred . . .

"Why don't you say something, Rachel?" her mother asked again, now as a reproach.

Rachel trembled, but not because of her mother's biting words; she realized that her hand was lying on her father's hand and quickly pulled it back as if she had touched a burr. Looking her mother straight in the eye, she quietly asked:

"Mama, what do the plaques in the green squares of grass mean?"

About a week later, Rachel's mother brought her father home, and five months later he died. Right after they came home from the cemetery on Staten Island, Rachel went to the beach. It was the end of September, but a light, warm breeze was blowing in her face, whether as a reminder of the hot, exhausting, humid July days or as a deceptive little joke sent by the angry, cold winds that were already on their way and would rage any day now along the entire shore. Whichever it might be, Rachel allowed herself to be seduced by the pleasurable breeze, which made her squint, and eagerly swallowed gulps of air. Suddenly something got stuck in her throat; it melted quickly and flowed over her gums, filling her mouth with a bittersweet, thick juice. She immediately understood what it was and looked around, seeking the place from which the spicy vanilla aroma could have reached her. No sign remained of the booth from which Rachel's father had long ago bought her little bags of roasted nuts drizzled with sugary syrup during their promenades on the boardwalk. The booth and the nut seller, "Gypsy," had long since disappeared from Brighton Beach. The time of her childhood had passed; it was as if the little girl in the tiny blue dress embroidered with red and yellow flowers, the red shoes, and the yellow beret on her head had dissolved in the fresh, transparent sea air, and that it was precisely today that the mischievous breeze had brought her the news.

The bittersweet sensation in her mouth ate into her throat, clawed at the soft tissue to the point of pain. It got hard for her to breathe, because at the same moment a bitter knot of tears uncoiled from the pit of her stomach up to her throat, erupted to the outside with a sob, and poured over her face. In the funeral home, and afterwards at the cemetery, she had not shed any tears. She had even heard her neighbor whispering: "A child doesn't weep for her deceased father?!" As she had never before wanted to do while he was alive, Rachel wanted to ask him a very important question, but she felt, while watching them lower the wooden casket with his body into the grave, that the territory that her mother so proudly called "family" had gotten narrower. And again she heard a grating sound next to her ear: "It's as if he had grown into the earth," but this time the words fell onto the lid of the coffin.

For quite a while after her father's death, Rachel didn't know what to do with herself. Actually, the problem had begun previously, right after her mother told her about the death of her father's first family. An image kept following her: Rachel, whose name she bore, quietly slipping out of the bunker carrying her crying little daughter. Furthermore she clearly pictured her own mother doing the same with her . . . That fearsome image made the question she hadn't managed to ask her father even more frightful: "Why had he let them go alone?!"

At that moment, Rachel felt the spiritual bond that had tied her and her father's fates so closely together start to loosen and unravel; she saw herself falling from a dangerous height, with her outstretched hand reaching to another hand, whose fingers had been locked together with hers just an instant before, but had been unable to hold on and had let her fall free. She looked down and saw beneath her feet, in their red shoes, a spurting wave that was just about to swallow her whole. At the last minute, before the catastrophe could occur, Rachel opened her eyes . . .

She was lying in her bed, uncovered and sweaty. Breathing easily after the groundless fears, she was now ready to jump out of bed, but then a new fright attacked her: she noticed a few red spots on her nightgown and also smeared on the sheet. She didn't understand where they had come from, and cried out: "Mama . . ."

Her mother was still in the house and she ran into Rachel's room. There she encountered her daughter's forlorn gaze, so she too looked at the bed. She immediately understood everything, and, now calm, she went up to Rachel, hugged her, and kissed her on the head.

"You don't have to be afraid, my child," she calmed her, "it's a normal thing at your age. Go into the bathroom and take a shower . . ."

Rachel's mother was now busy at work all day. Almost half a year after her husband's death, her Uncle Max also died. His will left quite a bit of money to his niece. At that point, she decided to buy the delicatessen on the corner of Coney Island Avenue and Avenue Z and convert it to a grocery/coffee shop with several tables where people could sit and have a cup of coffee and a sandwich or a delicious piece of pastry. In addition to Bolek, she hired another woman, a cook. But Bolek showed himself to be a person one could rely on: he was always wherever he was needed—you could find him in the kitchen, at the stove where he made his patented Polish pierogis, at the little tables with a platter in his hands, or behind the cash register. Once, Rachel's mother even told the cook, half-seriously, that she could leave the whole business to Bolek and go to Florida for the winter. In her comment there was something more than a compliment from a boss about her worker, but her daughter recalled that only some time later.

Rachel too, helped her mother, though her mother derived no joy from that. She felt that Rachel should stay at home and study, so that when she finished high school she could study to be a doctor or a lawyer.

"Why not? You have a good head, *keyn eyn hora*. Why else am I suffering here?!"

Rachel would listen to her mother's words quietly, without disagreeing with her. Her thoughts and dreams about her future, however, ran in a very different direction. She didn't dare to even verbalize them, so distant and fantastic did they appear even in her own eyes, to say nothing of her mother's ears. And perhaps Rachel kept them to herself because she didn't want to frighten her beautiful dreams away, the types of dreams many girls her age had.

In the evenings, before going to sleep, Rachel, already lying in bed, would pull one of her thick photo albums (she only had five altogether) out of her desk and leaf through the pages the way she had once looked with curiosity upon the faded cut-out pictures pasted to the walls of her half-dark alcove. Perhaps it was from that childhood fantasizing that her adolescent dream of becoming a movie star had emerged. Now Rachel, looking at the faces of her beloved actresses and actors, could tell you all their names and the names of the films they had appeared in.

Not infrequently she would stand in front of the mirror in her mother's bedroom—a tall mirror in which she could see herself from head to toe—and look at the fifteen-year-old girl, gazing with critical eyes at her long, skinny legs with their knobby knees, and her narrow, bony hips and very meager breasts, but, on the other hand, a long neck and two big, dark eyes, about which her father had once said that one could see the bottom of a well at night in them. What he meant by that, Rachel had not understood, but she had liked the way he said it. Girls in her class thought she resembled the famous Audrey Hepburn, though her nose was quite differently shaped, not so upturned . . .

Two years later, when she was finishing high school, she had seen many changes in herself that made her look femininely exciting. Her lips had already tasted their first boyish kisses—clumsy and long—while she and the boy were rubbing against each other in the half-darkness, enveloped in the sounds of the Beatles, or when, suddenly breaking apart, sweaty and overheated, they would break into a rock-and-roll dance moving as quickly as possible, as if they could thereby drive away their burgeoning lusts . . . Those were happy days and nights that got her dazed and confused without marijuana.

By then, Rachel was looking into the mirror with very different eyes. Of her previous dreams about the sparkling Hollywood skies there remained only a few sparks, and the photo albums with the stars had long since found their place in the attic, in the heavy wooden trunk, amid other discarded items, some even from Europe. The walls of the apartment where Rachel lived with her mother seemed to close in and narrow the area of their mutual existence. She often used to feel, especially after a noisy celebration, that she was falling into a dark hole of emptiness and exhaustion. Once she even thought that maybe it was a sort of bunker, similar to the one in which her father and twenty other Jews had survived. Each generation probably undergoes trials in such a bunker. Recently, she had seen her generation's bunkers in a television documentary about the Vietnam War: there are those who race out of their bunkers to save other people's lives with their own, and there are those who bury themselves alive within them . . .

On such melancholy days, Rachel would run to the beach. She had learned to listen to the seagulls and understand their sounds, extracting individual voices from their hundred-voice chorus as they sat on the gray-green water and rocked on the waves like white paper boats. One would weep and another one would complain about his fate; two others would fight over a bit of food, and a third one seemed to be cursing her friend because she had rejected her boyfriend; a mother gull would sob because her baby had hurt himself on a cliff, and another one, just the opposite, would go into raptures of joy because right before her eyes her son had circled in his first free flight . . .

Rachel decided to study to become a psychologist. She felt in herself an ability to listen to people and perhaps help them to understand themselves. If her father had had someone in whom to confide his feelings of lostness, what happened to him wouldn't have happened. She would try to explain it to her mother—helping people in that way was no less important than the help of a doctor or a lawyer. Her mother wouldn't oppose it, she was sure—in the brief hours that she had spent with her, Rachel had always felt a certain bright lightness coming from her and being transmitted to herself. Filled with that energy, she would go around for a while as if she had wings. Their closeness further increased after that morning when Rachel discovered the few red spots on her bed. It was as if a new and intimate relationship had been forged between mother and daughter, but now in a very different way—such as can only occur between two women. Her mother was the pulsing heart of their small family, and behind her talkativeness, which so grated on her father's nerves, was actually hidden a bitter loneliness. Rachel understood that much later, when she herself lacked a match to light up the road on which she was stranded.

It happened on a Saturday, a warm summer day that Rachel remembered very well. The day began with a clear blue sky. She had arranged with a girlfriend to meet on Manhattan Beach, to spend the beautiful day at the water. But, as often happens in New York, close to noon the sky grew cloudy, and it became clear that the weather would not permit them to continue to enjoy bathing and lying around on the beach. Her girlfriend proposed that they listen to the new Beatles album, *Sgt. Pepper's*, which she had borrowed for the day from her older brother.

Rachel, however, declined, not understanding why. She didn't know whether the sudden change of weather had also changed her mood, or if she wasn't in the mood to listen to music at that moment, or if it was just like her mother used to say to her at times: "Some sort of angry fly bit you." In any case, she went back home.

Rachel unlocked her door quietly—her mother might have gone to bed to rest a bit. Passing by her parents' bedroom, Rachel heard strange sounds coming from within: choked pieces of words—more like sobs. She quickly went to the door, which was not completely closed, and was about to pull it open, but she suddenly stopped because she felt heat coming through the open doorway—a fire that was driving her back from a dangerous spot. But she couldn't move—the narrow opening revealed an image that both frightened her and riveted her gaze with a shocking image: a man was on his knees, holding fleshy female hips against his skinny belly with his tanned, veiny hands. The two naked bodies seemed to be framed on all four sides—she didn't immediately understand that what she was seeing was only a reflection in the tall, narrow mirror that she herself used to look into. The rest of what was taking place on the bed was outside the frame of the mirror and hidden from her view. A spasm stopped her breathing for a moment, and it seemed to her that her heart had also stopped and that she had been standing at the doorway for a long time with her mouth open and her eyes staring. Her breath returned together with a cry. The reflection trembled as if the mirror were going to shatter, and two grimacing, overheated faces swam into view: Bolek's and her mother's.

Rachel ran back to her room and threw herself on her bed, facedown. She still heard the harsh sounds in her ear, but they quickly grew in volume and turned into hysterical laughter, as if someone were mocking her. Only seagulls could laugh that way, and Rachel immediately saw them before her eyes. They were slapping their pointy wings in the air, right in her face, and were densely covering the sun. She tried to tear through the living wall of wings, which had sharp hooks like barbed wire. She touched the steel barbs with her fingers and immediately pulled back her hands. It was her fate to die forgotten, surrounded and punished by precisely those birds whom she had so loved and to whom she had entrusted her greatest secrets. "They've betrayed me," thought Rachel, "and when relatives do that, there remains only to close one's eyes and say the last goodbye."

– Yasha –

An instant before Yasha opened his eyes, he felt the touch of her gaze on his eyelashes, or so he imagined. The old lady was sitting in her wheelchair, motionless, looking at him as he was lying on the sofa. The morning sunshine was falling on her face, emphasizing every wrinkle on her thin, pale skin, under which one could clearly see the projecting bones of her sunken temples, cheeks, and pointy chin. The long illness had sucked all the color of life from her body—only a few rare signs had been preserved on her shrunken, emaciated features, like reminders drawn on a portrait. They also came through the dark, deep eye-sockets and fell onto Yasha's eyelashes like warm drops.

He didn't move, as if the sickly image of the old woman, torn away from reality, were some sort of nuisance that was still following him from a bad dream. But no! Quite the contrary—Yasha seized upon the image with a fluttering heart; God forbid that he should drive it away and lose her again, this time forever, because only there, in his dreams, could the image find refuge.

"Mama," his lips mouthed the word soundlessly.

After the operation, they had all hoped that she would regain her strength. Her sisters never left her bedside for a minute. It was always that way when one of them got sick: they didn't eat and didn't sleep and didn't know what to do with themselves. That was also true when he, Yasha, would catch a cold. All three of them were a single body, and each felt the pain of the others, perhaps even more strongly than her own. Yasha was quietly astonished by that. He had told Clara about the three sisters when they had just begun dating, but Clara wasn't surprised. She found an explanation for it, which she referred to by a long modern word, probably some sort of medical concept, which Yasha promptly forgot. He would surely not have remembered it if not for the fact that all three of the sisters died within a single year.

That was the year he married Clara. Almost three months before the wedding, his mother took a turn for the worse. The doctors just waved their hands in futility—the disease wouldn't let go of her and it spread all through her body. It made no sense to keep her in the hospital any longer, and his mother herself pleaded for them to take her home. She sat on her bed, her feet covered with a blanket, leaning her back on two pillows. Her head, which she kept wrapped in a white kerchief, was bent to one side, exactly as in the picture in which she was photographed with Yasha when he first started school. The photographer had sat them down on a bench, putting several thick books under Yasha so he would look taller. Stepping back a few paces, he had considered them for a moment and then had bent their heads and pushed them together lightly. "Your heads, your heads!" he suddenly cried out, running to his box-camera on its tripod. "Another second . . . There, like that!"

His mother had asked the sisters to leave the room, and when they closed the door behind them, she drew the corners of her mouth back slightly.

"They'll have to forgive me for discussing secrets with you."

Yasha had taken her hand and tried to answer in the same tone:

"Are you sure, Mama, that you want to keep secrets from them?!"

"From them, maybe not, but don't interrupt me."

She was breathing hard and mumbled something, as if to a third person:

"I'm not destined to dance at your wedding . . ."

"Why are you talking like that, Mama?"

"Hear me out, Yasha—it's not good to postpone a celebration to another date; that's not the way Jews do things . . ."

"Mama . . ."

"Don't interrupt me . . . There, in the 'servant,' on the shelf with the Chinese Emperor, you'll find your father's address. It wouldn't be nice if you and Clare didn't invite him to your wedding . . . He's still your father, after all . . . And now call your aunts back in . . ."

Several days before going with Clara to register as husband and wife, Yasha suddenly remembered—the box! Truth be told, till then his mind hadn't been on fulfilling his mother's request. They hadn't postponed the wedding, but they had decided to make it a very modest affair, more like a dinner for close relatives and friends, and certainly without music. He took the porcelain toy, the Emperor, down from the shelf. It shook its head in dissatisfaction, as if to say "I'm the boss here!" Yasha immediately recognized the box his mother had mentioned. It looked like some kind of sea treasure, covered on all sides by tiny pieces of multicolored stones and shells, and on the lid, in the middle, there was a rose made of mother-of-pearl strips resembling long, pointy flower pedals. In the lower right-hand corner of the lid, on a flat, black, polished oval stone, there was engraved, with beautiful cursive letters, "Odessa, August 1954." His mother had gone there at that time on vacation from her work in a sanatorium, and little Yasha had been left at home with his aunts for three whole weeks. She came back from the seaside tanned and happy, and with gifts for each of them. For quite a while later his mother would recall how beautiful the city of Odessa was, and how warm the water of the Black Sea was.

He opened the box's lid. It contained his four medals won in chess tournaments, and two certificates: sports-master and a rectangular certificate enameled with Bordeaux color, with a golden seal of the Soviet Union in the center—he had received that, together with his diploma, when he graduated from university. Among themselves, the students had called the rectangular certificate "the little swimmer," perhaps because the university diploma made it possible for them to keep themselves afloat on the sea of life. There was another thing: a faded, square piece of oilcloth with a little hole in one corner, on which one could barely make out his surname; the day, month, and year of his birth; his sex and weight; and the number of the hospital ward where his mother had given birth. Yasha smiled—he recalled how his mother had once showed it to him. At that time a white gauze ribbon had still been attached to the little hole. "This is your first document," his mother had explained. "They attached it to your left foot in the obstetrics ward." And what's this?! His first baby tooth? It had been shaky for a long time but hadn't wanted to fall out. Yasha had been very annoyed by that because almost all the boys on his street had already lost a tooth. When his tooth finally fell out, his mother had taken it from Yasha to throw it out in the attic. "When we do that, we mustn't forget to say here, *mousie*—a milk tooth, and give Yasha an iron one instead." Yasha was sure at that time that his mother had actually done that. And now another thing that had once given him so much joy but ended up in bitter tears: after dozens of years in which it had lain in hiding, Yasha again held in his hand his dark-green fountain pen. Now he could read the inscription on its shiny surface himself: "Use it in good health! Your father." Simple words, but because of one word, father, he hadn't written a single letter with the fountain pen. What in the world had happened between two people, his father and mother, that had been capable of erecting a wall of alienation between them, one that had also walled him in for twenty-seven years? Could one explain and justify it just by the cloudy words "it was destined to be?" Who would explain it to him now?

At the very bottom of the box, he found a small, white sheet of paper, folded in half. Written on it in his mother's handwriting was the address and telephone number of Fima (Yefim), which was his father's name. Yasha had found that out for the first time when he first enrolled in school. His mother had led him to a table at which a woman sat who promptly extended her hand and said her name: "Lyudmila Antonovna." Yasha didn't get confused, and he called out his name loudly. The woman smiled, and taking her pen out of the inkwell, she bent over a fat book similar to his mother's bookkeeping ledgers. "This is the way we'll register you in the class journal: 'Yacov,'" said Lyudmila Antonovna. "Not Yacov but Yasha," he corrected her. She stopped writing and explained softly: "Yasha is your name at home, but your full name in Russian is Yakov," and she suddenly asked: "*Otsh-estvo?*" Yasha was hearing that word for the first time, and he raised his head toward his mother. He noticed that she got confused for a moment, but then quickly answered: "Yefimovich." He answered the rest of the questions that Lyudmila Antonovna put to him quickly and smoothly. The unfamiliar word again popped up that evening, when Yasha was already in bed. "Mama," he recalled asking, "what does *otshestvo* mean?" and his mother answered him briefly: "Patronymic. Go to sleep, son, it's already very late."

Yasha's father, as it turned out, lived in a different city, Tiraspol, which was across the Dniester from Bender. Yasha decided not to go there but to call his father on the phone and officially invite him to the wedding—to fulfill his mother's wish, so to speak. But when he did so, and heard, after a pause, a choked answer: "I'll be there, and good luck!" something seemed to tear inside him. It was like a belated echo of the few words that had been spoken at the school gate years before by the same voice with the same tremulousness. It even seemed to Yasha that he was once again feeling the stranger's touch on his shoulder. His father promised to come to the registration at the marriage palace (that's what they called the beautiful building in which they performed the solemn ceremony of registering the marriage.)

A considerable crowd was standing on the steps to the entrance, because aside from Yasha and Clara, a few other couples had gathered to solemnize the marriage. Clara held his arm and leaned slightly against him. Their friends surrounded them, joked, encouraged them, and whispered among themselves; Yasha smiled and answered something, but his eyes restlessly searched among the heads for a man whose face had whirled before his eyes once in his life and then disappeared. Could he have forgotten? Yasha's gaze, like a searchlight, highlighted various known and unknown faces from the crowd, and then quickly left them and shifted its focus to someone else. Suddenly he heard, very close to himself, someone calling out: "Yashanke!" He turned his head and finally saw the face he had sought so eagerly. At that moment, looking at the strange, elderly man who was awkwardly pressing a bouquet of flowers to his bosom, Yasha realized that the distance between the two of them was too great to be overcome.

He never saw his father again, but he saw his face before his eyes more than once, especially at the time of his separation from Clara, when his little daughter Marina ran up to him before leaving for

Boston and, hugging him, whispered in his ear: "I love you very, very much, Papa."

Yasha suddenly woke up. There was nobody next to the sofa, and he thought to himself: "This apartment has a rare ability to awaken memories. Apparently the walls and the objects here have absorbed a great deal of worry and pain from the people who've lived here." Yasha looked around, and his gaze again hit upon the painting that was hanging above the sofa. What attracted him to it so much? It depicted a complicated subject: the stormy ocean and the gray-black sky over it and the hustle bustle of seagulls between them were nothing new in such landscapes, but the little red shoe in the bird's beak injected a certain degree of drama.

He would probably have continued looking at the painting, satisfying his early morning fantasy, if Rachel hadn't come into the room.

"Good morning. You couldn't have been very comfortable sleeping on the sofa?"

Yasha became confused:

"Why would you say such a thing—I haven't slept very well in a long time. And first of all, excuse me for . . ."

Rachel interrupted him:

"You'll find your clothes in the bathroom."

Without another word, Yasha sidled out of the room, not taking his eyes off Rachel, like a little boy who had just done something mischievous. Looking at him, Rachel burst into laughter.

His clothes lay washed, pressed, and folded on the laundry basket, where he had found the silk pajamas the previous day. He quickly got washed and dressed, combed his sparse hair with his fingers, and went out to Rachel.

She was already expecting him in the living room, next to a low, mobile table on wheels, set for two people.

"I can't let you go without trying my patented coffee. Sit down, Yasha."

"Thank you very much, and excuse me again for my foolish behavior yesterday."

Rachel quickly poured the dark, thick, boiled liquid into the cups from the brass vessel that yesterday she had so proudly called by the Arabic word *finjan*.

Yasha felt more at home. Sitting down at the end of the sofa, he drew in deep breaths of air and exclaimed enthusiastically:

"Such an aroma must have come from the Shah's palace in Baghdad when the beautiful Scheherazade was serving him a small, white cup of coffee on a golden platter."

"You'll have to take it from my hands," said Rachel, handing him the coffee from the platter.

"With great pleasure, milady."

They broke out laughing, going along with the improvised drama.

"By the way, what you call *finjan* we in my home town of Bender called by the Turkish name *cezve*. To this day, there is still a fort in Bender left over from the Turks."

Yasha took a few more sips from the cup and added:

"True, I never saw such a thing as a *cezve* back in Bender—you couldn't find it in the stores. Perhaps because no one there drank Turkish coffee."

Rachel broke out laughing again. She put her tray down on the table and wiped away her tears with the napkin.

"I haven't had such a good laugh in a long time. Especially in the morning. My mother always used to say that it isn't good to laugh very early because the day may end in tears."

Her words delighted Yasha.

"You know, Rachel? My mother and my aunts also used to say exactly the same thing. Interesting . . ."

"They said it in Yiddish, no doubt, but I, unfortunately, have almost forgotten the language of my parents."

It got quiet for a moment. Those last words introduced a gnawing yearning for days long gone by, filled with very different sounds, aromas, and images, of which there is only a faint memory today; and they are hidden at that—and it is not at all clear whether that is because we want to keep them for ourselves or because we are ashamed of them.

"I wanted to ask you yesterday," Yasha carefully unraveled the silence. "What kind of painting is this?"

Rachel immediately turned her gaze toward the wall above Yasha's head.

"You like it?" and not waiting for an answer, she added: "I brought the picture from Israel. A local artist painted it there." And she grew silent.

"A white seagull . . . a red shoe," Yasha continued, drawing out the words as if he were trying to tease out the continuation of a story, and Rachel went along with him:

"I heard the story from a girl who had a rare talent for understanding what seagulls say to one another. She used to do that often, while sitting along the beach. One day she heard a beautiful, white seagull say that once upon a time there was a little girl whose name was Mirele. She was always cheerful and happy because she always felt the soft, warm hands of her mother on one side and the thick, firm fingers of her father on the other side. But there came a dark time when bad people appeared in their city. Then Mirele and her parents had to hide somewhere in a dark cellar. There were other people there too, frightened and hungry just like them. How long they sat there crowded together is hard to say, but suddenly Mirele felt hunger cramps in her belly and started crying. Her mother begged her to restrain herself for a while longer and not cry, but it didn't help. Then her mother whispered quietly in her ear that when they went out into the open air she would buy her a pair of beautiful red shoes, and they would all, all three of them, again stroll along their street. But Mirele's pain wouldn't leave her, so her mother picked her up and, holding her by the hand, pulled her after her. Mirele looked around, searched for her father with her eyes, and grabbed for his strong hand with her other hand, but her hand remained hanging in a dark emptiness. The fresh air lapped at her face, and it was so unbelievable that the little girl stopped crying. It was nighttime, but compared with the darkness in the cellar everything around them looked bright. Further, the sky was studded with stars, and each star was sparkling to the little girl. Suddenly they heard someone yelling at them. Her mother pulled her again, but strongly this time, and they started running down a narrow, abandoned little alley. Three men with rifles quickly caught up with them; they tore Mirele from her mother and attacked her mother. They beat her, screaming for her to show them the place where the others were hiding. Her mother remained silent, and the men began to tear her clothing off. Mirele was lying frightened on the paved gutter where she had fallen, and had already completely forgotten about her belly. The only thing that was whirling around in her head was the question, why was her father not with them? He was a strong and mighty person, after all—he wouldn't have allowed such things! And then the girl heard her mother screaming to her: 'Run, Mirele, run and don't look back!' And Mirele got up and started running. She didn't know where she was running to, but the piercing cry of a bird—short, like a gunshot—stopped her. She felt as if she were being dragged into a long, narrow tube. She closed her eyes, and opened them only when gusts of wind were rocking her on their flexible backs. She was flying . . ."

Rachel ended her story and added:

"The painter was the first person to whom I entrusted that story."

"Did you love him?" Yasha asked.

Rachel hadn't expected such a question. She again looked at the painting and said:

"That's an entirely different story, Yasha."

They said goodbye at the elevator. Yasha again felt confused and helpless; he shrugged his shoulders and kneaded his knitted cap with his fingers, as he had at their first meeting.

"I want to tell you, Rachel, that you are an unusual woman."

"Thanks, Yasha, but . . ."

"Don't interrupt me, please. My English is not good enough for me to say what I want to say . . . In your house, for the first time since I came to America, I felt calm and at peace, as if I had caught my breath after a long, exhausting journey and could now look back."

He was speaking and looking into Rachel's eyes. Her pupils gradually dilated, and her eyes came closer to his. He felt the moist touch of her lips on his.

The little doors of the elevator closed and he was gone.

"Oh, the ending is a good one," Rachel said—something she often used to hear from her mother. "He went away in the rain again without an umbrella."

– Rakhel –

The day continued in the same fixed order that had been in place between the two women for the last four years since Rachel had returned from Israel. She sat facing her mother and continued reading the book *Evergreen*. She saw that her mother was still upset; that night Rachel had awakened several times and had heard her mother weeping quietly. She had needed to go to her, sit at her feet, and lightly massage the soles—then her mother fell asleep again.

Rachel understood: her mother felt that something was happening in her house—that a third person, a stranger, was now present; Rachel became convinced of that when her mother awoke quite early and her gaze settled on the door, as if she were asking her daughter: "Who is there?" Rachel dressed her, seated her in the wheelchair, and wheeled her into the living room.

Yasha was sleeping on the same side as in the previous evening, when Rachel had covered him with the blanket; now the blanket was lying on the floor and Yasha's bare feet were sticking out comically from the long pajama pants. Rachel's mother couldn't take her eyes off the sleeping man. Her right hand began trembling slightly—a sign that she was upset. Rachel bent down, took her mother's hand in hers, and whispered softly into her ear: "Be calm, mother, this is Yasha— he is a good person . . . he will not do us any harm . . ." Her mother relaxed. Leaving her near the sofa for a while, Rachel went into the kitchen to prepare her food.

Now, as they read, Rachel, casting quick glances at her mother, suddenly realized that her mother, seeing a man sleeping on the sofa, had gotten so frightened because she was afraid that her unexpected guest would shatter her orderly existence with his intrusion into the narrow area of their day-to-day loneliness.

Rachel was reading a story about a first love that had remained eternally fresh and tender, like an eternal flower, after years of separation. Every word in the book sounded so natural and moving that she thought: Why, in real life, do those same words become so cheapened, so eroded, so darkened? Can such an emotion as love ever remain eternally green in real life? She recalled how Nati had once said to her that in a world in which people are killed every day, love cannot long survive.

Rachel had met Nati in Safed; she had gone there after a three-week stay in Ashdod, where her aunt, her mother's sister, lived. After her decision to leave New York—if for no other reason than to get away from everything that connected her with her past, with her nearly twenty years of life—Rachel had seized on her aunt's proposal to come for a visit to Israel, "and after that, as God wills," her aunt wrote. Her letters, with big, multicolored stamps pasted on them, used to come seldomly. Her aunt wrote in a mixture of Yiddish and Hebrew, such that her mother used to break her head before she could manage to read the letter through to the end. Soon after their liberation, her aunt had gone with a group of young people to Palestine, and her mother had had no communication with her for a rather long time. Only in the early '50s, also thanks to Uncle Max, did they find out where she was and what she was up to. Rachel's aunt had married a local young man and become pious.

Rachel had no great enthusiasm for staying with her aunt, but for the time being she saw no alternative. Furthermore, her mother had insisted that if she didn't stay with her aunt, she wouldn't let her go to Israel at all.

Rachel's suspicions were well founded. As it turned out, she had six cousins, and the youngest was not quite three years old. Her aunt was overjoyed with her American niece and immediately turned the little one over to her. The aunt, of course, knew no English, but the bit of Yiddish that Rachel had salvaged from her childhood years came in handy for her. In any case, she and her aunt were able to understand each other.

"Speak English to the boy," was her aunt's first advice to Rachel, "and he'll later speak English to you."

Her aunt did indeed look like her older sister, but looking at her was like looking at someone through an Oriental screen. What was contradictory, what made her very different from Rachel's mother, was not immediately obvious. She was heavy and slow-moving, and nothing in the house was in its proper place. She didn't work, and she spent almost her whole day preparing meals and looking after the younger children. At the same time, the radio never ceased blaring, because she was hard of hearing.

"As long as they, my children and all Jewish children, are healthy and know nothing of the troubles we lived through—they shouldn't know from such things here," she lectured her niece loudly, accompanying every word with a separate gesture: "With God's help, let no one in the land of Israel be lost."

All her remarks began with "Blessed be His name" and "With God's help." Rachel didn't understand all her aunt's words, and not only because of language difficulties—her words were always twisted, like something torn out of a prayer, repetitious in a way that was not suited to a simple conversation. Pious Jewish women had certainly not been a rarity in Brooklyn, but Rachel had always looked at them as outsiders who had almost no relation to her personally. She looked the same way at women from India or Pakistan, except with greater curiosity because of their exotic clothing.

Rachel felt completely lost in her aunt's house, having fallen into a very different reality and lifestyle. First of all, her aunt immediately started calling her Rakhel, and when Rachel resisted, her aunt answered with annoyance: "In my house, no one has a Gentile name!" Secondly, Rachel had to dress differently—to forget American wantonness—because "modesty is more bashful and has more pleasure," her aunt claimed. Actually, she was concerned about what her pious neighbors would think. And finally, though the three eldest children no longer lived with their parents, the crowded conditions in her aunt's apartment oppressed Rachel greatly.

On the other hand, however, when the whole family sat down at the Sabbath table on Friday evening—the aunt's elder sons used to come occasionally for the Sabbath—and the blessed, lit candles were burning in the middle of the table, the walls of the salon (as they called the living room) seemed to recede. At the head of the table, reclining slightly, sat the master of the house, a darkly charming man with a thatch of gray hair and a semicircular black beard that looked split. On the first day, Rachel's uncle had tried to ask her something in English, but after several disjointed words, he let the breath out of his capacious lungs, smiled helplessly, and said: "Good, very much good b'Yisrael!" He had no further conversations with Rachel and she saw him very seldom. Her aunt told her that he worked somewhere on a kibbutz, in a little factory that produced various fruit drinks.

Within a week of Rachel's arrival, her aunt had interjected, among other things, that girls of her age should already have a potential bridegroom.

"It's not good to be alone, even in Paradise!" her aunt shouted over the radio. "Take me, for example—I came here to no home and no close people, just comrades, friends, each one busy with himself. If not for the help of God . . . In Israel, no child goes lost, and we'll find a good young man for you too, Rakhel."

Rachel had tried to change the subject, but her aunt either did not hear her because of her deafness or didn't want to hear her because of her stubbornness.

"Your mother, may she be well, also looked for some support in life, poor thing, and found a broken soul, may my words not weigh heavily on him. What good things did she see in him?"

"Auntie . . ."

"Never mind," she interrupted Rachel.

The whole conversation was not to Rachel's liking. They were both sitting in the kitchen, at a low table, and were sorting rice. As her aunt had previously explained to her, that day she was going to make a delicious Mizrahi dish called *mujadara*—Rachel couldn't even pronounce the word.

"You needn't get mad," her aunt continued. She poured out another portion of rice from a little sack and spread it over the table with her palm. "You're like my own child, so would I give you bad advice? If you don't want to get married don't get married." Here her aunt threw in another piece of information: "For example, yesterday I heard on the radio that they've opened a new hospital in Safed and they need nurses there . . ."

"I'm not a nurse, and besides I don't know Hebrew . . ."

"You'll learn it—you have a good head, blessed be His name."

But it so happened that that advice pleased Rachel. For the time being, she would have to forget about becoming a psychologist, which she had long dreamed of doing. Her aunt was right: one has to stand on one's own feet, and for that reason one must have a trade. Besides, Safed was at the other end of the country, and she wanted to be alone, free as the wind.

Rachel stopped reading. Her mother leaned her head to one side and dozed off. She now recalled the restless night and the early morning. She covered her mother's feet with the blanket, which was still lying on the sofa, folded, as a reminder of the overnight guest. She herself was in a cold sweat, and threw a robe over her shoulders. Perhaps she could take advantage of the occasion and lie down for a while? On the other hand, on her hospital shift she never used to close her eyes for sixteen and sometimes twenty hours a day. Especially during the Yom Kippur War.

After taking courses in nursing for seven months, she began working in the hospital. Thus, unexpectedly—she had never thought or dreamed of such a career—did Rachel enter Israeli life. At work everyone called her Rakhel, as her aunt did, and by now it almost didn't bother her. Furthermore, she even interpreted it to herself as a sign of separation: a new place, a new name, a new way of life, and—who knows?—perhaps new luck. Her aunt had indeed said, when saying goodbye to her: "A new place, new luck."

She didn't fit in immediately in the ancient city, with its narrow, twisted alleys and stone steps. Brought up in and used to the long, carefully laid out, straight Brooklyn streets, all of which led to the ocean, she experienced the cramped streets of Safed as being driven into a twisted labyrinth. But it was only from the outside that the stone walls and quarters of the city looked gray, cold, and poor; precisely because of their frozen creases, the many-layered everyday aspects of human history and Jewish spirit had been engraved in their coarsely cut texture. Nati had helped her touch the surface of that history and feel, even if only with her fingertips, the hidden warmth of that spirit.

They had met at the Frankel's art gallery. Rachel had sought it out for no particular reason, just out of curiosity, as she used to do with other places as well; she considered it a way of getting used to living in the city. It didn't matter to her where she went, because she didn't know anyone there and nobody knew her. So Rachel had turned into the paved alley, which was like a corridor. The high stone walls on both sides were overgrown on top with thick bushes that stretched their branches, covered with tiny pink flowers, over the alley. She saw the sign over the entrance, written in Hebrew and English, and pushed the heavy door open.

Prepared to see pictures on the wall, as in the other galleries in the city, Rachel suddenly found herself in a rather large room that was full of smoke. Fancily dressed people with glass goblets in their hands were shuffling around on the stone floor or standing in circles and conversing loudly or laughing, and everyone was smoking. Feeling lost for a moment, Rachel quickly turned toward the door and was ready to sneak quietly back outside when she suddenly heard behind her, and in English at that: "You don't mind if I disappear with you?!"

A few moments later they had both found their way out of the alley.

"You spoke to me in English," Rachel said to the unknown man. "Do I look that much like a typical American?"

"On the contrary!" she heard. "You simply don't act like a Sabra. One of them would have immediately taken the occasion to remain in the happy company." And now he was already continuing in Hebrew. "My name is Nati—what's yours?"

That was how they met, and Rachel soon became convinced, by many examples, that disappearing was part of Nati's way of life.

"You know, Rakhel—it's definitely a good sign that we met during *bein hashmashot*."

"What does that mean?"

"It means the time between suns . . . when one sun is setting and the other one is about to rise."

He allowed the red-gold sunshine to strike his slender, tanned face and continued speaking:

"Look at this light—you can see it in only two places on Earth: Jerusalem and Safed. Blessed will be the painter who will someday be able to eternalize it on his canvas."

"Is that why they come here?" Rachel asked sarcastically.

"Who knows . . . Painters are crazy people: for a play of light and shadow, they are willing to sell their souls to the Devil."

"Are you a painter too?"

"I am also a crazy person . . ."

Rachel, standing now at the window of her New York apartment, smiled. She recollected further:

His residence was on a hilly little street, and as Nati told her, the district had once, before the War of Independence, been entirely inhabited by Arabs. Actually, his residence, or, as he used to call it, *my cave*, was more suited to being a studio than a home. It was a spacious room that, because of its Bohemian chaos, looked crowded and uncared for, but Rachel felt very much at home there. She grew to love the cave, which also became her cave, where the crowding brought them together on the narrow little sofa spread with a bearskin.

Nati loved to paint stones; you could find the image of a stone in all his pictures. And when Rachel asked him about that, he explained to her:

"Consider this . . . Man left histories of life on parchment, but his soul he entrusted to stone, to his gravestone. How was fire born if not between stones that God gave to Adam, and taught him how to strike a spark from them? The Almighty incised His gift to His people, the Ten Commandments, on stone tablets. True, stone is mute and lonely, perhaps because it has absorbed all the bloody histories of the human world, beginning with Cain and Abel, who was also killed with a stone . . ."

Rachel burrowed her cheek into his hairy chest, and remained lying there with her eyes closed, listening to the rhythmic beating of his heart.

"What do you hear there, Rakhel?" Nati asked quietly.

"Your heart tells me now that you will soon disappear."

"Listen carefully and it will also tell you how it already yearns for you and how it will hurry back to see you . . ."

He used to disappear, sometimes for two or three weeks, sometimes for several months; he explained to her that it had to do with his work, but she never asked him what his work was, perhaps because she realized that he wouldn't add anything to what he had already told her.

She had a key to his apartment, and more than once before going away he proposed that she move into their cave. She didn't do so because without him it made no sense; her loneliness would only have doubled there. And yet, Rachel used to pop in to the cave for a few hours after work almost every day; she would boil coffee in the *finjan*, the way Nati had taught her, and sitting on the sofa she would dig her feet into the bearskin while smacking her lips over the bitter drink. Afterwards she would take thick, artistic albums off the bookshelf— they were arranged there in a line from the stone floor to the ceiling, which was made of coarsely carved beams—and would thumb through them till it got dark. She would leave the last ones in a dark corner of the cave so they could bring light and warmth there again the following day.

The last time, when they were already saying goodbye, Nati embraced her and suddenly whispered in her ear:

"I'll be gone for a long time, Rakhel, but I beg of you—don't worry. Everything will be OK with me . . ."

Rachel turned toward him; Nati had never spoken to her that way. She had wanted to say something, or ask, but he put his finger to her lips as if to lock her mouth. He looked into her eyes as if he were looking for a support for his own gaze, and again said quietly:

"I'll come back at the time of *bein hashmashot* and I'll bring you a present—a pair of beautiful red shoes, just like the ones Mirele dreamed of having . . ."

That day, Nati told her a story about a Jewish boy from Poland, Noska, who had been almost the same age as Mirele. On a late autumn evening, in the house of his father, the local doctor, two monks had come in and said that they were going around the ghetto to rescue little children. His father knew them and was prepared to give both children into their hands—his son and his daughter, who was two years older than her little brother—but the guests only agreed to take the boy. He never saw his parents again, or his sister either. In the monastery, behind the thick stone walls, they changed the little one's name, and in about a week they hung a brass cross around his neck. He became a good Christian child and did everything they told him to do. He quickly learned to read, and could sit for hours over thick books, fascinated by the wonderful stories and mysteries of the saints. Sometimes he would encounter a picture in the margin of those books; entranced, the boy couldn't turn his eyes away. Furthermore, the picture would immediately come alive and talk to him in the words that he had previously read. But one day men with red stars on their caps came to the monastery. They collected all the boys that lived in the monastery, put them in a truck, and drove them to an orphanage. There they tore the brass cross off the boy's neck and once again changed his name. Two years passed, during which his new teachers did everything to knock out of his head all the things they had taught him in the monastery. One night, they woke up the boys they had previously brought from the monastery and took them away in a truck covered with a tarpaulin, on a very long trip across mountains and oceans. Later, when they finally got to their destination, they gave them all new names and ordered them to forget everything that had happened to them there "in the Diaspora." And so the boy grew up in his new home. He quickly got used to his new name and learned to speak the new language fluently; he would probably have also forgotten everything that had happened to him there, in the Diaspora, but the frequent wars didn't let him.

"What happened next to the boy?" Rachel couldn't restrain herself and asked.

Nati smiled to himself, but a certain mournfulness radiated from his eyes.

"It's only a story after all, Rakhel, and a story is only good to the extent that everyone can make up his own end to it . . ."

Rachel's shift fell precisely on Yom Kippur. Because of the holiday, there was limited staffing at the hospital. At about twelve noon, they told her to be ready for an emergency, and about two hours later they announced a new war.

The wounded began to arrive from the Golan in the first few hours. She felt that Nati's last, sudden trip was related to what had just happened; she was almost certain that he must be in the very thick of it. Weeks and months went by, because even after the victory, the battle between life and death continued in the hospital itself.

From time to time, she was able to get out for a few hours. She would climb the twisted, stony paths, and from just outside, two or three steps from her cave, she would sniff the air to see if there was the aroma of the coffee that only he knew how to make.

And one day it happened. Rachel didn't smell the familiar aroma, but she saw immediately that the door to the residence was partly ajar. Her heart was already there, inside, and only her legs barely dragged themselves, as if intentionally stubborn. She saw him standing next to the shelves with the albums, but it wasn't Nati; a stranger turned his head toward Rachel, and as soon as he saw her he took a step toward her.

"Excuse me—I wasn't able to get in touch with you previously."

He spoke to her in English, but she, interrupting him, asked him in Hebrew:

"How did you get in here? Do you have a key?"

The man extended his hand to her and, saying his name, he continued to speak in the same language as Rachel.

"I am Nati's comrade, and he gave me the key to his cave."

The guest had intentionally emphasized that last word, which was apparently supposed to help her understand that Nati wasn't just his comrade but a close friend. The imparted word, however, echoed in the room as if a hard rock had fallen down on the stone floor. And yet she calmly asked further:

"Is he OK?"

"Nati told me a lot about you . . . he loved you very much, Rakhel . . ."

Rachel slowly lowered her eyes to the little sofa, and resting her eyes on its emptiness, asked:

"How did it happen?"

She almost didn't hear his answer; by this time not one but many word stones had fallen onto the floor and had joined together into a hill that buried the cold truth beneath it. Only scraps of that truth reached her: "a secret assignment . . . killed . . . for now we can't say any more . . ."

The man was silent for a while, as if he were waiting for what had already been said to be put aside or to melt into the heavy silence.

"At my last meeting with Nati," his firm voice was heard again, "he asked me to give you this painting if he should be unable to do so himself . . ."

He pointed with his head at the easel that had till then been standing, lonely, in the middle of the room. Rachel, barely understanding what the man was saying, turned her gaze to the easel, and her eyes rested on a painting . . .

———

The ring of the telephone made Rachel shudder. Her mother too woke up and squinted, not understanding. The ringing seemed to have erected a wall between yesterday and today, between what was and what is. She picked up the receiver and heard Yasha's voice. He had called to tell her that he was going to Boston for a day; that he had to meet his daughter, Marina, and tell her everything . . .

"Children today understand more than we think," said Yasha, justifying himself. "After all, she is the closest person in the world to me. She and you, Rachel."

Late that evening, when her mother was already sleeping, Rachel went over to the window of the living room. The rain had stopped, and the full moon had playfully rolled out from behind a thin cloud. A streak of moonlight, plastered with myriad silver potsherds, spread across the water. "Tomorrow will be a beautiful day," thought Rachel.

January–October 2005
Brooklyn, New York

Karolino-Bugaz

– 1 –

Bella woke from sleep as if she had been driven out of it. She sat up and took short breaths, trying to restrain the rapid beating of her heart. Finally she stopped breathing for a moment and lay down calmly with her head on her pillow.

She closed her eyes and peered into the darkness, looking for the bench in the park where the young couple had just been sitting, furiously hugging and kissing, barely breathing in order not to have to tear their lips away from one another. She immediately recognized Mark and herself in the young couple. They had met in the park the day after coming back from Karolino-Bugaz. There, in the pretty little village on the shores of the Black Sea, not far from Odessa, they had gone to clear their heads before returning to study again.

Back then Bella had just finished her first year at the Pedagogical Institute in Kishinev; she was studying to become an English teacher. She had been to Karolino-Bugaz several times, but previously she had gone with her mother, under her strict supervision. This summer she had come by herself, though her mother was not very pleased by the idea. "Precisely because you're now a big girl," she had complained, "it would be better for me to stay near you." And then she had added, as if to explain to someone: "I know them, the boys these days . . ."

Mark, on the other hand, had come there for the first time, and not alone but with his friend Alik. Both were studying in Moscow at the Architectural Institute and considered themselves big-city boys who were traveling to the sticks to have a good time with the small-town girls.

Bella, as she had before, was staying at the Dolphin Suites bungalow colony. There were no special conveniences in the plywood bungalows, painted inside and out with dark-blue oil paint: two iron beds with a cubby between them; nailed to one wall a narrow shelf with four hangers, two for each occupant; and a narrow little window with a chintz curtain, bleached by the sun. The floor was covered with brown linoleum, worn away in spots, and from the ceiling, right in the middle, fastened to a white plastic lampshade, hung a narrow, sticky, coiled strip of paper—it looked like a spring that had just been pulled out of a jar of honey. That rather primitive thing had an important function: to catch flies and mosquitoes. More accurately, the poor flies and mosquitoes used to get stuck to the strip and find their end there.

It was hard to find the occupants inside during the day in such a summer cabin, whose construction was more reminiscent of a dog kennel sized for two bipedal creatures—the heat was suffocating; at night, however, when the wooden walls cooled off and absorbed the morning dampness from the sea air, they would sometimes have to shiver under the thin blankets.

To be sure, people didn't come to Karolino-Bugaz for comfort and luxury; such a gentle seashore, covered with thin, golden, powdery sand, was not to be found on the best beaches of Odessa. In addition, the place had not yet enjoyed much of an influx of people; it looked wild, overgrown here and there with short, spreading, prickly bushes that projected from the sandy dunes. But the most important thing, which at that time merged with the lively surroundings, was their youth—Bella's nineteen years and Mark's twenty-three.

Bella understood that the bench in the park with the two lovers was something she was seeing in a dream. She was standing in a corner of that dream and was listening to the short breaths between their kisses. Suddenly they tore their lips apart, but their gazes seemed to lock together, not allowing their eyes to turn away for even a second, as if they were playing a children's game: the one who blinks first loses. They both broke out laughing, and Bella heard Mark ask the young girl who was sitting across from him:

"Why did you start laughing, Bella?"

"And why did you, Mark?"

"I asked you first . . ."

"OK—I was remembering how you shoveled sand on Alik in the pit you dug in the sand so only his head with his straw hat stuck out . . ."

"True—he looked like a giant mushroom, and a little boy suddenly came up to the 'mushroom' and peed on it."

They hugged each other and kissed again.

Bella felt Mark's hot breath on her face, and at the same moment her gaze encountered a second gaze, alien and angrily piercing. She tried to turn her head away, the way you do when someone has thrown something at you, but the piercing gaze seemed to have locked itself onto her. Bella couldn't avoid it, and in addition her head seemed to be petrified and wouldn't move. From the dark glow, the figure of a black man emerged. "How did he come to be in this park?" a thought whirled in her mind. "In those days, a black man in Kishinev?" But she immediately realized that all this was taking place in a dream. The man was sitting on a bench across from her and was holding a bottle in his hand. He kept bringing it to his mouth and gulping down a mouthful of liquid, all the while not taking his eyes off her. In truth, he was looking at the young couple. Bella understood that when he suddenly put down the bottle, quickly grasped it by the neck, and slammed it against the edge of the bench. The bottle broke with a crash, and only a sharp-pointed sliver stuck out of the man's clenched fist. Tottering, he took his first step toward the happy couple.

The lovers didn't hear him or see him. Everything in space, aside from their locked arms, in that moment existed by itself without their participation, as if the two of them and the bench on which they were sitting were a separate island or a tiny planet in the enormous cosmos.

Bella wanted to cry out and warn them, but the choked sound remained stuck in her throat . . . She turned her eyes upward.

The early dawn filtered through the nylon curtain on the broad window of her bedroom. It colored the wall facing her with pastel red and yellow stripes. Bella thought to herself: How easy it is to separate sleep from reality—you just need one movement of your eyelids. A crazy dream . . . But it also disappeared immediately and just left a slight scratch on her memory.

Mark was sleeping with his back toward Bella. She smiled: Back then, thirty years ago, he had had thick black hair on his head, and now a bald pate shone there. On the other hand, his shoulders had now become covered by a thick, curly mop of hair. Mark himself had joked: "The hair from my head has slipped down to my shoulders. Let's hope it will go no farther."

Actually his hair had begun falling out after they came to America. And if it is true that the main reason for that is stress, he didn't lack for stress at that time. Yes, their wedding had been precisely thirty years ago. It was a beautiful summer day, though it had been pouring all week. On the day of their wedding, a Saturday, the sky cleared up as if it had poured out all its clouds and spread out a blue path for the sun. Mark's mother had even then, ostensibly joking, said to him: "You have a *nasher* for a wife!" "What makes you think that?" Mark had asked her, astonished. "When it rains a whole week before the wedding and the sun shines on your wedding day, that's a sign that the bride is a *nasher*!" she had answered. They had both broken out laughing, but it bothered Bella. One gets smarter as the years go by: now, when she herself was already a mother-in-law, she evaluated many things differently, but, as they say, it's easy to be smart in retrospect.

Bella touched her husband's back lightly, feeling the hairs that covered his body like "irritating elements," as Mark called them. And indeed, he reacted immediately from his sleep: he raised his shoulder as if he wanted to rid himself of something, drive it away, like a fly.

She took her hand away and again lay down on her back, looking at the sunlight shining through the window. Yes, now she had become an "irritating element," and previously? Previously, Mark used to be the first to begin the morning play while she was still asleep; he would snuggle up to her and touch her neck with his lips. At that time she wore her hair in a Care style—her hair was cropped short on her neck, her forehead was covered with bangs, and on the sides, over her ears, two long strands of hair hung down. The Care suited her very well, emphasizing her long neck.

Even before Mark touched her neck, Bella would already feel his hot breath. A glowing feeling would quickly flow from the spot where he had left his kiss, down her backbone all the way to her feet—and that was enough for her whole body to pull in his arms and keep them locked there.

Bella closed her eyes again. No, she didn't want to go back to sleep, though it was still very early, especially because today she could definitely have allowed herself to do so. It was, after all, thirty years since their marriage, her pearl wedding anniversary. She had read somewhere that pearls symbolized a neat and tidy love and fruitfulness. As for fruitfulness, they had a one and only son, David . . . To be sure, Bella had had three abortions—Mark hadn't wanted to have any more children. But God had sent them two grandchildren, and, as Bella had noticed recently, her daughter-in-law was again pregnant. And what about love . . . ?

The day after the wedding, the young couple had gone to Karolino-Bugaz. They had decided to have their honeymoon there, too, on the half-wild beaches where they had met. They had neither the time nor the money to take a month off for the honeymoon as was then the fashion.

Now the two of them owned the dark-blue plywood bungalow in the Dolphin Suites bungalow colony. The two separated iron beds had been moved together to make one sleeping place where Bella and Mark could satisfy their thirst for one another and the curiosity that kept raising new waves of emotion and enthusiasm to sample again the taste of love, which had, one would think, just a moment ago given them its last drop of honey.

They used to leave their "doghouse" only when it was impossible to stand the heat there. Like people driven out of the Garden of Eden, Bella and Mark would go down to the sea, and, holding each other's hand so as not to lose their closeness for even a moment, God forbid, would jump into the water. Refreshed and having gained new strength from the sea, they would fall down onto the wet sand so the onrushing waves, now weakened and exhausted from their race across the seas, could caress their feet with their moist tongues, arousing a new flow of feelings. Their gazes flowed together as if the lovers had suddenly realized that only now had the hidden love formula that nature had sent to them from its ancient depths been revealed to them. Given wings by that discovery, Bella and Mark would spring up and start running to their source of pleasure, as if they were afraid to forget the eternal secret that had just been entrusted to them.

About two weeks after returning from Karolino-Bugaz, they said their goodbyes: Mark went to Moscow to continue his studies and Bella remained alone in Kishinev. It was still a time of paper letters—you could hold a letter in your hand, carry it around, and pull it out of the envelope whenever you wanted and read it again—for the ump-teenth time, already—from the first word to the last.

Mark would write happy letters, and would almost always put in a joke at the end. Sometimes Bella would remember the joke during a lecture session and would unexpectedly laugh out loud. She kept the packet of letters in a shoebox in her cupboard for many years till their emigration to America. They moved from one rented apartment to another three times till they bought their own apartment in a co-op, and each time they packed their things Bella, when she came across the shoebox, would forget about everything she had to do and reread Mark's letters from that year of separation after their wedding. Mark himself used to joke, looking at the box of letters: "My epistolary legacy. After my death, you'll publish all these letters as a book and make a lot of money from it!" Bella would get angry at him: "Don't say that! The letters belong only to me and not to anyone else!" While they were packing for the last time before leaving the country, she was careful to make sure the box didn't get lost in the rush. They burned many papers at that time, especially the folders containing copies of his architectural projects and drawings, which they weren't allowed to take with them. "Big government secrets!" Mark smiled bitterly. "They haven't yet seen such projects in America!" So it had to happen that of the two chests full of baggage that they were allowed to send, precisely the chest in which the shoebox with Mark's epistolary legacy lay, was lost. Mark, with his jokes, had something to laugh about: "You see, Bella? Because of my invaluable letters they stole the whole chest!"

Now, remembering that lost packet of letters, one of those jokes swam up into her memory, like a greeting from that time. Bella practically saw before her eyes the straight lines of Mark's beautiful handwriting. "In the midst of a silver anniversary celebration, a witch suddenly appeared and said to the couple: 'If both of you tell me your dreams I will immediately make them come true.' So the wife said: 'I want a gold ring with a big diamond!' Instantly a diamond, set into a gold ring, was sparkling on her finger. No one had ever seen anything so beautiful. 'And what do you want?' the witch asked the husband. 'I dream of having a wife who's twenty-five years younger than I!', and at that very second, the husband became twenty-five years older."

Bella felt laughter rising within her, as used to happen to her during the lectures at the institute. She compressed her mouth with her hand, but the laughter virtually exploded in her belly and she gave a shake on her bed. Mark's shoulder again reacted, and he murmured an unhappy "M-m-m."

She had to get up, Bella concluded. Today would surely be a strenuous day: she had an appointment with Annette, her hairdresser, and then she had to pick up the cake she had ordered from the kosher bakery, and then she would have to go to the restaurant and finally confirm how many people were coming to their little gathering; it was, after all, thirty years—their pearl anniversary. Bella smiled and thought to herself: what would she ask of the generous witch if she showed up today and asked her what she wanted?

-2-

Bella threw her summer robe over her nightgown and quietly sneaked out of the bedroom, which was on the second story. She went down the stairs into the parlor, buttoning her nightgown along the way. The day had begun no differently from the early hours of other days. She would soon open the green silk drapes, open the window, and go into the kitchen to brew a pot of coffee. Bella did that the same way she had seen her father do it. He was a dyed-in-the-wool coffee drinker and had an especially respectful attitude both to the drink and to the process of preparing it. He kept Arabica coffee beans, wrapped in a parchment bag, in a special ceramic box on the top shelf of the kitchen cupboard, so no one, God forbid, could reach it. Bella was astonished by the whole thing: how did her father, an ordinary barber, come by such an aristocratic habit—brewing and drinking coffee? Every month, one of his clients, the bookkeeper at the central delicatessen, would bring him the special treat—300 grams of green coffee beans—and her father, with a pharmacist's precision, would divide the beans into thirty daily portions. He did it by eye, but never made a mistake, God forbid.

He would start by roasting the green, slightly bluish-tinged, coffee beans brought by the bookkeeper in a tin frying pan, the way one roasts sunflower seeds, and would then spread them out on a sheet of newspaper, each bean separately. After that he would pour them into the bag and hide them in the ceramic box. He would grind his morning portion to a powder in a special little mill and then pour it into his *turka*, as he called the brass vessel with a long, narrow handle. One could tell a whole separate story about that *turka*; Bella had heard it a hundred times: her father had brought the *turka* from Germany as a war trophy, and no matter whom he showed it to then, he couldn't give a sensible explanation as to why he needed the strange thing—it was just something to bring from there; but he, a Bessarabian Jew, who as a young man had worked for the manager of a cafeteria in Jassy, knew the true value of his only war trophy.

He brewed the coffee over an alcohol lamp, even after they had gotten gas in the house. He stood and mixed it, and waited till a brown foam appeared; after that, he held the *turka* over the heat for another second, and then, placing it on the table, he added a drop of cold water "so the grounds would settle." Finally, as a last touch: before he poured his enchanted drink into his cup he would throw in two salt crystals for taste.

If it is true that the home in which we grow up has its own smell, then for Bella that smell was the fragrance of her father's coffee. She herself brewed coffee every morning on the gas range, over the lowest fire, in the same *turka* that she had schlepped with her during her emigration across the ocean to New York, as a trophy of that abandoned life. Mark, with his wisecracks, couldn't miss that opportunity either: "You've brought your dowry to America."

Thanks to coffee, one might say, Mark found great favor with Bella's father, his future father-in-law. Bella's father encountered them accidentally one day at the very beginning of Bella and Mark's courtship. "Who was that hairy fellow who was with you?" he asked her that evening, and, not waiting for an answer, he added: "Tell him to come to me in my barber shop and I'll make a mensch out of him."

In one of her letters to Mark, Bella hinted that if he brought her father a few packages of Arabica coffee beans from Moscow, it would be "like a golden key to his heart." Her father appreciated the gift in his own way: "It's definitely Robusta, not Arabica, but we can't be picky these days!"

Bella and Mark were astonished by the expertise that the barber manifested. "What's the difference?" Mark asked. Bella's father answered him with no delay: "The Arabica type is milder and has a kind of aroma that stimulates all of one's feelings." He brought the opened package up to Mark's face and said, in an entirely different tone of voice: "And the Robusta type is strong and bitter . . ." He saw Mark's disappointment and pulled back a bit: "But it's no problem—good intentions are the best gift." After that, Bella's father was known by the nickname Robusta.

Bella sits in the wide armchair in the parlor, enjoying the tasty drink. On her knees she has a tray with several narrow strips of hard cheese—her daily breakfast. As a rule, she tunes her television to channel 704 and watches the NBC show *Today*. Of the four hosts she likes Matt Lauer, with his trustworthy soft voice and pleasant face, the best. "Women your age love such men," Mark remarked on one occasion. "You're right," Bella answered him, "we feel at ease with them."

Mark himself gets up later, but is the first to leave the house. Bella waits at the television till her husband takes a shower, gets dressed, and comes down to drink the already-cold glass of tea with lemon and sugar that Bella has prepared for him and eat his light sandwich: a piece of pumpernickel smeared with cream cheese. He has to take something before swallowing his pills for blood pressure and prostate trouble.

Passing Bella, he often stops to look at the television screen and ask: "What's today's sensation?" but he doesn't wait for an answer and immediately asks again: "Is it going to rain?" Bella tells him the weather forecast, and after wishing him a good day, she goes up alone to the second floor to do her morning ablutions. Today Bella didn't turn on the television; she thought to herself that it might wake her husband. Let him get a good sleep—they would surely come back late from the restaurant and the next day they would have to get up early again for work. Getting together in a restaurant to celebrate the exact date of their pearl wedding anniversary was Bella's idea. "Indeed—why not?" she thought. Living together for thirty years is not something to be dismissed with a wave of the hand! Five years previously, on their silver wedding anniversary, they hadn't been able to put their minds to that—Bella's mother had died that year. So why not do it now? They had lived through that portion of their life not easily but with dignity.

"Emigration," Bella's mother used to sigh, "is just like evacuation but without bombs." Like all immigrants, they had started anew, from nothing, but now, thank God, Mark was working at his profession as an architect and Bella was no longer sitting with her arms folded in her lap. Quite a few families they knew had fallen apart—immigration tests every family in its own way, and where there is a little crack it grows into a large chasm . . .

Mark didn't say yes, but he also didn't say no. He made do with a murmured "do whatever you think is right!" That definitely bothered Bella. The fact that they had shared their destined bit of joy and suffering for half a lifetime was so unimportant to him?! No, she didn't recognize him . . . Something was up with him lately. She remained silent, but the worm of doubt that had taken up residence beneath her heart quite a while ago tugged at her again after Mark's indifferent "do whatever you think is right!" Nevertheless, Bella did indeed do what she thought was right: she reserved the banquet hall at the Tatiana restaurant in Brighton Beach and invited their closest friends—sixteen people in all.

When she finished drinking her coffee, she turned the cup over on the saucer and sat a while deep in thought. A schoolmate of hers from Kishinev had liked to tell fortunes from the coffee grounds. "Do you see these two separate fine lines?" she would practically stick her near-sighted nose into the bottom of the cup that Bella handed her. "The broader one is yours and the narrower one is his—they come together, and then grow upward like the trunk of a tree." "What does that mean?" Bella had impatiently interrupted her friend. "It means, silly, that you will soon meet a boy, you'll marry him, you'll live together long and happily, and you'll die on the same day . . ."

Bella smiled now and picked up the cup. A dark brown spot was stuck to the bottom, and from it, as if from a root torn out of the ground, dried-out, twisty branches spread out over the porcelain sides of the cup. She peered at it and let her fantasy run free, trying to understand something, to explain it to herself: what does it mean, that picture "drawn by fate," as her schoolmate had explained to her long ago. Many years had passed since then. Bella had indeed met Mark shortly thereafter, and their lifelines had become entwined . . . What did she want to know now? Her tomorrow? Bella slowly turned the cup with her fingers, and suddenly the spot moved, began changing its form, forming a new face; the twisty lines separated and dissolved and the face of a man looked out very clearly from the bottom of the cup, a face with pale eyes and pearly white, projecting teeth . . ." It's the same face I saw in my crazy dream!" the scratch of that dream upon her memory again reminded her. She got up from the armchair, went over to the sink, and quickly washed out the cup and saucer under the faucet.

– 3 –

Bella went out around ten o'clock. She was supposed to be at her hairdresser's at ten thirty. At another time, she would have walked there—it wasn't far, on Sheepshead Bay Road—but this day she had quite a few things to take care of, and without her car she wouldn't be able to finish them all. It was a beautiful summer day, exactly like the one thirty years earlier, the day of their wedding. Yes, Mark's mother had predicted correctly—Bella was and remained a *nasher*, though lately she was restraining herself and refusing various tasty snacks. At the time of her wedding, she had weighed 103 pounds, and now she weighed 171.

Mark's mother had received her coolly; Bella had felt that more than she understood it. Perhaps her female ego was manifesting itself for the first time in her life. From the outside, she appeared pleasant, with a loving smile; they would sit and drink tea and eat pumpkin knishes. "Eat, Bella dear," she would repeat softly, and would then add: "Marky loves my knishes." A smile would indeed hang on her face, but the corners of her mouth would be clamped as if she were ready to flee at any moment. Also her voice, or more accurately, the tone of her voice, would get higher every time she wanted to emphasize: "It's taken so much out of us to get Mark into such a prestigious institute!"

His father would add meaningfully: "And not only that!"

"He needs to have a wife that is faithful to him, like a mother," Mark's mother would complain further, and once again his father would speak up: "And not only that!"

Mark himself would sit across from Bella and chew his mother's knishes in both cheeks. He would never take his eyes off Bella, seeming to send her signals not to get too excited about his parents' words. She could hardly wait till they left the house. She had heartburn, as if the knishes were filled not with pumpkin but with horseradish.

"Apparently," Bella tried to speak calmly, "your mother was expecting a princess, not a barber's daughter?" Mark stopped and hugged her. "Please . . . Jewish mothers. Each one thinks her son is the best in the world!" Bella suddenly broke out into tears. She thought to herself, almost swearing an oath, that if she got to be a mother-in-law someday she would never speak that way to her daughter-in-law . . .

She drove out of the parking lot and turned onto Bedford Avenue. Bella had learned how to drive a car in New York. The English she had learned at the Pedagogical Institute had indeed come in handy for her. She had taken an additional half-year course with Kaplan and now felt almost no self-consciousness about speaking to a customer. The first two years she had worked in a small real-estate agency, where she was a broker for apartments. At that time, the boss's business was going fairly well, and she would get a percentage for every apartment she sold or rented. Of course, she had never dreamed of changing from a teacher to a broker; Mark consoled her: "In America it is no shame when an English teacher becomes a broker; it's worse when a broker becomes an English teacher!" Without a car she couldn't have gone anywhere, so they bought an old Nissan for $1,500—their first car in America. Mark himself barely managed to find work drawing architectural plans in an architect's office all the way up in the Bronx. They paid him three dollars an hour and the train ride took him almost two hours each way. "It's a beginning," Bella consoled him. "Any architect can draw plans, but not everyone who draws plans can become an architect!" His boss, Mister Blank, quickly sensed whom he had for an architectural illustrator. Within about half a year, Mark was working as an equal with him, and two years later, after taking the licensing exam, he opened his own office in Brooklyn.

In the mornings, especially on Sunday, there was always enough room next to Annette's Salon for Bella to park her car. She had been a patron of Annette's almost since they came to New York nearly twenty years ago. Annette, or simply Anya, as Bella called her when they were face-to-face conversing with one another via the mirror, had worked several years for a boss, a local Italian woman; after that, she had gone into partnership with her, and several years ago she had bought out the whole business. Only then did Annette spread her wings: she rented another store next door; took down the wall; rebuilt everything brand new, with a modern interior; and hired three more hairdressers and a manicurist. Everything there sparkled. And on the outside, over the wide, high windows, there was a beautiful, full-width sign: Annette's Salon.

More than once Bella had heard her father tell her mother that a barber, when he cuts a client's hair, has to listen to everything that is troubling the client's heart. He even had one client who came to him so often that he didn't want to take any money from him because there was no hair left to cut. The client, poor fellow, complained that since they had closed the church in the city he didn't have anyone to whom he could unburden his heart. And her father used to add, half-seriously and half-smiling: "So now I've become a priest, too!"

Anya kept her clients' secrets. Herself tall and stately, with her dyed blond hair precisely gathered on her neck, she could have served as an example of how a woman in her mid-fifties should keep herself. They used to tell various stories about Anya; such a capable woman couldn't avoid sharp tongues, of which there was no lack in Brighton Beach. On the other hand, Anya was not one of those who need to hide her love affairs; actually she was a divorcee and didn't have to answer to anyone about "whom I sleep with and how many men I've had."

In any case, her career as a hairdresser had made it unnecessary for her "to lie down beneath anyone." She worked just like her coworkers, and one had to make an appointment with her two weeks in advance. She remembered the names of all her clients but called each one friend, which, like a universal key, unlocked the hidden chambers of a woman's soul.

The same with Bella: the moment she sat down in the chair and heard Anya's long drawn-out phrase: "Well, friend, what shall we do with your beautiful little head today?", which she said every time before starting work, it tugged at her heart.

Bella looked in the mirror and encountered Anya's gaze. She surrounded Bella's head with her fingertips and turned it slightly, first to one side and then to the other, as if measuring what one could do with that "little head."

"As always?" she asked.

Bella was already prepared with the answer; she had come there with it. And yet she squeezed it out somewhat uncertainly:

"Care . . ."

"What do you mean, 'Care'?" said Anya, looking her straight in the eyes. And as was her custom, not obsequiously, she said: "Friend— if you had said that twenty years ago, when I cut your hair for the first time, I would still have understood it, but now, with your neck, or more accurately, with what's left of it . . . It's a joke!"

She could have said it differently, not so directly, thought Bella, now herself turning her head—first in one direction and then in the other. Of course there was very little left of her beautiful long neck— those twenty years had squeezed it down into her shoulders. Nevertheless, Bella again, but now more firmly, called out the hairstyle she wanted: "Care."

Anya didn't answer her. She turned the chair around, with Bella in it, and tilted it to the wash basin, to rinse her hair first. The warm water and Anya's soft, long fingers, which moved with a light touch over Bella's shampooed head, quieted her tense nerves. Bella kept her eyes closed . . . Karolino-Bugaz—she had just come out of the ocean and was lying on her back on the sand, with her legs apart and her arms flung open as if she were preparing to embrace the sky. She placed her uncovered face beneath the sun. She felt the skin of her body tightening, absorbing the heat of the sun's rays, and every limb, in contrast, became weakened, allowed her body to tear itself away from the hot sand and remain hanging in the air like an empty vessel. She was rocking—whether the nap had grabbed her or whether the playful breeze had rumpled her hair . . .

A cool, moist kiss on the neck excited her, stimulated all her senses in a single moment . . . These words quietly rustled in her very ear:

If I could write the beauty of your eyes
And in fresh numbers number all your graces,
The age to come would say "This poet lies;
Such heavenly touches ne'er touch'd earthly faces."

"Mark?" Bella heard her own voice, as if from beside her.

"No. William Shakespeare. Sonnet number 17."

When Bella opened her eyes Anya was already finishing drying her hair with a towel. A disheveled woman with weary, sunken eyes looked back at her from the mirror. "Where did it go—her charm, her radiance?"—Bella thought to her herself, as if to send the words chasing the quickly fleeing vision.

"OK, my friend—let it be Care"—Anya gave in—"but my own interpretation of it."

She got to work, but first posed a question:

"Why did you suddenly latch on to this old-fashioned hairdo?"

Bella put her head down, as Anya required, and answered:

"Today is thirty years since Mark and I got married . . ."

Anya stopped cutting, raised Bella's head, and smiled. In the mirror, her smile looked somewhat crooked.

"Congratulations," Anya greeted her, and immediately added: "I don't see a celebratory face before me."

Bella didn't answer right away. She hung her head, as if she wanted to hide her eyes from herself, and said:

"I had a Care for our wedding—at that time it had just become fashionable, and Mark liked it very much. So I thought to myself—maybe now, too . . ."

Bella interrupted herself—what she was going to say after that was clear to Anya without words. Her own life experience and the dozens of confessions she had heard from her clients had taught her to understand women's unsaid words.

"Listen to what I am going to tell you, my friend," Anya declared calmly—"It's a natural thing: for us women, there is a time of waxing and a time of waning, but for men there is only a time of waxing; the bit of sperm they have hits them in the head so hard that they go crazy. They have only one thing in mind: to prove to themselves that they're still good for something. Pure masculine arrogance!"

Anya looked in the mirror for a moment, caught Bella's eyes as if she wanted to convince herself that her words were being correctly understood and that she could continue to speak.

"I have a few longtime clients who have the same problem with their husbands. One of them even got divorced not long ago. Why? A young Polish woman came to work here and kept an eye on my client's sick mother. She kept an eye on her so long that my client caught her husband and the Polish woman in bed together. It was a real production, let me tell you . . ."

She again grasped Bella's head on both sides with her fingers and pointed it toward the mirror. Looking at it for a moment and evaluating her work, Anya asked:

"Do you think he has someone on the side?"

Bella felt the blood draining from her head to her feet, which grew so heavy she couldn't move them from the spot, as if to confirm Anya's words about waxing and waning. Hadn't she asked herself the same question recently? But she used to immediately drive the thought away, didn't want to believe it. Her Mark exchange her for another woman?! Bella would have felt it. True, for the past few months he had been coming home from the office late in the evening, exhausted, and he had been going straight to the second floor; Bella would hear him go into the bathroom and then into the bedroom, where he would turn on the television, which would stay on till Bella turned it off and lay down to sleep in the other bedroom so as not to wake Mark, God forbid. They wouldn't exchange a word, as if she weren't in the house at all; the same on the weekends, Saturday and Sunday: he would finish eating his breakfast and head off to his office. She knew he worked a lot and had enough business, thank God—but she also knew that no matter how tired he was, he used to come downstairs after washing up, sit down next to her, and ask her how things were going at her work and how the children were doing. Now, having heard the question from Anya, she felt the weight of every word—as if it were biting into her body and sucking out the blood. Word leeches . . .

Bella shrugged her shoulders—she didn't have the strength to add anything to that.

"Are you going to the restaurant?" Anya thought it necessary to change the subject.

"Yes, to Tatiana . . ."

"Tatiana? The owner used to be a client of mine, but I haven't seen her for a long time. They say that she and her husband, Misha, have also built a new restaurant in Miami."

"True. In the beginning, they even came to Mark to make the plans for the restaurant."

"So what happened?"

"I don't remember exactly . . . Just at that time he had several extra projects to finish and they didn't want to wait."

"It's that Tatiana? The Hell you say! She's in charge there—Misha's only good for telling stories about Odessa. It's a joke!"

Anya turned on the blower and directed the stream of warm air at Bella's head. In a few minutes, she had finished her work.

"Well, my friend? How do you like my interpretation of your Care?"

Anya stood there holding a square mirror behind Bella, so she too could see how her coiffure looked on her neck.

"Very sexy!" she added in English, as if only in English could one appreciate the meaning of the two words. "I'm sure your Mark will like it . . ."

It may sound strange today, but thirty years ago the words "sex" and "sexy" had sounded vulgar to their ears, even immoral—introduced from the Wild West . . . Karolino-Bugaz, late at night, sitting at the very edge of the water, hugging one another. It's quiet—only the sea murmurs and washes their naked feet with its tiny waves, which in the moonlight look like the silvery scales of some giant fish. The moonlight shines a path before them. "You see?" she hears Mark's tremulous voice—"This is our road . . ." He gets up and takes her hand. "Come, Bella . . ." and she, as if enchanted, follows him, and the two of them go into the sea, exactly where the moon-beam begins and deceives them . . . It gets deeper, the beam sinks. Bella no longer feels the bottom. Frightened, she hugs Mark with her arms and legs and remains hanging on him. He starts to kiss her—on the lips, the eyes, the temples, the throat, the shoulders. She had in no way imagined that one could make love in the sparkling water and that it would be so delicious and sweet . . . Bella couldn't feel her body; she had merged with her beloved's body, with the sea, the moonshine, the night, which was pierced at that moment by two conjoined voices, rapturous with joy . . .

– 4 –

Bella was sitting in her car, ready to drive farther according to to-day's schedule, to Boro Park, to Stern Bakery; her son had rec-ommended that she buy her cake there. She straightened the narrow mirror over the steering wheel, which reflected her two worried-looking eyes. Bella thought to herself: Anya the hairdresser is prob-ably right—it's a natural thing, a biological process. One grows older, one's emotions, which had always conquered the temporary argu-ments and even battles between her and Mark, also grow older and cool off. Bella used to walk away quickly, and Mark used to come up to her from behind, hug her, and kiss her neck. Yes, even as recently as five years back, their bed had been the best place to soothe quite a few resentments.

What they call sex here was in that other life almost a forbid-den word, of which they were ashamed but which they didn't have to say out loud. Even on their honeymoon they had quickly learned to understand the language of the eyes, the lips, the fingers . . . Then, during the hot days in Karolino-Bugaz, everything was happening for the first time, as if it were something new. What had been locked away and hidden was suddenly revealed and spread open again. Mark was the guide, though, as he himself later admitted, he was more of a theo-retician than a practitioner in all those areas.

Bella never asked him whether he had had sex with anyone before her, not because she didn't want to know; she felt with her immature girlish feelings that it was enough for her that Mark himself never said ironically: "I'm some sexual gangster!" Even in later years, especially when he used to be sent on assignments, sometimes even for several months, it never occurred to her that he could carry on a flirtation there, as her own mother used to needle her: "Love-shmove . . . a man is a weak creature!" Bella understood that her mother was saying it with good intentions, to spare her daughter useless worry. It was indeed possible—after all, her mother herself claimed that "if God wills it, there's nothing human beings can do to prevent it." Bella was not one of those women who sniff their husband's shirts to see whether they smell of someone else's perfume. Especially not in those days, when the entire inventory of the Soviet perfume industry comprised just a few brand names.

Bella smiled crookedly: "It's really a joke!" and got into her car to continue today's route. Her thoughts, however, pulled her back to that late evening when she had to remain alone again and share her bed with her loneliness. Mark had been sent then to work in Bulgaria, to Plovdiv, the sister city of Kishinev. His architectural group at the Project Institute where he worked had won the competition to build a cultural center in Plovdiv, which comprised several buildings: a theater, a cinema, and an exhibition hall. It was certainly a big deal, but the bottom line was that Bella had had to stay alone with her child for two months. David was then almost two years old; Bella was working at the school, teaching English to the older classes. Naturally her mother helped her, babysat the child till Bella came home from work. The last half-year, Mark would stay in his office till late in the evening; the deadline for providing the plans was pressing. Weary, with his nerves twisted into a knot, he couldn't fall asleep . . . They would sit in the kitchen and David would fall asleep. Bella would already be falling off her feet, but Mark would keep telling stories. She knew that he needed her to sit next to him; it wasn't important whether she listened or not, whether she understood anything of what he was telling her with such intensity; Mark was a creative person, and if he entrusted her with his thoughts, she had to listen to him.

"He's a genius, that Semyon—he thinks up things they haven't even heard of in Moscow . . ."

"Open the window, Mark—you smoke too much . . ."

"It's a shame that such a project won't be accepted."

"Why are you so sure of that?"

"Is there any way a project whose chief architect is named Semyon Shoykhet could win?!"

And yet it did happen, and their joy was therefore all the greater.

There was no telephone in the apartment they had rented, and even if there had been, it was not so easy to reach someone abroad. Yes, Bulgaria was considered a sixteenth republic, but it was nevertheless beyond the borders of the Soviet Union, and to call there wasn't at all easy. Throughout his whole time there, Bella spoke to Mark only twice, prescheduling the call a week in advance, at the central telephone station, as was the procedure. She yearned for him, for his biting replies, for the smell of him, for his caresses and kisses . . .

It was already about ten at night. Her child was sleeping and Bella had just come out of the bathroom wearing a light robe, her hair still damp, ready to go to bed and read a bit till she fell asleep. Suddenly the doorbell rang.

"Who's there?"

"Guess, Bella . . ."

The voice sounded familiar. She opened the door as much as the chain allowed, and almost screamed: "Alik!" She was overjoyed to see him, though the hour was late, not one for receiving guests.

"Come in . . . It's so unexpected . . . How do you come to be in these parts?"

Alik, Mark's school friend, had stayed in Moscow after graduation. In his fifth year, a semester before defending his thesis, he had gotten married to a girl from Moscow. Mark joked about it even then: "Alik's a bold fellow. He's gotten hold of a girl with an unusual dowry—permission to live in Moscow!" Bella immediately answered: "Yes—your mother would certainly have been happier if you had captured a big-city princess!" The wordplay, which they used to engage in frequently, was nevertheless ended by Mark, with deep reverence: "On the other hand, I have a wife who translates all my English dreams for me."

As Mark would hear, Alik's career went quickly uphill, but not as an architect. His father-in-law was a highly placed big shot in the

Moscow city administration, and he found Alik a position as an architectural consultant.

"Excuse me, I meant to call you beforehand, but I realized that I didn't have your number."

"We don't have it either," Bella smiled. "Never mind—I'm glad you came."

They kissed each other.

"Excuse me, I've just come from the airport, and by the time I got settled in my hotel room it was already late. Fortunately I had kept your address, which Mark left me during his last visit in Moscow. By the way—where is he?"

"Mark has been in Bulgaria, in Plovdiv for almost two months now."

Alik got confused for a moment. He opened his leather briefcase and pulled out a beautiful, round cardboard box of Meteor candies and a bottle of Doina brandy.

"People come to Moscow from all over the country for special treats, so I brought you Moldavian candy and Moldavian brandy from there."

"A paradox of our reality."

They were still standing pensively in the narrow hallway when Bella suddenly snapped out of it:

"Go into the parlor . . . David is sleeping there," she pointed to a closed door. "You haven't seen him yet."

She went into the parlor first, took her things off the chair, and stuffed them under the broad sofa.

"Truth be told, I was already about to go to sleep . . ."

"I won't keep you long—I have to be at the municipal offices for a meeting tomorrow morning. I'm flying on to Kiev the day after tomorrow. It' really too bad that Mark isn't here . . ."

"Their project group won the competition for the best cultural center, so they exchange places every two months . . ."

"A fine fellow, Mark. He was the best student in our class!"

"Yes—work is the most important thing to him," Bella remarked regretfully. "He is virtually mesmerized by it."

She left the bottle of brandy and the box of candy on the low coffee table next to the sofa, went over to an old cabinet, and took out two goblets.

"We rented this apartment," she said, as if excusing herself, "and it wasn't worthwhile to buy new furniture for it . . . Though, truth be told, at this point there's nothing to buy . . ."

Alik opened the bottle and poured the golden liquid into the goblets. Bella noticed that he did it very quickly, with a certain flair, like a person who was experienced at it. Then he opened the candy box.

"I remember that you like sweets."

"Yes—my mother-in-law revealed that secret on the eve of our marriage."

Alik grasped the goblet, thought for a moment, and quietly said:

"You know, Bella—I envy Mark. Not only because he's a talented architect—that's another matter—but because he has a wife like you. I drink to the charming mistress of this rented apartment, to you, Bella."

Bella sipped the burning drink several times and felt the warmth spread throughout her body. After her bath and the bit of brandy, the weariness of the day was slowly leaving her—the troubling thoughts in her mind were fading.

"Tell me a little about yourself, about your big city life."

Alik had drunk up the first glass and had poured himself another one from the bottle.

"You mean, of course, my family life?" he pinpointed the matter. "One lives. So far, I have no children. Sveta, my wife, is a theater critic, as you know, so she gets lost in the theater nearly every evening. One night there's a premiere and the next it's a jubilee—Moscow has always been a theater city. In addition, she has a lot of friends among the actors and directors—the Bohemians, in other words . . ."

He drank up the brandy in big gulps. When he looked at Bella after that, no sign remained of his momentary thoughtfulness, as though the brandy had been capable of wiping it off his face.

"You'll laugh, but I frequently think back to that town on the seashore; it had such a funny name: Karolino . . ."

"Karolino-Bugaz . . ."

"Right! It seems like just yesterday . . . 'Yes, one day is longer than a century' . . ."

He filled up his glass again and proposed a toast:

"I propose a toast: To Karolino-Bugaz! To our youth!"

They clinked glasses and Bella drank up the remaining contents of her goblet in one gulp . . . She was feeling good now, she thought suddenly . . . Mark was somewhere far away but she felt his nearness, while Alik, by his unexpected visit, had brought a special mood to the regular night, had awakened almost forgotten memories, experiences . . .

It was obvious that the brandy had had a marked effect on Alik, despite its lightness, which he had emphasized. Bella even put her finger to her lips and pointed to the wall, on the other side of which her son was sleeping.

"I understand," Alik said, now whispering. "I too would like to have a son or a daughter already, but Sveta . . . She is totally involved in her theatrical life, to the point that she has forgotten about real life."

He picked up the bottle. Bella stretched out her hand with the empty goblet: "Me too—another few drops and that's all."

"Do you know, Bella, why I can't forgive myself?"

"Tell me and I'll know."

"That I didn't fall in love with you then."

Bella smiled. In those days of their first meeting in Karolino-Bugaz, she had definitely liked Alik more than Mark. An imposing figure, physically well put together, never tiring of telling jokes, he was one of those young fellows that girls swoon over. He, however, had his own approach to the squirmy question: he liked women who were older than he was and had already tasted the "fruits of the Garden of Eden," as Alik liked to put it. By his second day in Karolino-Bugaz, he was already flirting with a woman who was four or five years older than he was who had brought her child to breathe the fresh sea air. Years later, when Bella and Mark were reminiscing about those long-ago summer days of their youth, Mark had asked Bella casually: "And what indeed did you see in me—a skinny, foolish young man, and a nuisance as well? Compared with Alik, I was pitiful!" Bella remembers to this day what she answered: "Don't exaggerate . . . Though I was still inexperienced then and didn't even know how to kiss someone properly on the lips, I felt that you were someone I could trust, could rely on."

Alik took Bella's hand in his and touched his forehead to hers. For a moment, Bella was confused, instinctively wanted to pull free, but she almost involuntarily placed her other hand on Alik's head and stroked it. Alik began to whisper something, pulled her to him, and, still not raising his head, buried his face in her knees. Bella could barely hear her own voice, as if it were a distant echo from the past: "Alik—we shouldn't . . . It's late . . ." and she herself didn't understand what "late" meant: whether the hour was late or whether it was too late to change anything. The words bothered her—she got completely mixed up in them . . . She had to get free from them, and from thoughts, too—not think—not compare—just go along with the flow of the fumes that had made her body and her head so heavy. She remained lying face-up on the sofa with her eyes closed, and only her hands both opposed Alik's increasing urgency and immediately surrendered to him, pulled him toward her . . .

Suddenly she heard a voice weakly pushing its way through her clouded consciousness, like a slender, clean ray of light; the tip of the ray pierced into her ear and something seemed to burst there, so strongly that Bella trembled. A single word erupted from her mouth: "David!" She pushed Alik away with both hands and crept off the sofa.

"Little David is crying," Bella said, as if excusing herself . . .

She quickly buttoned up her robe. A moment later she was standing next to her child's little bed and calming him. She laid her palm on his forehead and convinced herself that he didn't have any fever, thank God! Alik followed into the room and stood next to Bella. The weak glow of the night light spread softly over the sleeping child.

"Mini Mark," said Alik quietly, looking at the little boy.

Bella nodded her head. Turning to Alik, she said:

"Excuse me, Alik—it's late already . . ."

"No, you excuse me . . ."

Nothing else happened between her and Alik. She might have completely forgotten the late night meeting—tucked it away in the

secret corners of her soul, such as every woman has—if Mark, returning one time from an assignment in Moscow, hadn't told her that he
had met Alik and that he had divorced his wife.

"Yes," Mark recalled, and took a round box packed in colored gift
wrap out of his suitcase. "Alik asked me to give this to you."

Bella tore off the paper and her heart skipped a beat—it was
Meteor candy.

– 5 –

Impatient honking came from behind the car that Bella was driving or, more accurately, standing still in. She realized that they were honking at her because the light had already changed from red to green and she still wasn't moving. A gray Subaru, which was traveling in the next lane, stopped next to her, and a man with a thin, dark face and a small black yarmulke on the top of his head stuck his head out of the window; Bella heard: "Missus, what are you waiting for? The green light will soon be gone!" She laughed—indeed, what was she waiting for? She was surely already in Boro Park. Bella turned onto 13th Avenue, the way David had explained to her, and she immediately saw, to her right, a big, blue sign that almost screamed Stern's Bakery.

Bella didn't stay in the bakery for very long. A very nice woman quickly brought out a big box and opened it so Bella could see the cake, which was beautifully decorated—in the middle, something was written, apparently in Hebrew. "These two letters mean thirty, and this is mazel tov," the woman said. Bella thanked her and asked her to wrap up another two cookies with multicolored sprinkles, for her grandchildren.

She left the bakery satisfied. Kosher it was—just let it be tasty. Mark definitely disliked all the "kosher delicacies," as he called them, but Bella knew very well that it wasn't a matter of "delicacies"—he couldn't come to terms with the idea that his son "had become a religious zealot, had gone over to a world from a hundred years ago!" "What sort of future awaits his children, my grandchildren?!" Bella had to listen to his complaints every time and come up with a neutral answer. It was better that Mark let out steam on her than that they lose their only son, God forbid. Once that almost happened—really, with all the cruelty involved . . .

When they came to America, David was not quite fifteen years old. They came with Bella's mother; her father, Robusta as Bella and Mark called him between themselves, had died in Europe. Bella's mother herself had said then that his death was a blessing—cancer had been torturing him for a year and a half, but he died suddenly, in a single instant, from a heart attack.

Her mother never complained—she consoled herself with the saying that "emigration is the same as evacuation, but without bombs," and added "Thank God for that!" On the other hand, she helped the children by means of her "privileges," to say nothing of the fact that the running of their rented apartment rested on her. She knew very well how to run a house thriftily so everyone would be well fed and satisfied. But the most important thing was that David, when he came home from school, had someone to take care of him and keep an eye on him. Bella and Mark, after all, would leave very early and come home late in the evening, exhausted, without a bit of strength . . .

The trouble came unexpectedly, as is appropriate for trouble, without a why or wherefore. One night Bella was awakened by severe groans coming from her son's room. The picture that was revealed to her remains before her eyes to this day. The blanket was on the floor and David, covered with sweat, was lying all curled up and thrashing about as if he were burning with fever.

He did not have a fever, and that frightened Bella even more, and also Mark, whom she had awakened. Calling an ambulance was something David didn't want. He gritted his teeth and was able to squeeze out a broken "no!" Could Bella and Mark have even imagined that their son was a drug addict? The words themselves were not part of their vocabulary; they were incomprehensible, they came from another world, they sounded like a curse, just like the word "homosexual." There, in that other life that they had tried hard to forget, they had hardly heard of such things as drugs and drug addicts. Only on television, when programs about the "rotten West" were shown, could they see groups of drug addicts. But they figured that to be part of the large amount of clumsily produced ideological propaganda, nothing more . . .

They called an ambulance all the same. The paramedic needed only a quick glance to know what was going on and he told them that David had taken drugs and would need to be hospitalized for some time. Bella closed the two forward little windows on the car and turned on the air conditioner. Her blood again pounded in her temples—"waxed and waned"; the news she had heard had sounded like a judgment pronounced in a criminal court. The life of their little family had barely gotten established, had found its way to a new reality: Mark was about to take his exams to get a license so he could work as a recognized American architect and Bella was taking courses that would permit her to establish a tourist agency; it looked as if their David, who was about to finish high school, had also decided to go to college, to study bioengineering, a very prestigious field, as he had once explained to his parents . . .

Bella's mother always claimed that those things happened because of a "good eye." People were envious, begrudged them—they thought that everything fell out of the sky for them! After the hospitalization, Bella and Mark wanted to immediately send David to a locked inpatient rehabilitation center. He resisted, threatened to throw himself off the top floor of a skyscraper. Mark, as was his custom, didn't pass up the occasion to make a cutting remark here too: "Why do you have to creep up so high when a five-story building would do?" Bella became even more depressed from all those words, threats, and jokes. They had to do something, and relying on someone else, even God, was something she couldn't do. After all, they were talking about her only son! So she decided to take David to Seattle, to her cousin, at least for two weeks, to get him away from his social circle. Maybe that would help him forget about the poison. And that's what she did: she got herself excused from her courses—they understood—and off they went.

After they came back from Seattle, they moved to a rented apartment in Queens. "A new place, new luck," Bella's mother received the news by saying. David changed schools and it appeared that her stubbornness had prevailed—she had dragged her son out of the deadly swamp . . . But her disappointment was even greater and bitterer with the subsequent revelation that her son was still using. Now it was she who was ready to throw herself off a skyscraper. Mark seemed to have removed himself completely from what was happening to his family, pretended not to notice, and avoided conversing with Bella, because all their conversations began and ended with the same words: "What will happen? We're losing him . . ." One time Mark said: "Perhaps if we hadn't left Kishinev we wouldn't have known such troubles?!"

If things had continued the same way it would soon have been too late; David needed a special program for drug addicts, and they entered him into it. Bella's mother couldn't be calmed: "You are no parents! To lock up your own child for a year, like in a prison!" Bella swallowed it, and indeed—could one explain it?!

David spent twelve months at the rehab and came out a different person. Bella never asked him what he had experienced there, and he told her only that he had been helped to clamber out of the dark hole not so much by the treatment but by the letters that he used to get from Leah.

Who was Leah? She is now his wife, the mother of their two girls, Bella's daughter-in-law. The strength of that girl, who was just a tiny thing, turned out to be the most effective medicine. David, who was his father's son, made a joke of it: "Our exchange of letters," he said "could be made the basis of an exclusive method for getting drug addicts to kick their habit." Leah's older brother, who was in the same refuge as David, was the one who introduced them. He had come from Israel "to become a millionaire in America," but he ended up in the drug rehab. He showed his friend his sister's picture, in which she was wearing a military uniform. For David, it was enough to make him fall in love with her—he asked her brother for her address and wrote her a letter. Oh, children, children! As it turned out, Bella met Mark in Karolino-Bugaz when she was the same age as Leah.

———

Bella remembered the words that had been said to her at the time of her first visit to Mark's parents. She kept them and their associated pain buried deeply within her, mostly for Mark's sake, but she never forgot the taste of those pumpkin knishes. The young couple lived in their house for half a year after the wedding; Bella and Mark had bought a house in Brooklyn by then, in Sheepshead Bay, which had enough room for all of them.

Bella got Leah a job at the tourist agency where she worked. It quickly became clear that the girl had been born for such work; after a while they created a separate division for her, which was devoted to running tours for Israelis visiting America and Canada and for Americans visiting Israel.

Entering into that life didn't come easy to David. He had to give up his youthful dreams about college and a subsequent career; now that he was married, circumstances required him to take concrete steps. In addition, Leah was soon far along in her pregnancy. David looked lost, full of doubts, and Bella was very much afraid lest his feelings of insecurity about himself push him again into that deep abyss.

She couldn't fall asleep at night—she kept needling Mark: "After all, you're his father—you have to help him!" At that time, Mark had drawn up plans for a shopping center for a client, a Lubavitcher Hasid, and he told him about David's history and asked him for advice. The Hasid listened, and told Mark to send his son to visit him at his office. Within a week, David was working for the man.

As would soon become apparent, working there David found not only a job but the community he had been lacking. He started wearing a knitted kippah. That didn't surprise Bella—after all, he was working among pious Jews. Then she noticed that he was permitting himself to grow a little beard and had exchanged the knitted kippah for a black yarmulke. She asked him, half-joking, whether he was planning to become pious? David took the question seriously, and answered yes—that he was thinking about it, that he had become very close to the boss's youngest son, who was a year older than him, and that he and Leah had been invited to their home for Sabbath dinner several times.

Bella looked at her son—how he was engrossed in telling about his new friend; his family; how beautifully and cozily they celebrated the Sabbath, accompanied by singing and putting on phylacteries; how everyone at the table, young and old, sang together. She saw in his eyes a spark of life that she hadn't seen in him for a long time. "Let it be that way," she thought to herself. "Perhaps that is indeed the price we must pay for his salvation . . ."

———

Bella looked at her watch: a quarter to two. She was late. No, she wouldn't be able to get to the restaurant—she would call them and explain everything to the manager. But first she would call Mark so he should at least lay out the shirt that he wanted to wear today so she could iron it. The prolonged ringing of the telephone that Bella heard made her doubtful. Had Mark gone into his office on such a day? It was bad enough that he did so every Saturday and Sunday so he wouldn't have to stay home. She again felt resentment pulsing through her. She was barely able to restrain herself from letting go of the wheel so she could rub her temples with her fingertips. No, she wouldn't call him on his cell phone. Enough—he was not a little child and she was not his mother . . .

She drove to her house. Mark's car, a dark blue Peugeot, was parked there, as always. Strange—perhaps one of his business partners had come for him? Bella pulled out the cake, locked the car, and ascended the several steps to the doorway. She was already calling her husband's name when she reached the doorway. But Mark didn't answer. Bella immediately went to the refrigerator to put the cake into it, and only afterwards did she walk upstairs to the second story.

She looked into the office and into the second bedroom. She called out again: "Mark." The silence evoked a mixed feeling of concern and anger. In the bedroom, where Bella had left her husband sleeping that morning, the bed was made precisely. No—she had certainly not hoped to find him there; her feet had brought her here, as if to a railroad station where she began each new day and ended it. She turned her head toward the alcove, the broad niche deep within which there stood a small, inlaid table on thin, elegant legs; above it, attached to the wall, hung a large oval mirror. Mark sarcastically called the alcove his "boudoir," using the French pronunciation of the word.

Bella encountered her reflection. She looked down and noticed a square sheet of paper on the little table that she hadn't left there. Her gaze seized on that piece of paper, which drew her to it.

Bella sat down on the soft, round stool holding the piece of paper in her hands, and looked over the straight lines of Mark's neat handwriting:

Dear Bella:

Please forgive me that precisely today on this our thirtieth anniversary I've decided to leave you. No, not for another woman—I don't have anyone! And not to leave life—God forbid! I am going away to find myself. Maybe that sounds strange, weird, or even insane. I feel, however, that if I don't do that today, I'll never do it. And then I will lose you for good.

The truth is that we have been drawing apart for quite a long time now. Perhaps because of the day-to-day hustle and bustle that has seized both of us and whirled us into a wild maelstrom; or perhaps because the string that was strung between us that used to sound a clear note to keep us together so we wouldn't fall by the wayside, and which made it possible for us to go on together on the road we chose thirty years ago, has ruptured.

Yes, we could probably excuse the emptiness that has filled the corners of our souls, where rare feelings, memories, smells, and sounds used to hug each other. Excuse it and calm it by citing what happens step by step with people of our age, especially our friends and acquaintances . . .

It had already been many years since they had come to America, since Bella had scanned the beautiful, pearly letters of her husband's handwriting. In moments of depression, she would reread his letters that had gotten lost somewhere between the two continents, as if between two parts of one life that had been torn apart, especially when Mark wasn't home for a long time because of his assignments or when they quarreled. The letters used to refresh her, as if she were dipping again into the waters of Karolino-Bugaz when they, Mark and Bella, sweaty and exhausted by their closeness, used to tear themselves away from one another for a few moments.

The sparse words of the little letter lay like pieces of ice beneath her heart, and were spreading damp coldness throughout her body:

I beg you — don't call me, don't look for me. I spoke to David on the phone and tried to explain everything to him so he would understand. Again— please forgive me if you can.

Mark

Bella tore her eyes away from the last word with difficulty. A young woman, looking very similar to herself thirty years ago, was looking back at her from the mirror. Bella looked with curiosity at her nakedness, as if searching for signs of the changes that would have had to appear after she was transformed from a girl into a woman. Unexpectedly, the dark shadow of Bella's dream from today rose up behind her narrow, white shoulders.

-6-

Mark stood on the top deck of the gigantic cruise ship *Carnival Dream*, which was slowly distancing itself from the city, as if a clod of earth had split off from the continent and, assuming the status of an independent island, had started swimming freely across the ocean. The sunset now clearly outlined a diagram of Manhattan on the dark blue heavenly canvas.

———

When Mark and Bella had finally decided to go to America, Mark's greatest dream had been to settle in New York; he imagined then that living in the great megalopolis would be like leafing every day through a magnificent edition of the *AIA Guide*, the guidebook issued by the American Institute of Architecture. Mark had bought an edition of the Guide in Moscow for a crazy price while he was still a student there, but had given it to a friend before setting out for America. His friend was jealous of him: "Now you'll be able to actually see every building . . ."

At first, Mark did indeed get on the train at the Sheepshead Bay station as if he were going to work, and would get lost in Manhattan for a whole day. He didn't need a guide—he knew the name and history of practically every building. The names of the neighborhoods like SoHo and Greenwich Village excited his ears and echoed in his brain, together with the ringing names of other cities and countries: Montmartre, the D'Orsay Museum, Guell Park, and Batllo House, which he had so far seen only in his dreams. Wandering around New York with his backpack, into which Bella had placed a few sandwiches and a small thermos of coffee, Mark realized one day that all these beautiful streets, buildings, squares, and parks, photographs or movies which used to elicit such enthusiasm in him, were in reality alien to him and removed from his life and his history, just like the hundreds of busy people around him.

Even during his first year as a student in Moscow, when he, a young man from the sticks, had come to the big city, he hadn't felt as lost as he suddenly felt in Manhattan during his "professional strolls." There it had been his community, with a common language and culture that he had grown up around and was steeped in, with all its ideology, thoughts, and way of life . . . Everything there had been understandable and familiar, and he, with youthful fascination, had actually dreamed of planning and someday building his building, or even an entire complex there, not only as an architect but indeed as a citizen of his city and country. He would be doing that for the people, he had thought, not for the authorities . . .

Sitting on a bench in Union Square Park and chewing Bella's sandwich, he suddenly understood the gigantic difference between that young specialist in the minutiae of architecture, full of hopes and plans, in love with the so-called international style, where the names of Le Corbusier, Ludwig Mies van der Rohe, Walter Gropius, and Phillip Johnson had resounded like the names of the Greek gods—and the wandering immigrant, without a language, without prospects for work . . . Mark recalled how they used to call New York the concrete jungle, and it turned out that he had become a lost Mowgli within it. Some joke!! He had felt as if something was stuck in his throat—not a piece of food but a lump of self-resentment. No, he was no Mowgli here and no Tarzan, because there in Brooklyn, in his rented apartment, three people looked forward to and expected substantive deeds from him. At that very moment, Mark decided that he would get to his goal, that he would continue in his trade here, no matter how difficult the road would be for him . . .

———

Mark took the elevator down to the promenade deck, which was on the fifth story and looked like a fancy street in a wealthy neighborhood, with stores, restaurants, night clubs, and a casino. Mark and Bella had taken their vacations several times on a cruise ship, though the first time Bella suggested that to him, Mark had been against it: "You know I prefer to walk around or drive around . . . We haven't seen anything together yet, after all!" Nevertheless, he had yielded to his wife, and he wasn't sorry later.

The highly curious passengers, or citizens of the floating city *Carnival Dream*, walked back and forth without a care in the world across their local piece of Times Square, stopped at the beautifully illuminated show windows, looked at the merchandise, got acquainted with the menus of the fine restaurants. Everything was still closed—only in the jazz club were a few musicians already playing. Mark sat down at a small round table and ordered a gin and tonic.

The soft sounds of the blues both lulled him and awakened him—lulled the daily hustle bustle and awakened memories . . . He had noticed recently that the older he got the faster he chased after his yesterdays, after a happy hour, after an unforgettable minute. He was seized by such remembrances, locked himself into them, and like a spider with a captured fly he crept quietly over the slender thread of time, sensing the taste of the previous encounter . . .

This was the first time in America that he was traveling somewhere alone, without Bella. She was the one who worried about where and when they should take their vacation, and not only because her work was related to the so-called entertainment industry; even in Russia, she had always been the family's motor—she took all the worries upon herself: about their child, their house, their way of life, the parents, because he, Mark, was a creative person, and "in his head he had to be free."

He had already gotten so used to that that when they got to America and faced a new reality he suddenly realized that he was useless in day-to-day life. No, he didn't sit around with empty hands—he tried to work here and there as long as he could bring in a few dollars. At night, Bella would drill into his head: "Go, study English! Don't waste your energy on casual jobs! Ask, search, get interested; you have a real profession, after all!"

The words "real profession" that Bella slipped in used to drive Mark crazy. Who needed his real profession here?! There weren't enough such specialists here?! He would get angry at her and they would quarrel and scream at one another; in the end, he did what Bella told him to do. It was she that drove him to Manhattan almost every day for his "professional strolls," and one day he met an acquaintance of his, an engineer with whom he had once worked together on a project, and that person did indeed put Mark in touch with Mister Blank, from whom Mark obtained his first job and who later became his partner . . .

The sweetish mild drink nevertheless contributed its bit of poison to Mark's mind, especially since he hadn't had lunch today. He didn't feel at all hungry and wasn't planning to go to the ship's dinner today, though from his previous experience he knew that they fed the passengers generously. How did they put it? "All inclusive!"

Gin and tonic also reminded him of a long-ago story, upon which Mark seized the moment it stirred in his memory. Bulgaria. Plovdiv. His first and last trip abroad. How old had he been then? Not quite twenty-eight. At that time it looked like a fantastic dream or an unbelievable success, and though it very soon became clear that Plovdiv was no less provincial than Kishinev, it was still—abroad. The Wild West infected the land of "Bratushki: with clear-cut signs of its differentness; even though they were trivialities, they struck one immediately: the American cigarettes Kent and Philip Morris; chewing gum; Coca-Cola in its elegant bottles, which were immediately recognizable, though till then he had seen them only in pictures; other delicious drinks, which everyone around called by the name Schweppes, which Mark immediately changed to "greps."

Toward the end of his assignment, which lasted more than two months, he met Sarigul. A dark, charming young woman, a translator of German and Russian, she was accompanying her boss, an architect from East Berlin, who was also participating in the big construction project. It had been at a party—he no longer remembered what and whom it was in honor of. They used to have parties fairly often, spontaneously as long as they could find some excuse. Mark was already feeling that the whole assignment was getting on his nerves; he missed Bella and his son. Considering how long he had been away, David might have forgotten what his father looked like. Sarigul came up to him holding two goblets in her hands that resembled a pair of glass funnels on long stems. She handed one of them, containing a cloudy liquid, to Mark.

"It's called gin and tonic," Sarigul explained, assuming a knowledgeable air. "Lately it's become a very popular cocktail all over Bulgaria."

She smiled and sat down next to Mark. She continued to speak, and her big, dark, somewhat slanted eyes sparkled merrily.

"My parents think that the various cocktails have been specially introduced from the West to demoralize our youth. A true Bulgarian patriot, they claim, should drink only our national drinks: Mastika, Rakia . . ."

Mark perked up his ears. A few days before he had left Kishinev for Bulgaria, a muscular young man had come to his office. It was not hard to figure out what bureau he served; their group had known in advance that a "man from there" would accompany them during the entire assignment, so his appearance and instructing was not a surprise for Mark and his colleagues. He did not give them a long lecture about "how a Soviet citizen should behave abroad"—Bulgaria, was, after all, a "brother Socialist country." He wanted to point out in general that he was made out of the same dough as everyone else, and at the end he added in a friendly way: "I am sure that everything will go very well; you just have to remember: Stay alert! And that's all."

Meanwhile, Sarigul was continuing to speak:

"I see you're married," she said with a nod toward his ring. "Do you have any children?"

"A son—David is his name. He's almost two years old."

"You miss him, of course?"

Mark sipped the cocktail and nodded his head as if to confirm it:

"Not bad. I drank gin once before, when I was still in Moscow, but tonic . . ."

"Separately I don't like them: gin is too strong for me and tonic is too bitter, but as a mixture, I like it."

She looked into his eyes and said:

"I too am sort of a biological cocktail: my father is an ethnic Turk and my mother is Jewish. My name too is a mixture: my mother wanted to name me Sarah, which was her grandmother's name, and my father wanted Gul, which was his mother's name. So they found a compromise, Sarigul, which means yellow rose in Turkish."

The biological cocktail temporarily relieved his tension, and the alcohol contributed as well:

"Now I understand why the Turkish half-moon and the Jewish stars shine from your eyes . . ."

"You're also a poet, Mark, like Andrei Voznesensky?"

"Do you like his poetry?"

"I've read several of his poems. I just know that he is an architect."

"Yes, I graduated from the same Moscow Architectural Institute as he did, but I don't write poems."

Sarigul got up from her armchair and unexpectedly said:

"Would you like to leave this boring party? I know a very pleasant place not far from here where they make unusually good Turkish coffee."

It was a warm evening with a clear sky sprinkled with stars. Hotel Renaissance, which they were leaving, was in an old quarter of the city. The stately lanterns, left over here from a long time ago, issued swatches of yellow light out of the darkness and spread them across the shiny stones of the gutter. Sarigul bent down and unbuttoned her high-heeled shoes.

"You won't mind if I take off my formal footwear?"

Mark shrugged his shoulders.

"If it's more comfortable for you. Aren't you afraid of stepping on a sharp stone, or . . ."

"No. After all, I grew up in this city and I know every little stone here . . ."

"I thought you lived in Sofia and came here with your German boss."

"Yes, I do indeed live in Sofia and my parents are there, but I grew up in my grandmother's house, in Plovdiv."

"I like this city—it reminds me of a sort of architectural cocktail made out of remnants of Roman ruins, proud Muslim mosques, and Orthodox churches, which seem to be grown into the ground . . ."

"That is indeed what happened: the Turks forbade the Bulgarians from building churches taller than their mosques," Sarigul added, with the tone of a skilled guide, "so they found a way—they built not upward but downward into the depths; you've probably noticed that when you go into a church you walk down a flight of stairs."

"I've noticed it, just as I've noticed that when Bulgarians say yes they shake their heads no."

"And you know, of course, why that is so?"

"I've been told that when the Turks forced the Bulgarians to convert to Islam, they put a knife to their throats, and if someone shook his head no, he would cut his own throat, so they nodded their heads yes, but it meant no."

"Who knows? In any case, it's a nice story."

They turned into a narrow alley, lit mostly by the glow from the windows. The walls of the one-story houses seemed to be built on high stone foundations and were resting on beautifully carved wooden supports. Sarigul and Mark stopped at a narrow door, decorated on both sides with flowerpots. Over the door hung a sign with the name of the café: Boga.

"Does that name mean God?" Mark asked.

Sarigul laughed:

"In Russian and Bulgarian, yes—but in Turkish the word *boga* means ox. Come in."

Sarigul felt at home in the crowded coffeehouse; she immediately went over to the tall counter from behind which there looked out a darkly charming man with puffy cheeks and thick, droopy, waxed mustachios around his mouth. On his hat was a red fez with a tassel, which added a certain costumed feel to his appearance. On the counter was a wide and deep brass tray filled with gray sand into which were inserted three or four brass *turkas*, exactly like the one Bella's father had had. Here they called it by the Turkish name *finjan*.

"Hi, Boga—this is my friend Mark and he is a connoisseur of coffee."

Mark raised his hand and nodded his head yes.

They sat down at one of the three little tables that were standing empty. Sarigul set her shoes down next to her and put them on again.

"Boga brews the best coffee in Plovdiv, and maybe in all of Bulgaria."

She said that deliberately loud so Boga, who was already puttering with his *finjan*, would also hear it.

Mark recalled his father-in-law, the real connoisseur of coffee, and smiled.

"I trust Boga will brew us Arabica coffee, not Robusta?" Mark said that loudly too, so it would reach the owner of the coffeehouse.

Sarigul was astonished, and turned her head toward Boga, who pretended that he hadn't understood what had been said in Russian. So she looked at Mark again:

"I see that I've really fallen into it—I know what Arabica is, but Robusta?"

Mark explained with a smile:

"It's a relative of mine who is the real expert in coffee beans, not I. I heard about the kinds of coffee from him."

"As I understand it," Sarigul asked, sensing the new turn of the conversation, "you are a Jew, too, though your name is Mark?"

"Mark is for my Soviet passport; my grandfather, who died in the ghetto, was named Mordecai."

"I don't know whether you've heard, but during the war the Bulgarians resisted the deportation of the local Jews. My grandmother survived because of that."

The aroma of fresh coffee, the stone walls, the floor of the half-lit room, and the quiet music with some sort of sad tune made the room feel even more crowded, seemed to compress it, so the two young people who had known each other for only a few hours would feel a closeness, which the night later provided to them.

———

The blues stopped and Mark returned from the brief journey back to his youth. He was still sitting at the little round table in the jazz club. The passengers, dressed up in evening clothes, satisfied by the more-than-sufficient dinner, went out onto the broad promenade, filling tables at the bars, sat at the game machines and green tables of the casino, took seats in the gigantic concert hall—in a word, they immersed themselves in the exuberant holiday of amusement and the high life that the Carnival cruise company had promised they would find here.

After three more gin and tonics, Mark felt that his place was now in the stateroom on the ninth deck. That would be enough attractions for today; it was time to sleep.

– 7 –

The bright sunlight and a slight rocking awakened Mark. He looked out from his broad bed, sat for a moment with his hands on the edge of the bed, still sleepy, with an unpleasant taste in his mouth. He gazed gloomily into the distance where one blueness merged with another one so that the line of the horizon could not be appreciated. He got up and took a step toward the blueness.

Opening the door to the balcony, Mark felt as if he were being washed with a cold, fresh breeze from head to toe. He looked out from the stateroom as if he were being liberated from confinement, and remained alone in the narrow space.

The ship was standing still in the middle of the ocean, a substantial distance away from a narrow strip of land, an island. Every three or four minutes, small motorboats, which had previously been hanging along both sides of the ship like toys, went down to the island. Mark looked at his wristwatch; it was already a quarter after nine. The watch hands seemed to be asking him "is it late or still early?" Whichever it might be, an inner turmoil, already deeply rooted in his day-to-day routine, was pushing him to hurry. In addition, his stomach was demanding its due—by this time it would normally have consumed the light breakfast that Bella always prepared for him.

Very quickly after his morning ablutions, conducted in an abbreviated fashion, Mark was ready to leave his temporary residence. He had decided that after breakfast he would not return to it but would immediately go down to the island. Wearing short hockey pants, a light green shirt, sandals, and a Yankees cap with a long brim, he inserted himself into the overall daily carnival, which had promised each resident of the ship city that it would make his or her personal dream come true.

Going up to the tenth deck, he looked for someplace to eat breakfast without wasting a lot of time. Apparently most of the passengers had already finished eating and had gone to the beach to sunbathe and then to eat again. After all, "it's all inclusive." Mark looked at the various dishes, and every time his eyes lingered on something that looked tasty, he heard Bella's voice as if she were standing behind him and whispering into his ear: "No—too fat!" "Fried food is just what you need for your cholesterol!" "Too salty for you!" "Too sweet!" "Carbohydrates—too many carbohydrates!" Mark waved his hand angrily back and forth next to his ear and placed samples of everything the voice had forbidden him to touch on his plastic plate. Nevertheless, when he was already sitting at his table he sighed heavily and pushed away the plate of oatmeal. As revenge against the voice, he drank his tea with two danishes.

As an experienced ship traveler, Mark quickly looked for the exit, and passing through the checkpoint he sat down in the motorboat. It didn't take more than ten or fifteen minutes for the boat to reach the wooden dock. Approaching the shore, Mark felt his heart start to beat faster, producing an uneasy feeling; for now, he couldn't explain whether it was a portent of good things or the reverse. He just thought to himself: what bad things could happen here on this island isolated from the whole world, to which almost the entire population of the ship city has gone, including the pleasant Filipino waitstaff who were following practically everyone and checking to make sure there wasn't something they wanted to eat?

His feet sank into the sandy beach, and the broiling heat came beating down, washing over his whole body. From a distance he heard a familiar song, which he used to hear thirty years ago through open windows on the streets, in the parks, on the beaches, on holidays and on ordinary days—a beautiful, romantic song that had flown off the movie screen and had flooded all the cities and villages from one end of the country to the other:

Everything is cloudy in the agitated world;
there remains only a moment, so hold me close.
There's only a moment between time and nothingness,
and that interval is called "Life"—remember that!

It had been years since Mark had last heard that once-popular song, and now, hearing the ringing sounds, he grabbed onto them, as he had earlier onto that thread of life that brings one to encounter happy moments in the night. He looked around and stood there, astonished. The fog had dissolved and a familiar picture revealed itself: an ocean beach and happy, laughing people who were whirling carefree before his eyes or lying motionless, stretched out on colorful covers, sheets, wide bulky towels, or just the sand. All of them had come here to grab their portion of sun and sea air, and all of them referred to themselves by the same name: vacationers.

Small children at the very edge of the water were using various-shaped tin cans to bake sand pies. Those who were somewhat older were building castles. Several happy boys were burying one of their friends with only his head sticking out. Mark recalled that he had done the same with his friend Alik, with whom he went to the seashore at that time; Alik had lost to him in a card game, and that was the forfeit in the game. A plump woman, one of the locals, was walking around among the vacationers with an enameled green pitcher in her hand, trying to sell them her goods: cooked ears of corn. Such merchandise has to be warm, so the pitcher was covered with a thick towel. When someone called her to him, she put the pitcher down next to her on the sand, dug around a bit under the towel, and pulled out a golden bargain: 10 cents an ear, including a tiny pinch of salt for taste.

Mark practically licked his chops; he could almost sense the exciting aroma of the corn ears and the soft, slippery kernels on his tongue. Bella didn't like corn, but for Mark's sake she would occasionally buy a few ears to cook and "refresh his little heart."

And now a photographer was striding along the water's edge. Short, with a sunburned Semitic face and a flat white cap on his head, he was wearing a multicolored short-sleeved shirt and short pants; a

Fed-2 camera was hanging from his neck and dangling in front of him. In one hand he was carrying a plywood date tree that was taller than he was, and on his shoulder was perched a live macaw with red-yellow-blue feathers. Its beak was the same shape as its master's nose, except that the human nose was a little longer.

Things immediately got lively: the children abandoned their games and ran to the photographer, teasing the parrot: "Polly, Polly!" and the photographer himself, trying to arouse interest among the overheated vacationers, yelling in his Odessa Jewish-Russian, as if it were a circus attraction: "The last guest appearance of the famous parrot Kesha before he retires! Don't pass up the opportunity to take a picture with him to keep forever!"

The excited children were already dragging their parents to be photographed, the sweaty women and men were waking up from their naps, and a line of people wanting to be eternalized with the "famous feathered actor Kesha" appeared. The date tree was now "planted" at the edge of the water, the clever bird was sitting on a branch, and the confused parents and their children were standing in place next to the exotic tree and smiling.

Mark thought to himself that perhaps dozens if not hundreds of now-faded pictures of such artificial palm trees and live parrots, with an inscription beneath them: Karolino-Bugaz, 197, are being saved to this day in family photo albums, as a remembrance of a short time when they were happy.

To one side of the crowds of people lying in the sun, there materialized a wide circle of boys and girls throwing a ball back and forth. Oh how many years it had been since Mark had stood in such a circle, carefree, playing a bit of volleyball! On the other hand, sports had never grabbed him—he liked painting better. He even finished art school, and one of his drawings was exhibited at a municipal exposition of young talent. But his mother dreamed that her eldest son would become a doctor, and no matter how many times Mark explained to her that the mere sight of blood made him feel faint, it made no impression on her. "You'll get used to it!" was her answer, and his father, as always, used to agree with her: "Only that? Of course!" Beginning in the ninth grade, Mark had started to secretly visit an old man, a former chemistry teacher who had graduated from the University of Liege.

Mark had graduated from school with a silver medal (he had won four, in sport), which gave him a chance, if he received an outstanding mark of five on the entrance exams, of being accepted without taking additional exams. The first exam at the Medical Institute was in chemistry, and all the calculations that Mark's parents had made came to fruition. There was one little problem: Mark's mother hadn't properly evaluated her son's character and stubbornness, which he had inherited from her. While they were still in Moscow, he had submitted applications to both the Medical Institute, for his mother's sake, and the Architectural Institute, as he had dreamed. On the first test at the Medical Institute, he received a four, and he didn't take any more exams there.

The sun was beating down as if it wanted to emit all of its heat onto the small island. Mark was still standing on the spot where his foot had taken its first step and was looking around. He saw a short but thickly branched wild olive tree that cast a short shadow, and he started to walk in that direction in order to leave his things there and go swim. At that very moment, he felt something hit him in the head. The blow wasn't severe, but it was strong enough for him to feel it— the ball that the volleyball players were using had left their circle and hit him. A girl left the group and ran to him after the ball.

When she was two or three steps away from Mark, he again felt the rapid heartbeat that he had felt ten or fifteen minutes earlier when the motorboat was approaching the shore. Now, however, he understood the reason—Bella was standing facing him, the way he had seen her the first time in his life.

"Excuse me," she called out, "my hands have holes in them!"

"It happens," Mark picked up the ball and held it out to the girl. "You're Bella, yes?"

The girl stood there, confused. One of the young group yelled out: "Bella—we're waiting for you!" She turned and threw the ball strongly in their direction, and then cried out: "Play without me!" and asked Mark:

"Do we know each other? I sort of remember something."

"You can't remember it for the time being."

She shrugged her shoulders, as when someone says something strange, and suggested:

"Perhaps we should go over to that little tree. At least there's some shade there."

"That's exactly where I was going when the ball caught up with me."

"Excuse me again . . . I'm not very good at these games."

"Imagine that! Me neither. But thanks to getting hit by the ball, I have run into you again."

"Again? And when was the first time?"

They walked over to the wild olive tree and sat down right on the sand beneath it. Mark took off his green shirt and threw off his sandals, but kept his shorts on. Though he had already put on his swim trunks while he was still in his stateroom something stopped him from taking his shorts off. Meanwhile, Bella was picking up handfuls of sand and letting them pour between her fingers in a thin stream. When Mark was finished, she reminded him of her question:

"So when did we meet for the first time?"

Mark looked into her eyes and answered:

"Thirty-one years ago."

Bella didn't turn her gaze away. On the contrary, she looked deeply at the man, as if trying to understand how far the joke was going. With a smile, she said:

"I see you like to make jokes and that they involve a lot of fantasy too."

"Exactly. Yesterday, for example, I played a fantastic little joke; I ran away from my own wedding anniversary . . ."

"Like Gogol's hero in the play 'Marriage'?" Bella played along with him.

"Almost. From my pearl wedding anniversary, which means after living together for thirty years."

"Are you serious?" Bella, astonished, dropped to her knees.

"As serious as a fantastic joke can be!"

"But how . . . How can something like that happen?"

"Very simple, Bella. One gets up in the morning, goes through all the morning rituals that he has been doing every day for many years, gets dressed, and suddenly . . ."

"What?"

"And suddenly there appears before him a generous witch who says: 'Tell me what you want, your fondest dream, and I will make it come true.' You then say you want to start everything over again from the beginning, as it was thirty years ago!"

"And the generous witch kept her word?"

"Of course . . . In her own way: my soulmate did indeed become thirty years younger, but I remained the same."

Bella laughed. She covered her eyes with her palms; only her nose remained uncovered, and she choked with sobs. Mark looked at her and recalled that when they first met he couldn't always tell right away whether she was laughing at a joke of his or whether his joke had insulted her somehow and she was crying. It had been a long time now since he had seen or heard his Bella laughing out loud.

Meanwhile the girl was wiping away her tears, and then said unexpectedly:

"I like you more and more . . . By the way, I still don't know your name."

"Excuse me . . . It's a very simple name: Mark."

She became excited. "You know—in the Dolphin Suites where I'm staying, there is also a young man by the name of Mark. He came here with his friend Alik."

"Very interesting. I even know that they are studying in Moscow at the Architectural Institute."

"Do you know them? From where?"

"I'll tell you later . . . Now I have to go and swim—if I don't I'll simply melt away."

"Come—I'll go with you."

−8−

Mark left the ocean out of breath but refreshed. He hopped on his left foot several times with his head tilted to that side, so that the water would come out of his ear. He looked around. Bella was splashing around not far from the shore, amid the yelling children and their stern parents who never took their eyes off them. The water came up to her blue and red brassiere with yellow flowers. Mark recalled that during the first days of their honeymoon Bella used to find excuses to avoid taking off her brassiere when Mark was near her; she was embarrassed to reveal her small girlish breasts, but the embarrassment soon passed.

Bella beckoned to Mark to come into the water, but he indicated that he would wait for her on the beach, near the olive tree, where he had left his things. He recalled how the whole time they had lived in Brooklyn, in Sheepshead Bay, actually just twenty minutes from Brighton Beach, he had only gone to the beach with Bella and David two or three times. Always busy, always immersed in his work . . . Was it really that important? Certainly if he had spent more time with his son, the catastrophe wouldn't have occurred. Truth be told, when Mark finally understood how bad things had gotten and how horrible the whole problem was, he simply gave up. It was as if the catastrophe cut him off from the dynamo that had given him his energy up till then. Just yesterday it had seemed to him that with a little more effort, a few steps more, he would reach his goal; he would achieve what he sought too, and precisely here, in this new and strange country, with unlimited possibilities as long as one had a license. To obtain the license to work at his trade independently, he was required to take six exams, in English of course, which didn't come at all easily to him, because he had studied French as his foreign language in school and at the Institute. During the day, he would be deeply immersed in his work in Mister Blank's office, and after that, at home, he would sit studying till late at night. That night, he had just fallen asleep when Bella woke him up to tell him that something was happening with David. Seeing his son curled up on his bed in pain, he thought he was having an attack of appendicitis. Would that he had been correct! Of course Mark had more than once heard the saying "burying your head in the sand, like an ostrich," and of course he knew what it meant, but he had never thought that it would happen to him: to bury his head in the sand of helplessness and hide from his very nearest and dearest.

Bella ran to the olive tree, arranged her swimsuit, and stood still for a moment, holding her hands and her face beneath the sun.

"I love to stand this way for a few minutes. Only then, with your body cooled off, can you feel the soft caresses of the sunbeams."

She said that with her eyes closed, because otherwise she would have seen how the gaze of her new acquaintance, the now far-from-young man, was tenderly caressing her damp face, moving down slowly from her chin over her long neck, stopping for a moment at a brown mole the size of a little raisin, and, as if rejected by it, straightening up and slipping over her rounded shoulders. Suddenly she turned her head to Mark and asked:

"Where are you staying?"

Mark didn't expect to hear that question. He began to stammer something, and finally squeezed out: "On a ship."

That apparently didn't surprise Bella. In addition, she was already immersed in her own plans, of which she made no secret.

"They're having a Neptune day here today, and I propose to celebrate it in our Dolphin Suites. I'm sure that it'll be fun!"

Neptune day! His head whirled as if he were looking at a movie of the summer events of his Soviet youth presided over by the sea god Neptune leaning on his gigantic trident. Demons, water-nymphs, pirates, and other mystical creatures accompanied him with song; they held pieces of wood, ostensibly remnants of sunken ships, and torn fishnets; trumpets blared, drums were beaten, and cymbals clashed— humming, screeching, everyone pouring water over everyone else, or, finding a victim and holding him by his feet and hands, dragging him to throw him into the water.

"Mark—why are you so quiet?"

Mark looked for an excuse to get out of the joyous masquerade.

"You know what, Bella? I'm no longer of an age to participate in such noisy events. Maybe, maybe we could find a quiet corner here, sit at a table, and drink a cup of coffee?"

Bella looked at him strangely. From her answer, it was easy to understand that she thought a normal person wouldn't have said such things.

"What!? Here, in this hole, a quiet corner? A cup of coffee? Did you fall from the sky?"

Mark stamped on the ground, as if he could bury himself in that spot up to his head, with only his Yankees cap with the long brim showing above as a sign for a little boy to come here and pee.

"I said something foolish, didn't I? I forgot where I was."

"It happens—especially on such a hot day," Bella made a joke out of it. "Nevertheless, there is such a quiet corner here, but without coffee . . . But it isn't near here—we'll have to put our legs in gear."

Mark put on his shirt, pulled his shorts over his swim trunks, and set out after the girl. They walked along the shoreline, up to their ankles in water, with their heads looking down as if they were searching for secret paths in the transparent water, each looking for his own: he, a path to his longed-for yesterday, and she, one to her untasted tomorrow. Long forgotten lines of poetry swam up straight out of his past, lost in the course of time like that box of letters to Bella from the first year after their marriage. And quietly, with his bare feet seeming to feel that path to another happy period in his life, he brought these lines to his lips:

I love to kiss your palms—
their touch heals and burns.
It can throw a beam of light
into the darkness of the abyss.

I love to hear your words,
their good sense refreshes and buries.
The dreams at night give me joy
after the truth of the week deceives me.

Why are you hiding your palms in yesterday,
and letting your gaze wander to somewhere far, far away?
The wind has carried away your words
and left the dreams in today.

The footprints left behind them in the sand—his, broad and deep, hers short and shallow—were quickly washed away by the wanton little waves so no one, God forbid, could catch them, find them; except for a seagull that flew along low above their heads, whistling like a boomerang thrown in their direction by the stiff hand of reality.

"I was listening to your voice," Bella said, "and I suddenly realized that it was familiar to me. True, the other fellow sounded"—she looked for a suitable word and Mark supplied it:

"Younger, firmer . . ."

"Right! And I can't recall whose voice it was."

She paused for a moment, as if expecting to hear the answer from Mark, and asked:

"Is that your poem?"

Mark smiled, looking down at his feet:

"My old friend wrote those lines years ago. At that time, he was in love with a girl he later married . . ."

"Read me some more of his poems."

"I don't remember any more—they've just fallen out of my head, together with my hair," and he raised his cap. "Actually it seems to me that after the wedding he didn't write any poems at all."

"And how did things go in his family life?"

"Ordinary—as with many people of my generation: they worked from Monday to Friday; on Saturday and Sunday they went out to see a new movie or a play, or dropped in on some of their friends; they celebrated his and her birthday every year, and three years after the wedding a boy was born to them—they called him David."

"David?" she interrupted him for the first time. "My grandfather's name was David. I loved him very much. He lived in the outskirts of the city, in a district with the strange name Old Post. I later learned that almost the first post office in Kishinev had been located there. He had his own cottage there, built of clay bricks carefully whitewashed and shingled. The spacious courtyard was surrounded by a tall, strongly built fence made of thick boards. My grandfather lived there with my aunt, my mother's younger sister. I don't remember my grandmother— she died half a year before I was born. Actually, I bear her name."

Bella stopped talking, apparently remembering that Mark had been talking when she interrupted with her grandfather.

"Excuse me Mark—I interrupted you."

"Not at all—it was very moving. Tell me more, please."

Bella continued with her recollections—she wanted to tell this near stranger more and more about herself, as if it were critical to her for him to know.

"Every Friday morning, my mother and I used to take the number 10 bus from the central market to the last station, and from there we would walk another 10–15 minutes to my grandfather's house. In his courtyard, several hens would be thrashing about, and a handsome rooster would be parading around them. My grandfather would be looking forward to seeing me. He always wore his sleeveless fur jacket—always the same, summer and winter—with his crushed hat on his head, sitting on a chair and leaning with his back against the wall. When he saw me come through the courtyard gate, he would slap his knee, which was supposed to mean: come here! He didn't need to do it twice—in a minute I would be sitting on his lap."

"'Well, little Bella, are you settled there?' he would ask with a gravelly voice that was hoarse from smoking. 'Now I'll show you some hocus pocus.'"

"I already knew that hocus pocus, which he would repeat each time: he would pull a raw egg out of his pocket, poke a hole in the tip with the pin that had been holding together the two sides of his fur jacket, and bring the egg to my mouth. I would turn my head away—I hate raw eggs to this day. But my grandfather knew how to get around me. Would you like to hear a story? Yes? Then drink! I would begin to suck the nauseating liquid from the hole in the egg and my grandfather would begin to tell the promised story, about a shepherd boy and his sheep, which . . ."

Mark finished the sentence:

"Which the evil witch carried off with the storm wind."

"You've heard that story too?"

"Yes, from my wife. She always used to constantly tell it to our little son when she was raising him."

"If I ever have a son," Bella said dreamily, "I'll call him David, too, in memory of my grandfather."

The breeze, which was lightly caressing her face, brought with it a delicious aroma of boiled fish with garlic. Further along their path—it was already visible—Bella and Mark saw a broken-down hut. Black fishnets were hanging out to dry on high, thin poles.

"Ok—here's your quiet corner," said Bella proudly. "It belongs to the fisherman Kuzmitsh."

Mark inhaled the delicious aroma, and suddenly realized that he was very hungry. They had now reached the bonfire over which a large iron cauldron was cooking a real fisherman's fish soup. Two blond young fellows, sunburned and heavily muscled—one of them a head taller than the other one—were puttering around at the fire. Bella obviously knew them, because she called them by name: the taller one was Mitia and the shorter one was Yura; they were the fisherman's sons.

"And this is Mark—we met today on the beach."

While they were talking, the fisherman Kuzmitsh himself appeared from the hut. He was short and wore a sailor's undershirt and a pair of faded military trousers cinched by a narrow belt, with his feet sticking out. When he saw the guests, he came toward them with a waddling gait.

"Good guests need not be invited—they're always welcome," he said in his bass voice, and added: "As we say, 'if we have good guests, we can enjoy ourselves with them.'"

He went over to the cauldron, pulled a spoon out of his pocket and tasted the dish. Squinting, he smacked his lips and rendered his conclusion:

"For delicious fish you don't need a table," and now with a commanding tone, he added: "Mitia, pull out our golden fish."

The tall Mitia lazily got up from the sand and went down toward the ocean. When he got to the water, he grasped a string attached to a piece of iron stuck into the ground, and began pulling something out. A net basket came to the surface, and Mitia pulled out the "golden fish," a bottle of vodka.

Mark rejoiced silently, so no one would notice. His joy was not so much because of the vodka itself as because of the way in which it was cooled. He recalled how they, the students in the dormitory, used to hang just such a net basket full of products out the window in the winter. Somehow they did without refrigerators too.

There was actually no real table, but several turned-over empty wooden boxes served the function very well. They all sat down right on the sand and Yura brought each of them an aluminum bowl of fish-soup. Bread, salt, and a few hard red peppers lay right on the blackened boards of the improvised table. Meanwhile Mitia brought spoons and small, polished glasses out of the hut. It was clear that they were always ready for guests.

Old Kuzmitsh was now holding his golden fish in his hands. Grasping the tab of its tinfoil seal with two fat fingers, he quickly tore it off the bottle. He systematically poured a shot of vodka into each glass and proposed a toast: "To those who now lie in the sea!" Pouring the vodka down his throat in two gulps, he turned his attention to his bowl of fish soup.

Mark also drank up his shot and looked at Bella, who had put her lips to the edge of the glass. She made a face and put the glass down next to her on the sand. Mark winked at her, as if to say "I won't tell anyone!" For him it was nothing new that Bella didn't touch hard liquor. Wine, yes—she liked a bit of good wine. When David's first girl was born, she and her coworkers celebrated the event with champagne. Mark had still been in his office when they rang him up on the telephone. What was the matter? He had to bring home the new grandmother—she had overdone it.

The fragrant and fatty fish soup, right from the fire, burned his mouth, but still Mark turned eagerly to the simple food. Biting off a piece of black bread from the chunk that Mitia had previously torn off the loaf for each person, he chewed a piece of red pepper and quickly washed it down with a few spoonfuls of the fish soup. Bella was sitting across from him, and now and then he cast a brief look at her, as if he were waiting to hear: "Don't rush so! Too fat! Too much bread!" But she was silent, unhurriedly taking spoonfuls of soup from the bowl and bringing them to her mouth.

After the second glass, which only Mark shared with him, Kuzmitsh forgot about him too, and now by himself, keeping the bottle near him, kept pouring into his glass. Every time he drank a shot, his thin, waxy face developed a sad, depressed look.

Everyone had finished eating and was waiting till the water in the big, sooty teakettle, which Mitia had previously put on the fire, would boil to make the tea. The old fisherman was looking forward to that moment. His sailor's soul, dazed by the vodka, was dying for a simple human word; he put his hand on Mark's shoulder and asked:

"Were you in the war?"

Mark felt his face start to burn. What could he say to Kuzmitsh? Actually, he, Mark, was now not much younger than Kuzmitsh, so he just shrugged his shoulders. But the fisherman didn't really need Mark's answer—he had apparently asked the question in order to answer it himself.

"I was," he declared, and gave the details, as if he were reporting. "I fought the Fascists on the Black Sea, as a sailor on the battle torpedo cutter TK 63!"

"Really?" Mitia exclaimed. "You're starting again? Everyone already knows that you were a brave sailor."

"Be silent when war veterans speak, you wet-behind-the-ears boy!" his father interrupted him angrily. "What do you know about those dark times?!"

Mitia didn't answer. He quietly started to gather the utensils and lay them in the empty cauldron. His brother also got up and went into the hut. Bella wanted to help Mitia out with the utensils, perhaps wash them, but he refused.

"Thank you, Kuzmitsh. Your fish soup was delicious, as usual. I could lick my fingers."

Mark was ready to express his delight with a "delicious!" but at the last minute he choked down the word and just nodded his head. He was eager to get up from his place, but Kuzmitsh held him by the hand with fishermanly skill, as if he were a large fish just pulled out of the ocean. Mark understood that he had been caught in the fisherman's net.

"I'll wait for you near the water," said Bella, coming to his aid. "I hope that Kuzmitsh won't keep you long."

The fisherman's gaze accompanied her, and he asked Mark:

"Your daughter? A good girl—she's friends with my guys. I have two additional older children, a boy and a girl—she's already a mother herself."

He poured himself another glass and moved the bottle to Mark's empty glass. Mark did not refuse.

"To our victory!" Kuzmitsh toasted, and added: "May our children know nothing of war!"

Having drunk up and bitten off the end of the pepper, he asked:

"Do you have other children?"

"A son and two grandchildren."

"In that case, we have to drink to them separately."

The remainder of the conversation went smoothly. Mark felt that in the simple, hospitable, hard-working man who hadn't even asked what his name was and had immediately invited him to his table and had shared his bread and whisky with him, he had now found a sincere friend such as he hadn't met till now in America and probably would never meet. He could unburden his heart to him.

"You understand, Kuzmitsh—I've run away from my wife on the eve of my wedding anniversary, after thirty years of living together."

"There's something I don't understand: You lived and had children with her without being officially registered?"

"No, it was our pearl wedding anniversary, I'm telling you—it's been thirty years."

"Now I understand," he nodded his head. "You're an admirable fellow! I've now lived with my wife for nearly forty years, and I can't do it because I'm a weak person. But I love her anyway!"

"I love mine too, but recently I feel that we are drifting apart. She talks to me like a doctor to a patient who is getting senile. We often even sleep in separate rooms. True, there's a reason—I snore. So what? Didn't I snore before? Maybe not as loudly."

"Before you didn't only snore less loudly," Kuzmitsh offered his conclusion. "Before you used to kiss your lover thoroughly and do something more, no?" and he gave Mark a sly wink.

"True—you're right. And now our sex is more like a medical procedure."

"My brother," Kuzmitsh interpreted it in his own way, "what can we expect in that area by now? As they say—your youth is gone, the tomatoes have withered."

Just then, Yura brought some green enamel pitchers and a tin box with sugar out of the hut and placed them on the table.

"Bella," he called, "come drink some tea."

Mitia took the teakettle off the fire and poured the now-boiled water into the pitchers.

The group sat down again, each one in his place, and sipped loudly. Bella left her pitcher standing on the table so the tea would cool off. Meanwhile she sorted the beautiful mother-of-pearl seashells that she had found near the ocean while Mark and Kuzmitsh had been unburdening their hearts, and threaded individual seashells on a thin fishing line to make a necklace.

Kuzmitsh, finished with his tea, got up heavily from his seat and announced:

"I have to go lie down, because I have the watch again tonight."

Waddling from side to side even more, as if he had just finished rowing in the ocean to catch mackerel, he dragged himself off toward his hut. Mark sat for a moment, following him with his eyes, and then suddenly stood up, caught up to the fisherman, and taking his American cap off his head he put it on Kuzmitsh's head. They hugged each other.

"Cut out those intelligentsia tricks of yours," said Kuzmitsh, looking Mark straight in the eye. "Go back to your wife. You won't find anything better anyway!"

The sun was descending toward the horizon when Bella and Mark set out on the same road, but this time to go back. A cool breeze was blowing from the ocean, and Mark, pulling off his shirt, threw it onto Bella's shoulders. She thanked him and put it on properly, with the sleeves, and buttoned all the buttons.

During the first years they lived together, Bella, especially on holidays, liked to jump out of bed in the morning and put one of Mark's shirts on her naked body, roll up the sleeves, and walk around that way in the kitchen. Mark definitely liked that, and he often used to grab Bella by the hand and pull her back into the bedroom.

"Does it suit me?" she asked in a deliberately flirtatious manner.

"Very sexy . . . Tomorrow that will become the local fashion."

Bella took his arm and pulled him to her.

"How much longer will you be here?"

"I return today."

"When?"

"After the third signal from my ship."

"Why after the third one?"

"That's how it goes in all stories; that was the condition imposed by the generous witch."

"What's the name of your ship?"

"*Carnival Dream.*"

"Recently I keep having a certain dream—a terrible nightmare."

"Tell it to me. They say that after you tell a dream to someone else, you forget it."

"Some terrible person, or a black shadow, is running after me brandishing a sliver from a broken bottle, and any minute he will catch up to me."

"Such a thing will never happen. I know a spell to drive away even the worst dreams."

"What do I have to say?"

"Very simple—first you have to spin seven times to the left and then seven times to the right; then you have to spit three times into the ocean and say: 'Black shadow, angry face, disappear from my dream!'"

"And that will help?"

"Of course it will help. It always helps me."

Bella stood still for a moment, then started spinning the way Mark had just said. When she was finished spinning, she turned her face toward the ocean, spat three times, and repeated the spell precisely, word for word: "Black shadow, angry face, disappear from my dream!"

"Now everything will be OK!" said Mark quietly, as if he were afraid to disrupt something.

Bella, still standing with her back to him, asked:

"Will you come here again?"

Mark was silent for a moment, in order to answer calmly, and then said:

"I don't know . . . But if it does happen, I'll always search for you here."

Bella came close to Mark. She stood on tiptoes and kissed him on the lips.

The two of them now stood that way, as if petrified—the aged Mark and the young Bella—and kissed, as the stubborn roaring of three signals—two short ones and one long one, resounded over the island.

The taste of the kiss still lay on his lips, and the long farewell signal of the voyaging *Carnival Dream* was slowly fading away, together with the dream. Mark looked at the clock that stood on the small table next to his bed. The green electronic numerals showed a quarter to twelve. "It seems that I slept longer today than ever before," he thought to himself. "Bella has left and I didn't even hear her. She was planning to go to her hairdresser to get a beautiful hairdo, and then to go pick up the kosher cake, and then something else . . . Women are stubborn—a party!"

He got up and saw a light green shirt and hockey shorts lying on the floor. "How did they get here?" he asked, astonished, and bent down to pick up the shirt. A string of beads—mother-of-pearl, rough seashells—slipped out of the upper pocket and fell down to his bare feet.

The End.

July–September 2012
Brooklyn

Boris Sandler is one of the leading Yiddish fiction writers of the postwar generation and has received every major contemporary Yiddish literary award for his work. He served as the editor in chief of the *Yiddish Forward* from 1998 to 2016. Mr. Sandler's work has been translated into English, Hebrew, Russian, German, and Romanian.

A prolific translator of Yiddish literature, **Barnett Zumoff** has published twenty-four volumes of poetry and prose in translation. He has served as president of the Forward Association and the Workmen's Circle, and in 2009 was awarded the Mlotek Prize in Yiddish Culture. He is also a professor of endocrinology at the Icahn School of Medicine at Mount Sinai.